PLAYS

BY

MRS. W. K. CLIFFORD

BY THE SAME AUTHOR

THE LIKENESS OF THE NIGHT
(Four Acts)

A LONG DUEL (Comedy, Four Acts)

THE SEARCHLIGHT (One Act)

BADELEINE (One Act)

PLAYS:

HAMILTON'S SECOND MARRIAGE
THOMAS AND THE PRINCESS
THE MODERN WAY

BY

MRS. W. K. CLIFFORD

NEW YORK
MITCHELL KENNERLEY
MCMX

AUTHOR'S   NOTE.

*Of these three plays, only the first has been pro-
duced.*

*"The Modern Way" takes its title from a volume
by the same author published two years ago, and is
adapted from a story contained therein.*

*Any inquiries regarding the dramatic rights of
"Hamilton's Second Marriage" should be addressed
to Miss Alice Kauser, 1402 Broadway, New York, and
for the other two plays to Miss Elisabeth Marbury,
1430 Broadway.*

*These plays are copyrighted in the United States of
America, and all rights are reserved.*

7 CHILWORTH STREET,
   HYDE PARK, LONDON, W.
      January, 1910.

CONTENTS

HAMILTON'S SECOND MARRIAGE

A PLAY IN FOUR ACTS

PRODUCED AT THE COURT THEATRE,
LONDON, OCTOBER, 1907, BY

MR. OTHO STUART,

WITH

MR. DAWSON MILWARD, MR. E. M. GARDEN, MR. GRAHAM
BROWNE, MISS FRANCES DILLON, AND MISS ALEXANDRA
CARLISLE IN THE CHIEF PARTS

DRAMATIS PERSONÆ

SIR HENRY CALLENDER
MAURICE HAMILTON, *ex-Civil servant*
COLONEL DEMPSTER, *his friend*
GUY ARMITAGE
JUDSON, *butler to Sir H. Callender*
BECKER, *Hamilton's servant*

LADY CALLENDER
SYLVIA, *daughter to Sir H. and Lady Callender*
MADAME BUNSEN, *a riding mistress*

TIME: Present.

ACT I

SCENE.—LADY CALLENDER'S *drawing-room on Camden Hill. French windows opening on to garden and lawn seen beyond. Fireplace* R, *door* L. *Grand piano (open)* C. *Flowers about, &c. Pleasant, home-like room of well-off people.*

TIME.—*Early afternoon.*

> [*When the curtain rises* SIR HENRY CAL-LENDER *is standing by the bell, which he rings rather impetuously. He is elderly, lively and mannered.*

Enter SERVANT (JUDSON), *with note on tray, held down by his side.*

SIR H. Where is Lady Callender?

JUDSON. Her Ladyship is lying down, Sir Henry.

SIR H. Oh! [*He always says " Oh!" in the same short tone.*] And Miss Sylvia?

JUDSON. Miss Sylvia is out.

SIR H. Oh! What's that——

> [*Looking down at tray.*

JUDSON. [*Handing note.*] Mr. Hamilton's servant brought it this morning—just after you had gone, and was to wait for an answer.

> [SIR HENRY *reads it with some excitement.*

SIR H. Oh! [*To* JUDSON, *who is about to go.*] Judson—wait. [*Reads note again.*] I—I want a telegram to go immediately. [*Sits down at writing-table,* R.] No—stop—I won't send it—I'll telephone—— [*Exit* JUDSON.] [*Looking at note again.*] Of course.   [*Exit.*

[*Stage empty for a minute.*
[*Re-enter* JUDSON, *showing in* GUY ARMITAGE— *young, boyish in manner, good-looking.*

JUDSON. Miss Sylvia is out, sir, but I'll see if her Ladyship is about yet.

GUY. Don't disturb her if she's lying down— I mean—er—taking her little siesta—or going out.

JUDSON. No sir.   [*Exit.*

[GUY *alone makes business—looks round room—whistles the tune of the song he afterwards plays, drifts to piano, and plays and sings softly to himself.*

[*Sings*] "Did you ever see the devil
          With his wooden pail and shovel,
          Digging taters by the bushel
          With his tail cocked up
          .   .   .   tail cocked up
          Did you ever see the devil
          With his wooden pail——"

Enter LADY CALLENDER (46), *handsome, rather austere-looking, but sweet-mannered—a little firm in manner, as of a woman whose preju-*

dices, in spite of her sweetness, it would be difficult to conquer.

LADY C. My dear Guy—that tune again! Don't you know any other?

GUY. Nothing so beautiful, Aunt Peggy. But I hope I haven't disturbed you?

LADY C. No, dear; I had finished my little siesta.

GUY. [With a little, merry, backward shake of his leg at LADY C.'s last word.] I came to see if Sylvia would stroll round to the riding school, and have a look at Clara—she's getting on splendidly.

LADY C. Sylvia is at her Debating Society. [Sits.

GUY. Debating Society! Lord!—all girls under twenty-five, aren't they?

LADY C. Yes; I think so.

GUY. What on earth do they debate about?

LADY C. Well, last time it was Women's Suffrage and——

GUY. [Quickly.] Which side did she take?

LADY C. Against it—of course.

GUY. [Relieved.] That's all right. What's it about to-day?

LADY C. She didn't tell me—sit down, dear.

GUY. Does she do much talking?

[Sits down at piano again, facing LADY C.

LADY C. I don't know, of course; but she has keen views on most subjects—for a girl.

GUY. [*With a little sigh.*] She never airs them to me.

LADY C. Perhaps she's afraid you would laugh at her. I think it takes an older companion—if it's a man—to bring her out.

GUY. Ah! the immaculate Hamilton, for instance.

LADY C. He said, the other day, that he enjoyed a talk with her immensely.

GUY. [*Good-humouredly.*] Indeed? Very kind of him. Well—well—shall I sing you a verse, Aunt Peggy?

[*Begins to sing and play mournfully.*
" Did you ever see the devil
With his wooden pail and shovel."
[*Stopping abruptly.*] There's nothing like the devil for a beggar who's in love.

LADY C. [*Amused.*] Are you in love?

GUY. Oh, no; not at all, thank you—I thought I was, but I find I'm not—for the present. [*Plays for a minute, stops.*] What a funny chap Hamilton is! Your Anglo-Indian is always a little—well, you know.

LADY C. He wasn't long in India; he threw up his post twelve years ago, when his wife died——

GUY. Oh, he's a widower, is he?

LADY C. Didn't you know?

GUY. Never thought about it, Aunt Peggotty —or I should have said he was a bachelor; he has the cut of one. . . . Wasn't it he who put Sylvia up to having more riding lessons?

LADY C. He said they would be good for her. She had never ridden in London at all, and not much in the country——

GUY. She didn't seem to care about it before he worried round.

LADY C. I don't think she knew how lovely Bexted was till he came——

GUY. I wonder what made him go there. It is rather off the beaten track.

LADY C. He saw Briary Way advertised, and it sounded like the sort of thing he wanted.

GUY. [*Thoughtfully.*] You see, he's rather elderly.

LADY C. He's only forty-two.

GUY. I believe he's gone on Sylvia. They take it badly at that age.

LADY C. [*Who evidently dislikes slang.*] What makes you think he's " gone " on her?

GUY. Rather difficult to explain the symptoms, but I know 'em—wonder if it's any good. He had a good pull all that time in the country. Still, she isn't a girl to be snapped up easily.

LADY C. [*A little severely.*] I hope she regards marriage too seriously to be "snapped up."

GUY. Beg pardon, Aunt Peggotty, didn't mean to be rude. Well, I must get back to my little sister going round and round on her gee-gee.

LADY C. Are there many girls at Madame Bunsen's?

GUY. A good many. Best riding-school in London now. Rummy thing for a woman to do, isn't it?

LADY C. Very. I wonder what her history is?

GUY. I should think she was in a circus from the way she rides—no one can touch her. Some one said she came from Mexico.

LADY C. She seems to like Sylvia.

GUY. Shouldn't wonder—a good many people do. [*Thoughtfully, after absently playing for a minute or two.*] I think I shall go to Japan and have a squint at the world in general, for a year.

LADY C. [*Surprised.*] My dear Guy—what for?

Enter SERVANT, *with telegram*

[*Opens and reads it.*] No answer. [*Exit* SERVANT.

LADY C. How tiresome! Colonel Dempster can't dine to-night. Could *you* come, dear?

GUY. Should love it, but I'm engaged—worse luck.

Re-enter SIR HENRY CALLENDER.

SIR H. [*To* GUY.] Oh, is that you? [*To* LADY C.] I say what the deuce are they doing with the library—I particularly want it this afternoon.

LADY C. My dear Harry, the place simply reeked of tobacco.

SIR H. Why shouldn't it? Excellent tobacco!

LADY C. But I couldn't let people take their cloaks off there till I had it turned out. They've taken down the curtains to fumigate, opened the windows, washed everything with carbolic——

SIR H. The devil——

GUY. [*Quickly cuts in singing.*] "With his wooden pail and shovel"——

LADY C. Be quiet, Guy. [*To* SIR H.] They are going to burn some pastiles, and when Sylvia comes in I shall ask her to arrange some of those tall lilies there.

SIR H. [*Rather amused.*] Oh! is that all. . . And where *is* Sylvia?

LADY C. She'll be here very soon now. She went to the Debating Society at Lady Redcar's.

SIR H. And what's that? [*Pointing to the telegram.*] Some one thrown us over for to-night?

LADY C. Colonel Dempster. I asked Guy to take his place, but he can't.

SIR H. Oh! [*To* GUY.] Why can't you?

Guy. Wish I could, but I'm going to dine with Buckles—Empire afterwards—they've got a dancer——

Sir H. I know—Wish I were going—best thing in town.

Guy. Rather! [*Quickly.*] I say!—Clara will wonder what's become of me. Good-bye, Aunt Peggotty.

Sir H. We'll go to the Empire together one night, shall we?

Guy. Should like it—awfully. [*Exit* Guy.

Sir H. [*Evidently glad he's gone. Turning to* Lady C.] Sylvia won't be back just yet?

Lady C. No.

Sir H. That's all right. . . . Now!—What about to-night? Would Hamilton do?

Lady C. Yes, he'd do. But I don't think we ought to ask him again—just yet.

Sir H. Because—Oh, nonsense—give him time. He is not the man to rush things—only just got his London house—wants to see if he can afford to marry again, perhaps.

Lady C. But I am certain Sylvia is fond of him. We ought to have put an end of it before —only I didn't see why we should.

Sir H. Neither did I—[*With an inward chuckle which he tries to hide.*] You are quite sure you would like him for her?

Lady C. Quite—he is the sort of man she

ought to marry . . . and she would be next
us at Bexted——

SIR H. Not too old?

LADY C. Why no. . . . I'm sorry for
Guy, but he'll get over it——

SIR H. H'm! Hamilton is a good fellow—
Dempster, who has known him all his life, was
saying so the other day—behaved well over some
crisis—he didn't say what. . . . I like him
—did from the first. He's a widower, of
course——

LADY C. But there are no children, and his
wife died long ago. . . . I'm certain Sylvia
cares for him.

SIR H. [*Triumphantly.*] Well, look at this
then. [*Pulls out note and hands it to her.*] Came
this morning——

LADY C. [*Reading.*] "Could you see me alone
—this afternoon?"—Of course it's that. [*Face
brightening.*] What have you done?

SIR H. Telephoned. He was out—but had
left word he'd be back at four punctually. Said
I'd ring him up again. [*Looking towards clock.*]
Must go in five minutes. Shall tell him to come
immediately.—Lucky he lives so near, eh? And
you've turned out the library at the very moment
when I ought to receive my future son-in-law
there and do the heavy father.

LADY C. You must see him here.

Sir H. It's the sort of interview no one has in a drawing-room. A drawing-room is a woman's place.

Lady C. I'll go before he comes. . . . Why didn't you tell me before?

Sir H. Only just had it, been at the Law Courts all day, mere fluke that I came in now.

Lady C. Harry! [*Laughing.*] What with wanting to take Guy to a music-hall, and going to the Law Courts when there's a case unfit for publication——

Sir H. That's why—that's why——

Lady C. [*Shaking her head.*] You'll never be any better——

Sir H. Never, my dear, but you are good enough for us both. [*Pause.*] . . . I want to tell you something else. [*Hesitates.*] I ran against Florence Cathcart to-day.

Lady C. [*Stiffly.*] Oh! Did you speak to her?

Sir H. Yes—of course I did.

Lady C. How did she look?

Sir H. Not very well, poor thing—and rather forlorn. [*Hesitates a minute.*] I felt sorry for her.

Lady C. A pretty woman always gets you on her side.

Sir H. I married one.

Lady C. *shakes her head at the compliment.*

Don't you think we could let her come and see us now and then, on the quiet, you know. I wouldn't say anything till I had spoken to you—

LADY C. [*Quickly.*] No——

SIR H. It's years ago——

LADY C. It doesn't make any difference. It is giving way and condoning, that makes these things possible. No one who has figured in the Divorce Court shall come here with my consent——

SIR H. " Forgive us our trespasses "—they do up there. [*Half grave, half joking.*]

LADY C. I do. But I can't let her come.

SIR H. Then what's the good of forgiving? —won't do her an ounce of good.

LADY C. A difference must be made. It is only by holding the marriage tie sacred that you will keep it unbroken.

SIR H. Still, you might make an exception.

LADY C. It's the exceptions that do the mischief.

SIR H. I'm afraid she hoped——

LADY C. [*Passionately but firmly.*] I can't help it. I'm sorry.

SIR H. [*Looks at her in dismay, shrugs his shoulders, and then as if he gives up the subject, says*] Well, I'll go back to the telephone.

[*Exit.*

LADY CALLENDER *alone, enter* JUDSON.

JUDSON. I thought Sir Henry was here, my
lady. Madame Bunsen has called.

LADY C. He will be—directly. Madame
Bunsen?—er—er—ask her—ask her to come in.

[*Exit* JUDSON.

Re-enters a minute later, announcing
Madame Bunsen.   [*Exit.*

[MADAME BUNSEN *is in a riding habit.
Her manner is slightly foreign, a little stiff and distant; there is a note
in her voice as if uncertain of her
position.*

LADY C. Oh! I didn't know you were riding,
or I wouldn't have asked you to come in, Madame
Bunsen. How do you do?

MADAME B. How do you do? . . . I
was passing and thought I would leave a message for Sir Henry. He spoke to me about a
mare for your daughter. Just now I heard of
one that a pupil may want to sell.

LADY C. He will be here directly. Won't you
sit down? [MADAME B. *shakes her head.*] I
should like to thank you for all the trouble you
have taken with my—Sylvia. [*Hesitates before
the last word, looks at* MADAME B., *and then
says it as if satisfied by the inspection.*]

MADAME B. [*With a quick smile; she has been
grave before.*] But I love her—best of all—
she is charming.

MADAME C. I'm delighted to hear you say so.

MADAME B. And so fresh—so innocent.

LADY C. She enjoys her rides immensely.

MADAME B. I always keep her beside me when it is possible. We have ridden many miles between green hedges this spring. [*Then with a more formal manner.*] I fear I must not wait. Sir Henry isn't at home?

LADY C. [*Rings.*] Yes, he is at home. . . . I'm glad your school is doing so well.

Enter SERVANT.

Ask Sir Henry to come at once. [*Exit* SERVANT.

MADAME B. It is doing splendidly. More and more come every week.

LADY C. It is a remarkable thing for a woman to do.

MADAME B. [*With a shrug.*] It's the only thing I *can* do—I'm not clever.

LADY C. [*A little curiously.*] And you *have* to do something?

MADAME B. [*Distantly.*] Oh, yes.

LADY C. [*Sympathetically, evidently warming to her.*] You have no husband or child?

MADAME B. No, I am alone. [*With a change of tone, looking towards garden.*] How beautiful those lilies are—how good to have that garden—and in London.

Enter SIR HENRY.

Sir H.   My dear Madame Bunsen—this is a surprise.   [*Shakes hands.*]

Madame B.   I heard of a mare—one minute ago.   I think it is just what you want.   Could you come and see it on Friday?   It belongs to a pupil who will be at the school that day.

Sir H.   Why, certainly—with pleasure—delighted.

Madame B.   You'll not decide on anything else till then, she is so anxious to find a good home for it?

Sir H.   Of course I won't—I'll come and see it on Friday—make a point of it.

Madame B.   That is excellent.   [*Turns to* Lady C., *and says rather distantly.*]   Thank you so much for your reception.   [*About to go.*]

Lady C.   I'm very glad to have seen you.   [*Seeing that* Madame B. *has looked again towards the garden.*]   I should like to give you some flowers—but you couldn't carry them now.   I'll send you some by Sylvia to-morrow—if I may?

Madame B.   [*Surprised.*]   Oh, how kind you are! and it is so charming here.   [*Shakes hands.*]   I am glad I came——

Lady C.   So am I.

Sir H.   I'll see you off.   [*Exeunt* both.

   [Lady C. *goes to window* l., *as if to see her mount.*

Re-enter SIR HENRY.

LADY C. [*Evidently looking after her.*] What an interesting woman. I wonder who she is? She said she was alone—it seems strange. Why is it do you suppose?

SIR H. Been projected into space without any belongings, perhaps. . . . Well, I caught Hamilton, he'd just come in.

LADY C. And——?

SIR H. He'll be here directly. [*Looks at his watch.*] In two minutes. You'd better go, my dear, he mustn't see you beforehand. Be quite wrong, you know.

LADY C. There he is! [*Listening and laughing.*] I'll go this way.   [*Exit by garden.*

Enter SERVANT *announcing*
Mr. Maurice Hamilton.

[*Exit* SERVANT.

Enter HAMILTON (42), *distinguished looking, hair slightly touched with grey; he must have charm and magnetism; a little soldierly in his bearing.*

SIR H. How do you do? Glad to see you.

HAMILTON. How do you do?

[*Looks rather anxiously towards the window.*

SIR H. Sylvia's out, the wife's busy, so I thought I'd see you here.

HAMIL. [*Evidently awkward.*] Very good of you——

SIR H. They are making an infernal havoc in the library because it smelt a little of tobacco smoke, and some women are going to take off their cloaks there to-night.

HAMIL. [*Trying not to be awkward.*] I should have thought it would remind them of their own cigarettes.

SIR H. Not a bit of it . . . sit down. . . . Had your note.

HAMIL. I thought it would be the best way.
[*Sits down—pause.*

SIR H. Anything I can do for *you?* [*Looks at him half puzzled.*] Up a tree? Down a hole?

HAMIL. [*With a smile.*] Both, and you can do a great deal for me——

SIR H. Both?

HAMIL. I'd better make a plunge and be done with it. I'm head and ears in love with your daughter.

SIR H. Ah! I'm not surprised—frankly, not surprised. . . . Have you spoken to her?

HAMIL. No, I wanted to see you first.

SIR H. Oh! [*A little doubtfully.*] It's the girl who settles the matter in these days, and the father has to give in, ask what you have a year, and express a hope that there are no past irregularities.

HAMIL. I know. But there are irregularities, though not of the usual sort——

SIR H. Oh! Money, perhaps; the——

HAMIL. No, not money. There's no difficulty in that direction. . . . I should have spoken a month ago, but a chance remark fell from Lady Callender and opened my eyes. I should go away altogether, but—I'm hard hit—I'm a conceited ass perhaps to think that I've a chance—but——

SIR H. Well? Is there any good reason why there shouldn't be? Out with it, Hamilton, what is it?

HAMIL. You think I'm a widower—I'm not.

SIR H. Not?

HAMIL. The woman I married is alive. I divorced her.

SIR H. The deuce! [*After a pause.*] You divorced *her?*

HAMIL. Yes. Two years after marriage.

SIR H. Oh! Well; this is a pretty kettle of fish—divorce—any mention of it *is* the deuce in this house.

HAMIL. I was afraid so.

SIR H. [*Getting up and walking about in his agitation.*] I think you ought to have told us before—when you came to the neighbourhood, or when we knew you first, at any rate.

HAMIL. It never occurred to me that you

didn't know—but it was a subject you would naturally avoid—and it wasn't a matter of which *I* was likely to speak.

SIR H.   How did it happen?   Was she very young?

HAMIL.   She was nineteen; I was eight years older.

SIR H.   Humph! . . . Dempster was talking of you the other day at the club.   Does he know?

HAMIL.   Of course, and probably thought that you did.   He was in India at the time—knew her—ask him about it—anything you please.

[*Pause.*

SIR H.   Poor chap—two years——

HAMIL.   Not quite two—three before the decree was made absolute.   The other man married her, and they vanished—went to the other side of the world, I was told.   It's twelve years ago.

SIR H.   [*Feelingly.*]   What did you do?

HAMIL.   Chucked my appointment—travelled —came back.   For a long time I didn't dare to think of her at all.   Then I tried to imagine her dead; it was better than the other thing—she *is* dead to me, and has been for years. . . . She had to be if I was to live. . . . I tried to get interested in politics—but I preferred to keep in the background—I've always believed in work.

SIR H.   Quite right—quite right.   [*Tentatively.*]   When did you fall in love with my little girl?

HAMIL.   The first hour I saw her.

SIR H.   Oh!

HAMIL.   She's too young for me, I know that. She is——

SIR H.   Twenty-three.   Her mother is eighteen years younger than I am.

HAMIL.   [*With a rueful smile.*]   Still she may regard me as a fogey.   I'm forty-two.   But if she doesn't—would it be plain sailing, if I can win her—when she knows what I have told you?

SIR H.   My dear chap, I'll be frank with you.   I would rather things had been different; but if she asks me, I'll not stand in your way— in fact, you may count on *me;* but her mother will no more hear of it under the circumstances than she will fly.   She has strong views on marriage, and a horror of divorce—guilty or innocent, it's all the same to her, and Sylvia is much more under her influence than under mine.   Upon my life, I believe she'd be as shocked as her mother.

HAMIL.   Will you let me put the facts before her?   Could you put them before Lady Callender?

SIR H.   [*Getting up and walking up and*

down.] Of course I could—and a nice time I should have. I'm sorry—for I like you.

HAMIL.   Thank you.

SIR H.   [*Pause.*] You're quite sure the other woman isn't dead?

HAMIL.   I know absolutely nothing about her.

SIR H.   When did you hear of her last?

HAMIL.   Twelve years ago—she went to the antipodes with the man who is now her husband.

SIR H.   Why shouldn't we assume that she's dead; she's dead to you, let her be so to us?

HAMIL.   [*Firmly.*]   No—I couldn't do that.
[*He turns away.*

SIR H.   [*Cordially.*]   Quite right.   But it's a precious *cul de sac.* . . . I wonder you didn't tell Sylvia about it before you confided in me.

HAMIL.   I didn't think it would be fair—besides it's not a pleasant story.   I hoped if you were on my side that you would tell it her—your views might influence hers.

SIR H.   Not a bit.   Women have such confounded opinions of their own in these days.

HAMIL.   It's one of the things I like in her.
[*Pause.*

SIR H.   Tell her yourself—after all, she'll take it better from you; but let her think it over before she answers.   You'll be sent away with a flea in your ear, I'm afraid.

HAMIL. I'll risk the flea. And in the meantime?

SIR H. You want me to get one on mine?

HAMIL. Well——

SIR H. I'll risk it too—and tackle the mother—which is a difficult business, I can tell you—half a dozen fleas wouldn't be equal to that.

HAMIL. You're splendid. [*Grasping* SIR HENRY's *hand.*]

SIR H. And we'll do it at once—— [*Ringing the bell.*] No time like the present.

HAMIL. That is what I want——

Enter SERVANT.

SIR H. Has Miss Sylvia come in yet?

SERVANT. Just now, Sir Henry.

SIR H. Ask her if she would come to me here.

[*Exit* SERVANT.

And, my dear Hamilton, you mustn't think that her mother is ungenerous, or anything of that sort—she comes of a good old-fashioned family, that would have been shocked at divorce and—other modern inventions——

HAMIL. It's hardly modern.

SIR H. Of course not. Henry VIII. and all kinds of people—but there wasn't much to be said for some of the old usages—I think I'm rather muddling it up; what I mean to say is that she's rather for high thinking and clean living, and that kind of thing——

HAMIL. So am I—we all are.

SIR H. Of course—— [*Trying to remember.*] Or is it is in *good* living? . . . That would cut both ways, eh? [*Laughs.*]   Here she is.

Enter SYLVIA (23), *graceful and pretty.*

SIR H. [*Going towards her, and in a somewhat unsteady voice.*] My dear, Mr. Hamilton wants to have—er—a little talk with you——

[*Exit* SIR HENRY.

SYLVIA. [*Who is surprised and awkward.*] How do you do? I've just come from the Debating Society—I told you about it the other day in the garden.

HAMIL. I remember—and pray what did you debate to-day?

SYLVIA. Well—we had a really good subject. I should like to tell you about it——

HAMIL. [*Impetuously.*] I don't want to hear —I want to tell *you* something—on which all my happiness depends—I love you—you know I love you—it is uppermost—I must say it first of all —I love you——

SYLVIA. Oh!——

[*Holds out her hands; he kisses and drops them.*

HAMIL. I don't want you to speak yet, dear, till you've heard—a fact of my life that—even

if you could love me—may make you send me
away for ever——

SYLVIA. Send you away for ever——

HAMIL. I thought you knew it till a month or
two ago—or I should have taken care that you
did before I came to-day—but, knowing I love
you—will help you, in any case, to deal with me
gently.

SYLVIA. [*Bewildered; with a little smile.*]   It
can't be anything serious—and if it is——

HAMIL. [*Walking up and down.*]   I want to
play the game fairly—not to urge you—to put
my case before you dispassionately.

SYLVIA. Tell me what it is——

HAMIL. It is about my first marriage——

SYLVIA. Yes——

HAMIL. I was twenty-seven, and home from
India on six months' leave. A month before my
time was up I met a beautiful girl of nineteen
—the daughter of an Italian General who had
married an Englishwoman—he was dead. I dis-
liked the mother, but Juliet——

SYLVIA. Juliet?—it's such a lovely name——

HAMIL. [*Nodding.*]   And she was fit for it.
She swept me off my feet—she was like no one
I had ever met. I loved her, I was infatuated,
I don't want to disguise that from you. . . .
We were married and on board ship before either
of us realised what we were about——

SYLVIA. And then?

HAMIL. She was a beautiful, passionate, uneasy creature—impulsive, and so young—that is the excuse I make for her.

SYLVIA. Excuse—what did she do? Weren't you happy?

HAMIL. I was; but, looking back, I fear she was not. My work occupied me a great deal—she was thrown on her own resources.

SYLVIA. But she had friends?

HAMIL. Yes, of the sort one makes in India—and a host of admirers always hanging about her. I thought there was safety in numbers, and I am not a jealous or suspicious man—I don't think I had any reason to be till the last. It was impossible to keep her down in the heat—she went up to Simla with Mrs. Sinclair, the wife of one of my colleagues; that was the year after our marriage. There was a man called Farance up there——

SYLVIA. Yes——

HAMIL. He had come out for a holiday, from England. It never occurred to me that he was bent on mischief—he hung about her as others did—not more, as far as I knew. When I went up to Simla she told me she had ridden with him sometimes in the early morning—she rode like the wind in a storm—but she seemed delighted to go with me, too. I was pre-occupied;

there was a threat of cholera below and it worried me—perhaps I didn't notice things as much as I ought to have done—I knew vaguely that she danced with him a good deal, still I never suspected. One day—[*A gesture as if he had not yet got over the pain and the surprise of it*]— she went off with him.

SYLVIA. Went off with him?——

HAMIL. She left the usual note saying she had gone with a man who loved her more than I did.—More! [*As if oblivious of* SYLVIA.] It was so incomprehensible—for she knew that I adored her, and I thought she cared for *me*—I suppose I was mistaken.

SYLVIA. What did you do?

HAMIL. I did the only thing possible to help her—got a divorce—set her free——

SYLVIA. Oh!——

HAMIL. And the other man married her when the formalities were complete. They went to Auckland twelve years ago.

SYLVIA. But where is she now?

HAMIL. I don't know. I know nothing about her.

SYLVIA. She's living?

HAMIL. I suppose so. If she were dead I think I should have heard. There's nothing else you need know—my marriage ended more completely than if death had taken it in hand—

it's over and finished—and she's another man's
wife——

SYLVIA. [*With a shudder.*] Oh, how dreadful—and you loved her so very much?

HAMIL. Yes—I did—[*With a pause*]—but
that is over and finished too, she is dead to me—
more than dead. For years I was dazed and
cared for nothing—I worked desperately—work
is generally a good physician. Then I went to
Bexted—a new world—it woke a new life in me,
and you came into my heart—without knowing it; gradually you filled every hour of the
day—I loved you—loved you—as I had imagined it would never be possible to love any
woman again. I thought you knew my position
—that your people, at any rate, did—then something your mother said made me realise that you
didn't, and that divorce was a horrible thing to
her——

SYLVIA. But it is to every one, surely—though
I see that it was the only thing you could do.

HAMIL. It's strange to find people feeling so
strongly about it in these days——

SYLVIA. Perhaps we don't belong to these days.
To us marriage is the most sacred tie in the world
—it can only end with death——

HAMIL. Dearest, marriage is not a ceremony
said over two people in a church—it is much more
than that. She broke away from all that it

meant, or she never had it to give *me*—it has
gone to the other man. She is not in my life any
more. *You* are in my life—I think you love me
a little——

SYLVIA. Love you a little—I love you with
all my heart—but this makes it impossible. [*With
a little shudder*].

HAMIL. Don't say that yet, Sylvia—I entreat
you to think it over—to take into your heart and
soul the story I have told you—the love I have
for you—and all that yours would mean to me.
Don't let a thing that is ended—that no longer
exists—come between us, though if it must be so
I will respect your feeling—I will go away and
you shall never see me again——

SYLVIA. [*Slowly*]. I'll think it over—I couldn't
answer now——

HAMIL. That is what I want, dear, I wouldn't
even take an answer—the one I most desire,
now. Send for me, for good or ill, when you
are sure—I don't feel that I can wait very pa-
tiently—let me know my fate soon. [*Takes her
hands and kisses them. Goes towards the door.
Looks round and says*] I will wait.

> [SYLVIA *nods as if unable to speak, and
> sits looking dazed, and straight before
> her.*

CURTAIN.

ACT II

Time.—*Four days later. Afternoon.*

Sir Henry Callender *is standing with his back to the mantelpiece.* Lady Callender *is sitting rather bolt upright in an arm-chair—evidently dismayed. There is silence for a minute or two.* Sir Henry *pulls out a large white silk handkerchief, and gives a gasp or two; but he is brisk and lively as usual.* Lady Callender *gets up, crosses the room, and stands as if waiting for him to speak.*

Sir H. [*Looking up.*] Well, my dear?

Lady C. It has been a dreadful shock.

Sir H. I thought it would be.

Lady C. I wanted it so much.

Sir H. [*Soothingly.*] You make too much fuss about it. It's such a usual thing in these days. If we hadn't been country cousins we should have taken it for granted that if his wife wasn't dead he had divorced her—or she him——

Lady C. [*Shocked.*] Oh no——

33

Sir H.　My dear, divorce is becoming as common as—as motor-racing or appendicitis or—anything of that sort—only it hasn't come our way any more than—living a mile from the main road—motors come our way—it will, depend on it and other things, too.

Lady C.　You do run on so.

Sir H.　So does the world—it won't stop where it was, or is, never did—new ideas, different ways of thought come along—can't prevent it.

Lady C.　I wish you had said it was impossible —that you had not allowed him to see her.

Sir H.　Well, but after all, Sylvia is the person it most concerns.　She's three and twenty and it's only fair play that she should decide—fair play to them both.　I expect we've given them that, for I've said everything I could for it—felt bound to, he's such a good chap—you probably said everything you could against it, so there you are.

Lady C.　But if he hadn't seen her—if she had been told of the impossibility——

Sir H.　Humph—she might have broken her heart—I don't think it would have done, I don't really—she's been very sensible, thought it over, taken three days—and if she decides for him we must make the best of it. . . . After all I shouldn't be surprised if the other woman's dead —she ought to be—the least she could do in fact is to be dead.—Have you any idea what she is going to do—Sylvia, I mean?

LADY C. No. She begged me not to speak to her about it again.

SIR H. So she did me.

LADY C. She listened to all my arguments.

SIR H. And to all mine—we have done everything we can—and she's had a pretty time of it, between us.

LADY C. He should have told us before.

SIR H. But he thought we knew, till lately. If we had been in London before this year, and he had been seen at our house, some one might have mentioned it—though things are forgotten so soon, even that might not have happened. People often think you know more about them than you do. Look at the Senior Wrangler who went to the theatre just after taking his degree, and when the audience cheered the play he thought —but you know that story. I daresay Hamilton thought we knew all about *him,* and looked at the facts of his life with—with sympathy.

LADY C. I wonder what Sylvia means to do.

SIR H. If she accepts him—so must we—the younger generation to which she belongs and the new world—and the new ways of thought are different from the old ones, and we mustn't behave like fogies—at least I mustn't though I am one.

Lady C. Or I like a frump?

Sir H. You couldn't—any more than you could look like one.

Lady C. Here she is.

Enter Sylvia. *She looks proud and gravely happy.*

Sir H. Well, my dear?

Sylvia. I want to see you before Mr. Hamilton comes—I wrote to him—he will be here directly.

Lady C. And—and have you decided——

Sylvia. [*Looking at her mother and putting out her hands to them.*] Oh, I am afraid to tell you. . . . Yes, my darlings, I have decided— and I am so happy—so glad——

Lady C. Glad!

Sylvia. That the chance is given me to mend that broken life. I think it was splendid of him to have it out with father before he spoke to me —and he didn't urge me—or not more than he could help, he only told me that he loved me and insisted that I should think it all over before I said yes or no. And I have—I have!

Lady C. You don't feel that he is still married?

Sylvia. [*With a thrill in her voice.*] No—o—o, mother. That marriage is more completely at an end than if she were dead.

Lady C. Sylvia!

SIR H. You're quite right—in my opinion, quite right.

SYLVIA. For then he might have been thinking of her—loving her all these years. Dreaming of an eternity with her by-and-by.

SIR H. Naturally.

SYLVIA. It would be far worse to marry him, and worse in *him* to marry again, if she had loved him to the last moment of her life; it would mean forgetfulness, or seem like playing her false because she wasn't here any longer. But this is different.

SIR H. Quite right. Unless you have good reasons you ought never to marry again—or marry at all in fact. I think there *are* reasons why people *may* marry twice—but I daresay it will lead to embarrassments in the next world— at least it may——

LADY C. [*Distressed but affectionate.*] Oh, you do talk such nonsense, Harry.

SIR H.—But as you say this is different.

SYLVIA. She killed his love for her.

SIR H. There was nothing to hold them together in fact but the marriage ceremony.

SYLVIA. And the law annulled that.

LADY C. It was a marriage in the sight of God. And she promised to be faithful to him all her life.

SYLVIA. And in the sight of God she broke

that promise, and the law recognised that she had broken it. They became strangers again. She married another man, and she's that man's wife—not Mr. Hamilton's.

SIR H.   I should think you made a very good debater, Sylvia. And in this instance there's been that most eloquent counsel—a woman's heart—to plead his cause.

SYLVIA.   Oh, father, but I've used my head, too. I've argued with myself, leaving my heart out of the question. I have put all the reasons against it before myself——

SIR H.   Oh!

SYLVIA.   I didn't want to be weak just because——

SIR H.   Of course not—you have taken counsel —as I say.

LADY C.   [*Slowly.*]   And if this woman were in London—if you met her?

SYLVIA.   [*Drawing back as if she had not considered this.*]   But she's not——

SIR H.   She's on the other side of the world —he doesn't know where, he hasn't seen her for twelve years—more—not since the decree was made absolute and she married the other.

[LADY C. *gives a little shudder at* " Decree."

SYLVIA.   Surely God and man alike have set him free?

LADY C. And suppose one day you met her, face to face?

SYLVIA. I hope I may never do that!

LADY C. But you must realise it—it's quite possible.

SYLVIA. [*Slowly.*] I don't think I should mind—I should know that in heart and thought they were strangers. If he cared, it would be different. [*Turns away distressed.*] It's no good, I can't give him up—be kind to me—help me——

SIR H. [*Caressingly.*] Kind to you, my dear —why we couldn't be anything else. . . . I'll leave you with your mother, she wants you to be happy—it's the thing she wants most in the world —that's why she hesitates so—that's why.

[*Exit to garden.*

SYLVIA. [*Turning to* LADY C.] Mother, he's the whole world to me. Won't you face it, won't you see it as I do? She's more than dead to him; she went out of his life years ago and into another man's. He is free. And you like him? You liked him so much at Bexted——

LADY C. He is the only man I ever hoped you would marry—till I knew this. [*Evidently has a long struggle with herself.*] But I will try and look at it with you and your father, since you don't feel as I do about it. [SYLVIA *kisses her hand gratefully.*] I'll do anything that will make

you happy. . . . [SYLVIA *gives almost a sob
of relief.*] He'll be here directly.

SYLVIA. Yes, he'll be here—— [SIR HENRY *is
seen near the window.*] When he comes send him
to me—tell him I shall be by the lavender bushes.
I would rather see him out there.

[*Exit by garden, passing her father, who re-enters.*

[LADY C. *makes a little gesture and is about to
speak when* SERVANT *enters, followed by*
COLONEL DEMPSTER. *a military-looking man
of about five and forty; all through the interview it is evident that he has great regard
for* HAMILTON.

SERVANT. Colonel Dempster. [*Exit* SERVANT.
[*The* CALLENDERS *look rather put out for
a moment, but recover quickly.*

SIR H. Oh, how do you do?

COL. D. How do you do? [*Turning to* LADY
C.] I came to apologise for my absence the other
night.

SIR H. Don't mention it—that sort of thing
will occur at the best-regulated dinner-parties
you know. [*Pause.*] We are expecting—er—
Hamilton.

COL. D. I saw him at the Club yesterday—he
seemed rather preoccupied.

LADY C. You've known him a long time, Colonel Dempster?

Col. D. A very long time.

Lady C. And you like him?

Col. D. I've the greatest regard and respect for him.

Sir H. [*To his wife.*] You hear that.

Col. D. [*Looking round.*] Is there [*with a smile*] some special reason for this question?

Enter Servant *announcing.*

Servant. Mr. Maurice Hamilton.

Sir H. [*Going forward.*] Ah, there you are —how do you do? Heard you were coming.

Hamil. [*A little awkwardly, after shaking hands with* Sir Henry.] How do you do, Lady Callender?

[*She shakes hands and says nothing.*

Hamil. I didn't expect to find you here.

Col. D. I've only come for five minutes—with an apology. I am going directly. [*Significantly.*

Hamil. [*With a smile.*] You needn't. . . . [*In a low eager tone to* Lady C.] I had a note telling me I might come.

Lady C. I know.

Hamil. She's not here?

Sir H. [*With a merry nod.*] She's in the garden.

Hamil. [*To* Lady C.] May I go to her?

Sir H. She's waiting for you.

Hamil. [*Turning quickly to the window— when he gets there stops, looks round with a happy*

face, and says to Sir H., *nodding at* Dempster.]
Tell him. He is the best friend I have.

Col. D. I think I can make a good guess. As
a matter of fact, I have expected it since I saw
them together last month. He's a fine fellow—
I'm very glad.

Lady C. I'm miserable about it——

Col. D. My dear lady! Miserable? She'll
be immensely happy.

Lady C. But the divorce? We knew nothing
of it till three days ago.

Col. D. Well, but he was on the right side.

Lady C. [*Shuddering.*] I *hate* divorce.

Sir H. And I maintain that it is a very wise
provision. A man has a wife who doesn't care
for him—or has changed her mind—likes somebody else—is unfaithful—best thing he can do
is to let her *go* to the other man—in fact, what
else is he to do with her? Unless he shoots her—
and then he'd be hanged. [*To his wife.*] I assure you, my dear, that to object to it only shows
that you are old-fashioned and—and early Vic-
torian. [*Appealing to* Colonel D.] I believe
that's one of the worst things that any one can
be called.

Col. D. Quite. Almost fatal. So bad that
it ought to be libellous, whether it's true or not.
[*Turning to* Lady C.] Believe me, my dear lady,
you've nothing to be uneasy about.

LADY C. [*With a little smile and shrug.*] I've given way. They are together now. [*Looking towards the garden.*]

SIR H. It's an excellent thing to sweep out prejudices. Besides, I always vote for doing the best one can for everybody—especially for a pretty woman, or a man who is a good fellow; it makes the world easier and pleasanter. . . . Now tell us something about Hamilton. You knew him in India?

COL. D. Oh, yes—and before that—knew all his people.

LADY C. Did you know his wife?

COL. D. I did, indeed.

LADY C. And her people?

COL. D. Only the mother—who wasn't much good to her—in a rackety set, and took lovers as the natural accompaniment of marriage, of life, even in middle age. When I knew her she was a widow——

SIR H. Of course, they always are. Girl badly brought up, no doubt—what was *she* like?

COL. D. A strange, beautiful creature. I didn't see much of her in India. It all happened up at Simla.

LADY C. [*A little cynically.*] Like a Kipling story.

SIR H. Those stories shouldn't be encouraged—you see they come true, sometimes. But they're

amusing to read—I thoroughly enjoy them—
especially when they—well—when they go a little
bit off the rails.

LADY C. Oh! [*Impatiently shaking her head,
but amused and indulgent, as she always is with
her husband.*]

COL. D. People were very sorry for him. He
was frightfully cut up.

SIR H. Of course—of course. Should be myself. What was the other man, Farence—yes, it
was Farence—like?

COL. D. Good-looking, and women liked him.
She bolted with him quite suddenly, no one suspected anything till it was done.

LADY C. Was Mr. Hamilton fond of her?

COL. D. Devoted—but he was fearfully over-
worked and harassed. He got a divorce—wanted
to settle money on her, but she refused it.

SIR H. That was decent of her.

COL. D. Oh, yes—and no matter what she did,
she was a charming girl, with nothing vicious
about her. She and Farence disappeared, and
nobody heard anything more of them—or of
Hamilton either, except through the papers,
though there was no reason why he should bur-
row out of sight.

LADY C. He was sensitive, of course. I like
him for it.

SIR H. He took a little place next to us at

Bexted a year or two ago. Used to take long, lonely rides—saved me from a nasty spill one day—that's how we came across him. He didn't want to know anybody, we had to force ourselves on him.

COL. D. Oh, that was it. [*Getting up and making a movement of departure.*] Look here, I'll go before these young people re-appear. I should feel *de trop*.

SIR H. Not a bit of it. You can congratulate them.

COL. D. I think I'll do it another time, if you'll let me. [*Shaking hands with* LADY CALLENDER.] I am glad I came in, if it has given you any comfort. If I had a girl, I should be only too delighted if he married her.

SIR H. [*Going towards the door with him.*] And so will she be. [*Outside the door.*] Very glad to have seen you.   [*Re-enters.*]

[LADY C. *is standing by the sofa, looking out towards the garden.*

SIR H. Well, is that all right? [*She nods and he puts his hand on her arm.*] You know, the fact is you didn't like being worsted after setting up a fine moral fence and saying no one shall get over it.

LADY C. [*Smiling.*] Perhaps that had something to do with it.

SIR H. It never does to make a hard and fast

rule, it's sure to get some knocks or be kicked aside. An open road to walk on—an open mind to live with, and you are safe.

LADY C. I know.

SIR H. [*Following direction of her eyes.*] Here they come. She's radiant! What a nice chap he looks—I don't wonder—should do it myself if I were a woman—Ah! [*Sound of satisfaction.*]

> [HAMILTON *and* SYLVIA *appear at window. They hesitate for a minute and then enter.* SYLVIA *goes up to her mother*

SYLVIA [*Joyfully.*] Mother, dear! [LADY C. *folds her to her heart and kisses her.*] And Maurice——

SIR H. It's evidently all right. [*Wrings* HAMILTON's *hand.*] My dear fellow, may you indeed be happy. God bless her!—[*Putting his arm round* SYLVIA]—and make her so.

HAMIL. I will—I promise you I will. [*Turning to* LADY C.] And *you* will trust me?

LADY C. [*Brightening up a little.*] Yes, I give her to you—I trust her to you. [*Gives him her hand.*]

SYLVIA. [*Shy, but radiant.*] I want to tell you both—that your child is the happiest, proudest girl in the world.

HAMIL. That's good hearing for me.

Enter GUY ARMITAGE. *There is a little hesita-*

*tion and awkwardness which he perceives and
evidently does not know how to account for.*

GUY. [*Hesitating by the door.*] How do you
do, every one.

SIR H. Oh!—Come in, Guy——

SYLVIA. How do you do.

[*Nods to him and turns to* HAMILTON.

GUY. [*Looking round.*] Anything going on?

SIR H. Oh! Well——

LADY C. Guy, dear, come in.

[GUY *comes forward and evidently takes
in the situation. Pause.*

SIR H. Well——

GUY. [*Constrained, and looking at* HAMILTON
and SYLVIA, *who are standing together.*] The
Governor sent me round. Clara's a bit dull, and
he thought we might get up a party and go somewhere.

SIR H. Capital! We ought to do something
to-night—don't you think so—[*looking towards*
SYLVIA *and* HAMILTON]—just the time?

SYLVIA. Not to-night—I couldn't, dear.

[*Turns to* HAMILTON *again.*

LADY C. [*To* GUY.] And I don't think *I*
could. You must tell your father that—that——

SIR H. Why shouldn't you all come and dine
here? That's a good idea, eh? What do you say,
Sylvia?

SYLVIA. [*Who has been talking beamingly to*

HAMILTON.] Yes? Say to what? I didn't hear.
[*To* GUY.] I'm dreadfully rude—do forgive me.

SIR H. [*To* LADY C.] Look here—is it going to be any sort of secret?

LADY C. You must ask Sylvia.

SYLVIA. Why should it be a secret? Especially from Guy. [*Looking up at* HAMILTON.]
He has always been one of us.

> [GUY *evidently perceives what is coming,
> and pulls himself together.*

LADY C. Yes—and always shall be.

> [*Evidently fond of him.*

SYLVIA. [*Going forward to him.*] Guy, dear, wish me—wish us both—happiness. I'm engaged to Maurice Hamilton.

GUY. [*Rather ruefully for a moment.*] Thought there was something in the air when I came in.
[*Recovering.*] I wish you everything—everything in the world that's good. You know it—dear old girl. Hamilton [*holding out his hand*] you're in luck.

HAMIL. Yes, I'm in luck.

GUY. [*Unconsciously retreating backwards towards the piano.*] When did it happen?

SYLVIA. Just now.

SIR H. No one knows it yet outside this room. You came in at the—the, what do'ye call it, psychological moment.

GUY. When's it to be?

Sir H. Nothing like Guy for coming straight to the point, eh?

Hamil. It's to be soon—as soon as possible; there's nothing to wait for.

Sylvia. Oh, I didn't say that.

Sir H. Trousseau, finery? As much as you like, my dear.

Guy. It's rough on me, anyhow.

Lady C. Rough on you?

Guy. I sha'n't be here to pew-open at the wedding.

Sir H. Oh! Not here?

Guy. I told the Governor this morning—going to make tracks for Japan——

Sylvia. Tracks for Japan?

Guy. That's it. I want to see what the world's like the other way up.

Sir H. Oh!

Guy. [*Solemnly.*] But I don't know how you'll get through it without me.

Sylvia. Neither do I. Couldn't you put the Japanese off for a bit?

Guy. [*Backing towards the piano—looks round him with somewhat forced merriment.*] I fear not. It's now or never for the little Japanese— the time has come and the Governor's willing— so we'll have a little tune.   [*Begins to play.*
    " Did you ever see the devil——"
    [Lady C. *makes a little gesture.*]

LADY C.   That everlasting song!

SIR H.   He'd sing it in church if he came, wouldn't he?

GUY.   Rather.   [*Sings*

[SYLVIA, *laughing, goes a step nearer the piano.*

SIR H. [*Joins in lustily.*]

" Did you ever see the devil
   With his wooden pail and shovel——"

   Enter SERVANT *with a note, hands it to* SIR HENRY.   GUY *continues to play softly.*

SIR H. [*Reading note.*]   It's from Madame Bunsen.

GUY. [*Stops.*]   Oh, yes, I forgot, I meant to tell you she's going away for a bit—this afternoon.

SYLVIA.   What does she say, father?

SIR H.   Says she has to go to the country suddenly; will I wait a week or ten days about the mare?   Of course I will.

GUY.   By George, you should have seen her this morning whirling round that school——

SYLVIA.   Isn't she wonderful?   I do like her so.   You know she came here the other day, Guy?

GUY.   No; I didn't hear that—came here?

SYLVIA.   And mother fell in love with her—sent her some flowers yesterday—Madame Bunsen was so pleased—she almost wept.

LADY C. I should like to know her history—there was something very attractive in her.

SIR H. Handsome woman—you've seen her—haven't you, Hamilton?

HAMIL. No; but I should like to—can't think why I haven't—she goes out with her pupils, doesn't she?

SYLVIA. Yes; but she always takes us outside London, right into the country, as fast as possible. You *must* see her—Maurice.

[*In a tone that shows the name is new to her.*

HAMIL. I want to see her.

SYLVIA. [*To* HAMILTON.] You might come to the school and look on at me, too.

HAMIL. [*Nods to her with a tender smile.*] I will.

[GUY *begins to play again, the Lohengrin Wedding March, and looks up at* SYLVIA *half-derisive, half-pathetic.*

SYLVIA. [*Laughing and confused.*] You horrid boy!

[*Lifts his hand from the keyboard.* HAMILTON, *who is standing well away from them, looks amused, and says nothing.*

LADY C. Some people won't have that March; they say it's unlucky.

SIR H. [*Who is looking at* MADAME BUNSEN'S *letter, turning to* HAMILTON.] Can't make out her name. Is it Julia—no Suzette?—curious hand she writes?

> [*Hands letter to* HAMILTON.
>
> [GUY, *who has got his hand free from* SYLVIA, *triumphantly launches into the Wedding March again.*

SIR H. You young scoundrel!

> [*Laughing, turns from* HAMILTON, *and going towards* GUY. SYLVIA *takes* GUY'S *hands off the piano again, with a happy laugh.*

HAMIL. [*Whom no one notices, looks at the letter as if transfixed.*] Juliet!

SIR H. Let's have the devil again. [*Begins to sing.*

> [GUY *plays it again, the group at the piano sing it.* HAMILTON *stands alone, petrified—the letter falls from his hand.*

CURTAIN.

ACT III

SCENE.—SYLVIA'S *sitting-room—a pretty white room with flowers, etc.—mullion window.*

TIME.—*Ten days later, morning.*

HAMILTON *and* SYLVIA *discovered sitting together.* SYLVIA *is happy all through this scene— confident in the future.* HAMILTON *is moody and absent, jerky and happy all by turns.*

SYLVIA. But, Maurice, dear, I thought you wanted to be in London. I have always lived in the country, except for three months every spring, and don't mind how quiet it is, nor how far away—I shall have you and that is all I want.

HAMIL. [*He lifts her hands and kisses them.*] And you won't miss the Debating Society?

SYLVIA. No, I shall miss nothing, and the Debating Society won't have married people. . . I long to explore the library at Briary Way— there are such lovely rows and rows of books—I should like to have a little writing-table of my own there——

HAMIL. You shall explore as much as you like—you shall have six writing-tables——

Sylvia. No, thank you, one will do. . . .
But I am certain to make all manner of changes.
I shall love to fuss about the house as mother
does—I look forward to it as part of—of——

Hamil. Part of the show? [*Amused.*] You
shall fuss to your heart's content.

Sylvia. I can't believe that I shall be living
there with you, in a little while. I think we ought
to have loose chintz covers in the drawing-room
—those brocaded ones are handsome—I only saw
them once of course—but——

Hamil. You shall have covers and curtains and
everything else you like, my dear. I was wonder-
ing to-day if you would care for some ponies to
drive. I might get you a pair.

Sylvia. I should love them—but we will ride
too—long rides? I can take them now—or all my
lessons will have been thrown away. You will let
me ride?

Hamil. Yes. [*With a little change in his manner.*]—If you like——

Sylvia. Madame Bunsen will be quite cut up
at your stopping my lessons. She was so kind to
me. She didn't say much, you know—she never
talked to the pupils—but she generally kept me
beside her on all those long rides into the country
this spring—[*with a little happy sigh.*] Oh! it
was lovely! I think she knew how much I liked
being near her.

HAMIL. [*Trying to hide his dismay.*] Did she?

SYLVIA. [*Nods.*] I used to find myself looking in her direction and listening to the least word she said. I mean to go and see her when she comes back.

HAMIL. Why should you—better not.

SYLVIA. Oh, but I should like to—and to tell her about you.

HAMIL. I would rather you didn't——

SYLVIA. [*Surprised but unsuspicious.*] Then I won't. She is not back yet.

HAMIL. I know—[*This is evidently a slip and he adds quickly.*] I inquired—I was passing—Perhaps you might send her a note of apology—that would be enough—and we shall be far away soon.

[*Pause, he crosses the room.*

SYLVIA. Do you know, Maurice, I think you have taken a dislike to your house in Kensington Square?

HAMIL. No, but I don't want to live there—at present.

SYLVIA. [*Quite unsuspiciously.*] I wonder you took a house at London.

HAMIL. I bought it on an impulse from Fisher, who was going off to Vienna. That day at Bexted when he stayed behind instead of going to hear your father's speech—I thought, for the first time, that perhaps you cared—— [*Sits*

SYLVIA. [*Softly.*]   I did!

HAMIL.   I was always a castle builder, and
when I saw that house, I had a vision of your going up and downstairs—lately I've sometimes fan-
cied I could hear your dress rustle and see you
coming down ready for the theatre or the Opera—
you told me once that you would like to go often
to the Opera [*she nods*]—you shall.

SYLVIA.   What else have you imagined, Mr.
Dreamer?

HAMIL.   Quiet evenings in the winter, sitting
by our fireside—you and I——

SYLVIA.   Opposite each other like Darby and
Joan?

HAMIL.   Perhaps sometimes they sat on the
same side?

SYLVIA.   I wonder——

HAMIL.   I think it's probable. . . . You
don't want dinner-parties or to know crowds of
people?

SYLVIA.   No, I don't. . . . [*Tenderly.*] All
the castles you have built shall stand and the
dreams come true.   Oh, we'll be so happy, but—
[*A little puzzled*] I don't think you believe it yet.

HAMIL.   Sometimes I don't . . . [*Gets up
and walks about, then stops suddenly.*]   I can't
. . . Say that it will go on—that you love me.

SYLVIA.   I love you.   I have said that a good
many times lately——

HAMIL. And the old mistake—my mistake, makes no difference—you are sure?

SYLVIA. I will make up to you for it——

HAMIL. And *nothing* shall come between us? You've gripped the facts—you know what you are doing?

SYLVIA. I gripped them that first day, and I have thought it all out since—I know what I am doing, *nothing* shall come between us.

HAMIL. [*With his arms round her.*] And you don't mind the quiet marriage?

SYLVIA. I like it better, there will be more *you* in it, and less crowd, than there would have been if we had the usual fuss.

HAMIL. And then we'll go away to the other side of the world.

SYLVIA. [*Quickly.*] Not to the *other* side of the world—we'll keep to this side, *our* side.

HAMIL. We will—*our* side—France and Spain.

SYLVIA. Or Italy—I've never been——

HAMIL. [*Uneasily.*] Not Italy. But we'll go to heaps of beautiful places——

SYLVIA. That you've never seen with any one else. [*With more meaning than she knows in her voice.*]

HAMIL. [*Repeating tenderly.*] That I've never seen with any one else. [*Passionately.*] Oh! Once more—it's too good to be true. I'm not too old for you, too battered, too grumpy and moody?

SYLVIA. No! And battered? You are *not* battered.

HAMIL. [*Taking her hands and kissing them.*]
I love you.

SYLVIA. [*Looking at her own hands which he
still holds.*] When is my ring coming back? I
wish it hadn't been too big, I want to wear it.

HAMIL. To-morrow. [*With a change of manner.*] By the way I've something else for you; I'd
forgotten that, what a ruffian I am! [*Feels in his
pocket.*] But where is it?

SYLVIA. Oh!

HAMIL. Oh! [*Mimicking her in fun.*] You
said that just like your father. [*Kisses her.*]

SYLVIA. [*Laughing.*] Did I?

HAMIL. [*Quite happy and gay.*] Where the
deuce is it? [*Feeling in his pockets.*] By Jove!
What did I do with it? What an ass I am, it's
not there—I can't have lost it.

SYLVIA. What is it? Do tell me.

HAMIL. It's something in a little case——

SYLVIA. Another ring?

HAMIL. [*Still busy with his pockets.*] No, not
another ring—yet—something else—to wear round
your neck. Oh! I suppose it's all right——

[*Sits down.*

SYLVIA. [*Laughing.*] What have you done with
it? Tell me what it's like.

Enter SERVANT *with little package on tray.*

HAMIL. By Jove! Is this it—perhaps I dropped it— Oh, no, it's too big.

SYLVLA. [*Taking package. Exit* SERVANT.] Why! It's Guy's writing. He's coming in this afternoon to say good-bye. [*Opens it.*] What a lovely bangle! It's a wedding gift. Oh, Maurice! a wedding gift, the first one I've had.

HAMIL. They'll come——

SYLVIA. [*Opens a note and reads.*] "Dear Sylvia, I'm not going to see you this afternoon, I've funked saying 'Good-bye,' and I'm off. Every good wish. Wear this sometimes in remembrance. Renewed congratulations to Hamilton. Your affectionate old playfellow, Guy." —Guy's gone! . . . Oh, I am so sorry!— I shall miss him.

HAMIL. He's a good chap—what an awfully nice bangle. [*Business.*

SYLVIA. [*Business with it.*] Isn't it a dear? But why—why didn't he come—I'm so sorry not to see him again—you can't think what he has been—all my life. His mother was my mother's greatest friend—that's why he calls her Aunt Peggotty.

HAMIL. I know, and you are all very fond of him—I'm awfully sorry for him, poor chap. . . . I say, do you mind if I rush back to the House and see if that thing is there? I might have left it in the cab and if so, I'll telephone to Scotland Yard—I'm rather uneasy about it. I shouldn't be more than a quarter of an hour gone. [*Gets up suddenly.*] Let's go together. Come with me—in a taxi.

SYLVIA. No. Go alone if you don't mind, I'll wait for you here. You'll be quicker without me, and I'm rather upset at not seeing Guy again.

HAMIL. [*With a little sympathetic sound.*] Of course you are! I'll be back in a quarter of an hour. [*Turns to go, then suddenly comes back, takes her face between his hands and looks at it gravely.*] My dearest, I love you!

[*Exit* HAMILTON.

[SYLVIA *alone, sits thinking, then gets up and makes business about the room. Looks at her bangle, rings the bell.*

Enter SERVANT.

SYLVIA. Judson, has the dressmaker sent?

JUDSON. No, miss.

SYLVIA. Let me know if she does.

JUDSON. Yes, miss. [*Exit.*

[SYLVIA *looks at her bangle again, puts it in the case, says "Dear old Guy"—goes to piano—plays a full minute or two.*

Enter JUDSON.

JUDSON. Could you see Madame Bunsen, Miss?

SYLVIA. Madame Bunsen? Oh, yes, certainly. Ask her to come in.

Enter MADAME BUNSEN *in walking dress.*

SYLVIA [*Going forward and holding out her hand.*] Madame Bunsen, I thought you were away still——

MADAME B. I have came back suddenly—sooner than I expected—I only went on business—I cannot bear the country, unless I am riding with my pupils.

[*Sits on chair Sylvia indicates.*

SYLVIA. Oh! But it's lovely—you seemed to like it on all those rides this Spring.

MADAME B. That was different. . . . Just as I was starting to come back I had a telegram—that is why I am here.

SYLVIA. A telegram?

MADAME B. I heard of a mare before I went away—I told Sir Henry. It belongs to one of my pupils who is going to Egypt. He promised to wait before deciding on anything.

SYLVIA. Yes, but——

MADAME B. She is going sooner than she expected, and telegraphed to the school. It was sent on to me. I got it this morning at the station—then ran from the house with it—she is so anxious to sell the mare—I think it is just what you want—don't say you have one.

SYLVIA.   I haven't—here, that is—but——

MADAME B.   Sir Henry told me the one you had in the country was no good for London— that it had a mouth like a money-lender's conscience——

SYLVIA.   I haven't—here, that is—but——

MADAME B.   He hasn't bought you one?

SYLVIA.   No, but I don't want one—now. I am going abroad, perhaps. Didn't you get my father's letter?

MADAME B.   Oh, no; has he written about it?

SYLVIA.   Yes, to the school.

MADAME B.   They only sent on the telegram, I haven't been there yet—I hurried here first. What did he say?

SYLVIA.   He wrote to tell you that—it is quite sad [*with a happy smile*]—I'm not coming to the school any more.

MADAME B.   Oh, I am so sorry—you are the pupil I have liked best—I shall miss you so. Why is it?

SYLVIA.   I fear there will be no time for any more lessons just at present—I'm—I'm going to be married—quite soon.

MADAME B.   [*Impulsively holding out her hands.*]   But that is good news, I'm delighted. I have looked at you sometimes and felt you would be so much loved—and now it has come true.

SYLVIA. Thank you, dear Madame Bunsen.
Yes, I am much loved——

MADAME B. That is why you look so happy!
I am not surprised, of course. I thought it was
coming. I knew it.

SYLVIA. But why?

MADAME B. Oh—h—I could see it—he's devoted to you.

SYLVIA. You don't know him?

MADAME B. But I have seen him very often
lately, and any one could tell that he loved you;
it was in his face——

SYLVIA. He went to ask if you were back
this morning, but he didn't say he knew you.
[*Puzzled.*] I wonder——

MADAME B. Oh, but he doesn't really, he
wouldn't call it knowing. He's delightful.
You've known him a long time?

SYLVIA. A little for a long time, but inti-
mately—only—not quite a year. He is our neigh-
bour in the country.

MADAME B. Not quite a year—but that *is*
a long time—unless you are cold—unless you are
insensible—and you are so tender. You have had
time to love him—to adore him. A year! A
lifetime can be lived in a year.

SYLVIA. [*Carried away by the other's emotion.*] It doesn't seem long, it has gone so
quickly.

MADAME B. [*Not noticing* SYLVIA'*s remark and going on quickly.*] I married—for the first time—a man I'd only known a month.

SYLVIA. For the first time! You've been married twice?

MADAME B. Yes, twice. And the first time I might have been happy, I could have been—[*in a low voice*]—but it was all a sad mistake—for him and me, too—and the second time I was miserable, because—[*with a shudder*]—but he's dead—one mustn't speak ill of the dead—and I oughtn't to speak of these things at all—you must forgive me. [*Rising, and her manner becomes a little distant and strained, as if she remembered that intimacy was not desirable.*] Let me give you my congratulations. It's not likely that we shall meet again—unless you come back after you are married. I am glad I came to-day—and that I came the other day, too, and saw your mother—she was very kind to me.

SYLVIA. She liked seeing you so much.

MADAME B. And now I know what you look like in your home.

SYLVIA. This is my own little sitting-room.

MADAME B. [*Walking round it.*] It looks like you. . . . I shall think of you here. [*Stopping by the window.*] There is the garden, I shall imagine you walking in it with your bridegroom——

SYLVIA. I hadn't thought of him by that name. I notice that you so often use words that seem almost foreign, and you make your sentences sometimes as if you were not English.

MADAME B. My father was Italian, and I suppose even modes of speech descend to one.

SYLVIA. [*Vaguely.*] Italian?

MADAME B. Yes, Italian. . . . Well, I'm glad I came—I wonder if ever I shall see you again—perhaps not. Good-bye. I hope you will be very happy—that he loves you—loves you—not a little, but with all his heart, before all things—before his work—before everything.

SYLVIA. He does—I know he does.

MADAME B. Dear child, I am glad—it must be such joy—and may you give him as much as he does you.

SYLVIA. I do—I will.

MADAME B. [*With a sigh.*] Good-bye.

> [*Takes her hand, holds it, and then impulsively and yet half afraid kisses her.*

SYLVIA. Dear Madame Bunsen, I shall never forget you. I hope you will be happy, too—in the future—you must have had so much trouble, and yet you look so young.

MADAME B. I'm thirty-three.

SYLVIA. And you've been married twice!

MADAME B. [*As she half turns to go.*] Twice.

The first time at nineteen—and the second time
when I was twenty-two.

SYLVIA.   The second time when you were
twenty-two! But how soon your happiness was
over—the first time.

MADAME B.   It hardly came—I waited for it
—but it never came.

SYLVIA.   He died so soon?

MADAME B.   He didn't die.

SYLVIA.   He didn't die.——   [*Looking at her
doubtfully.*

MADAME B.   He divorced me.

SYLVIA.   Oh! [*Slowly.*] He divorced you?
        [*An almost unconscious suspicion takes
            possession of her.*

MADAME B.   Ah! I oughtn't have said it—
you are shocked. Why did I? You mustn't repeat it, not to any one in the world.

SYLVIA.   I am sorry, and I will not repeat it.
        [*She has grown cold, and almost fright-
            ened, she is watching* MADAME BUN-
            SEN, *who goes towards the door, then
            stops again.*

MADAME B.   Good-bye. My congratulations
to Mr. Armitage.

SYLVIA.   To Mr. Armitage? He has gone
away. Didn't his sister tell you?

MADAME B.   No. [*With a smile and forced
brightness.*] He'll be back soon, of course?

SYLVIA. Not for a year.

MADAME B. Not for a year! But—it's Mr. Armitage you're going to marry?

SYLVIA. Oh, no! You've made a mistake. It is Mr. Maurice Hamilton.

MADAME B. [*With a cry, staggers back.*] Maurice!

> [*She tries to smother the name.*

SYLVIA. [*Bewildered and hardly able to speak.*] You know him?

MADAME B. [*Trying to control herself.*] I did—a long time ago—he is very clever—he is like no one else in the world—and you love him —you will make him happy——

SYLVIA. [*Holds out her hand to prevent her from going away.*] Madame Bunsen, were you —was it *you* he divorced?

> [*They look at each other for a moment, before* MADAME B. *can make herself answer.*

MADAME B. Yes, he divorced me. I deserved it; it was my fault, not his. You knew—he had divorced some one?

SYLVIA. Yes. [*Rigidly.*] He told me you were on the other side of the world.

MADAME B. [*With a little harsh laugh.*] And I thought he was there—I never dreamt he was back in England—and here! You must let me go—I would give my life not to have come here

to-day. It was as if something irresistible drove
me—to you—to this house.

> [*Goes towards the door.*
>
> *Enter* HAMILTON.
>
> [*They stare at each other for a moment
> in silence,* SYLVIA *unconsciously re-
> treats, pale and stony.*

HAMIL. [*Looking at* MADAME BUNSEN, *stag-
gered.*] Juliet!

MADAME B. Yes, Maurice, it is I.

HAMIL. What are you doing here?

MADAME B. It was chance, it was fate, it
was not intentional——

HAMIL. What did you come for? What does
it mean?

MADAME B. You must let her tell you. [*Bows
her head as if stricken.*]

> [*Exit* MADAME BUNSEN.
>
> [SYLVIA *and* HAMILTON *are left staring
> at each other aghast and silent.*

HAMIL. What did she come for?

SYLVIA. It *is* Madame Bunsen?

HAMIL. Yes.

SYLVIA. But you knew before; why didn't you
tell me?

HAMIL. I couldn't.

SYLVIA. You went to try and find her this
morning——

HAMIL. I sent—to ask if she had returned—
I couldn't explain then——

SYLVIA. Why did you say she was on the
other side of the world?

HAMIL. I thought she was—till the hour we
were engaged.

SYLVIA. Till the hour we were engaged?

HAMIL. We were at the piano—do you remember Guy came in—while he was playing a
note was brought to your father?

SYLVIA. Yes——

HAMIL. He gave it to me to read. I recognised her writing—her name, Juliet.

SYLVIA. Oh, how cruel! This is why you
have been so strange at times?

HAMIL. Yes.

SYLVIA. You should have told me.

HAMIL. I couldn't. I have not known an
hour's peace since—even with you——

[*A long pause.*

SYLVIA. [*Slowly.*] Maurice. It's no good
—I can't do it——

HAMIL. What do you mean?

SYLVIA. It undoes it—it puts an end to it all.

HAMIL. Why should it put an end to it all?
What did she say?

SYLVIA. It's nothing that she said. But can't
you see that it's different—it's different alto-

gether. When I thought she was thousands of miles away, when I had never seen her, or heard her voice—when I knew nothing about her—then she was an abstraction, a legend, she was dead, she was more than dead, but now—I couldn't do it—couldn't—couldn't.

HAMIL. We will go away—we will go to the farthest ends of the earth if you like.

SYLVIA. It would make no difference. I've known her, taken her hand, she's a living woman —I can't do it.

HAMIL. Why should that make such a difference? She's another man's wife.

SYLVIA. The other man is dead!

HAMIL. Dead! [*Goes back a step.*]

SYLVIA. Didn't you know?

HAMIL. I knew nothing about her. Nothing since the day I heard she was married to Farence and had gone back to Auckland with him. I sent my lawyer to the school this morning, and told him to offer her any sum of money I could manage—to say and do anything that was possible to induce her to go back—to go anywhere —out of Europe—that can be done still.

[*Pause.*

SYLVIA. It would be no good, I couldn't do it—Maurice, it is all over——

HAMIL. But explain, why should you throw me over now?

SYLVIA. [*Passionately.*] How could I marry a man knowing that another woman whom I'd seen and heard, remembered his loving *her,* remembered his kisses—his caresses just as now I had them—remembered their wedding day—and knew by her own memories all that he said to me—that she went over it all in her thoughts—sat alone—by her fireside, imagining the very manner in which we sat by ours—even the things we said—oh—no, no.

HAMIL. It was the other man she cared for —she wouldn't feel all this——

SYLVIA. She would—she would—a woman knows. If she were dead it would be different——

HAMIL. You said when we had our talk in the garden, that you felt she was less my wife than if she were in her grave, and she and I had loved each other to the end. For then there might have been times when I wondered if in some other existence she knew of the new life I had made—and felt that I had forgotten *her*——

SYLVIA. [*Hopelessly.*] Yes—I said it.

HAMIL. But now that is impossible—she and I are absolutely apart.

SYLVIA. I know—I meant it—I had thought it all out, but I'd not been put to the test. Now I know it would be easier to marry you remembering her dead—than as it is. I argued

to the contrary with my mother—I had an answer
to all her arguments—but words are only sounds,
and theories are dry husks——

HAMIL. Dry husks! [*With a miserable half-
laugh.*] It sounds like the Debating Society.

SYLVIA. Oh, yes, if you like—and the Debating Society is no good. Nothing is any good but
human experience, then one knows—one's instinct
—one's heart tells one. It isn't as if I had seen
her just this once—though even that would be
enough—I saw her every day for weeks. She
kept me beside her as we rode into the country
twice a week this spring. Once I went early
to school and met her by the entrance; she held
my hand for a minute—just now she kissed me
—it went through me—thrilled me—there was
meaning in it all—it was this.

HAMIL. And you are not made of the stuff,
you've not the courage to throw everything to
the winds for the man you love, as thousands
of women do?

SYLVIA. She did, I suppose, for the other
man—and brought misery on you. I've not *that*
courage. I believe I would go down a precipice
for you, but not if it dragged you down. But
this is beside the point—it's no question of courage.

HAMIL. Have you no thought of my happiness, no consideration for my point of view?

SYLVIA. Oh, I have, but I can't do it—it's no good, Maurice, I can't: it's the penalty of the sin that she committed.

HAMIL. And why should it be visited on me?

SYLVIA. [*Staring at him, and speaking as if she were listening to some one, or to some higher self.*] But that is the mystery of it all. The wrong thing is done, the crooked deed put into the world, and shame and misery hang on to it and trail after it on and on, ever so far, through generations perhaps—so many wrong things are done, and innocent people suffer for them— that is the tragedy of the world. I've thought it out so often—it's the Debating Society, you'll say again—no matter what it is—it is wrecking us.

HAMIL. [*Impatiently, desperately.*] Cast everything to the winds and come to me. We love each other.

SYLVIA. I can't, I can't do it, Maurice, now that I've seen her. I even love you differently —I shall love you always and think of you— but differently.

HAMIL. Oh, it's madness, it's folly.

SYLVIA. Yes, it may be. But the great events in our lives are shaped by folly as well as by wisdom, I can't do it—I can't, indeed. I could never feel your arms round me again, and not remember the woman who, perhaps, was think-ing of us—of all she had lost—that I had——

HAMIL. Heaps of women marry men who have divorced their wives.

SYLVIA. Other women may, I can't. My own happiness is wrecked on this discovery as well as yours—and somehow I'm so sorry for her—for a moment I saw into her heart and soul as she stood there. Can't you understand how im-possible it has all become? We are not all made alike. It is no good blaming me for what I am, or blaming her perhaps for what she is—*I* am so made that I cannot be or do all that was my dearest hope an hour ago.

HAMIL. It's useless, I see it. I say it—to my desolation and misery. I scout it, and am desperate. I tell myself that what you say is nonsense, but I feel the truth of it. Give me your hands once more [*bends over her hands*] my dear—it has been too good a dream to come true. But I shall be better for it all my life. Forgive me all the pain I've caused you. I sup-pose I went too far away from the world in which men and women live now in my search for happiness—but it's over—and I've left you where I can never reach you. [*Goes toward door.*

SYLVIA. [*With a sob.*] Maurice! Maurice! What will you do—where will you go?

HAMIL. [*A gesture of dismay—despair—*

then turns and hesitates.]   Kiss me once more,
Sylvia!

SYLVIA.   I can't—[*Retreating a step.*]—it is
different—it would feel strange—and wrong——

HAMIL.   [*Bitterly.*]   You are right—it is different. . . .   Good-bye.   [*Exit* HAMILTON.

SYLVIA.   [*Desperately, holding out her arms,
with a cry, to the closed door.*]   He's gone!—
He's gone.

CURTAIN.

ACT IV.

SCENE.—HAMILTON'S *study in Kensington Square.
A comfortable room, with books, writing-
table, easy chairs, &c. Writing-table to* R.
C. *Fire burning in grate which faces audience. Door* L. C. *Window* R. *Lamp on
table, &c.*

TIME.—*Eight months have elapsed. Late afternoon.*

HAMILTON *discovered sitting at a writing-table,
he arranges papers, &c. Business.*

Enter BECKER *with letters on tray and evening
paper, which he puts on the writing-table.*

HAMIL. Oh—thank you.
[*Takes letters, throws paper on writing-
table.*
[BECKER *makes business at the fire—puts
on wood, &c.*

HAMIL. [*Looking up from letter and speaking with animation.*] Oh, Becker, I want to
tell you that this house is sold, the matter was
concluded this afternoon. I shall be going abroad

again in a month, and everything here will be finished up. Tell the servants—I wish them to know as soon as possible. Of course I shall do anything I can for them.

BECKER. Yes, sir. They'll be very sorry. We all hoped that as the house didn't go off while you were away that perhaps you would settle down a bit.

HAMIL. Not in England.

BECKER. It's remarkable it should sell directly you come back, sir, and it didn't all the time you were away.

HAMIL. Perhaps the agents weren't energetic enough.

BECKER. There was a good many come after it, too. One lady came every month, with an agent's order—but she wouldn't look at it till you were back. I'd like to know if it is her that's bought it.

HAMIL. No, it's a parson. A lady, what sort of a lady?

BECKER. Well, quite a lady, sir—Mrs. Enfield her name was; she came again to-day. I told her you were back, and she said she'd call again to-morrow. You see I didn't know it was sold.

HAMIL. Curious thing. . . . Well, the parson has it, Becker, so I'm afraid she can't. You'll tell the servants what I've said.

[*He turns to the table.*

[*Exit* BECKER.

[HAMILTON *looks at his letters again and puts them aside, gets up, takes up paper, stops, puts it down, pokes the fire, lights a cigarette, sits down doggedly as if determined to shut out everything.*

Enter BECKER.

BECKER. Colonel Dempster has called, Sir; will you see him?

HAMIL. [*Looks over his shoulder as* BECKER *enters.*] Ah! [*Jumps up quickly at the name.*] Certainly. Ask him to come in.

[*Exit and re-enter* BECKER.

BECKER. Colonel Dempster.

Enter COL. DEMPSTER. [*Exit* BECKER.

COL. D. My dear fellow, I'm so glad to have caught you.

HAMIL. [*Going forward.*] I'm awfully glad to see you.   [*Grasping his hand.*

COL. D. Was vexed to be away when you returned. However, here I am. [*Takes off his coat.*] You got back a week ago, I hear! Glad to be in England again? [*They sit.*]

HAMIL. No, only came back for some business—and to see you—going away again, directly things are tidied up here.

COL. D. H'm, sorry for that—hoped you were

thinking better of it, was afraid you weren't though, when I saw the board up outside.

HAMIL. It will be pulled down to-morrow. The house is sold—matter concluded to-day——

COL. D. [*With a grunt.*] What are you going to do?

HAMIL. Don't know——

[*Pause, hands the cigarettes.*

COL. D. [*Lights one.*] Not made up your mind?

HAMIL. Some idea of going to Egypt for the fag-end of the winter—wish you'd come with me——

COL. D. Can't, I'm afraid. I should like it. . . . Seen any one since you came back?

HAMIL. No. . . . Have you seen any one lately?

COL. D. Everybody, been here all the time.

HAMIL. [*Uneasily.*] You know what I mean.

COL. D. Of course I do, but I was afraid to mention it.

HAMIL. You needn't, so go on. I'm not a sentimental fool—that's all over—though I curse myself at intervals for having disturbed her life.

COL. D. Well, she's got over it pretty quickly. [HAMILTON *looks up.*] You don't seem to know?

HAMIL. What?

COL. D. She's going to marry that boy.

HAMIL. You mean Armitage? [*Sound of dismay.*] Well, he's a lucky chap.

COL. D. Am not sure that I agree with you, I was rather disgusted to tell you the truth, might have waited a year, at least.

HAMIL. My dear Dempster, she's the sweetest girl on earth. A heart's often caught in the rebound. I am glad that I didn't cost her as much as I feared. [*Pause.*] I don't feel sure that at the back of her head or the back of her heart, she wasn't always in love with him—but nothing occurred to make her aware of it, till I upset her peace.

COL. D. Well, I must say I thought she was fond of you from the look of matters.

HAMIL. She was. And she's a clever girl, or thinks herself one, and she liked talking to a man a good deal older than herself, liked winning him. She was probably a little bit in love with the situation, and a good deal more with her own splendid courage and compassion.

COL. D. Humph. Where do the splendid courage and compassion come in?

HAMIL. Compassion for the mull I'd made of my life—courage when she'd reasoned it out with herself and took me in spite of all the prejudice against divorce in which she had been brought up—and the opposition of the mother.

COL. D. She should have stuck to you.

HAMIL. She would, but for—what happened. I perfectly understand her point of view.

COL. D. Well, I don't—I dined there a fortnight ago. Am glad to say I wasn't put next the young lady, or I mightn't have been very agreeable.

HAMIL. I wonder if she ever thinks of me?

COL. D. I'm coming to that. After we went upstairs, she managed to get me into a corner, and asked after you.

HAMIL. What did she say?

COL. D. Wanted to know when you were coming home.

HAMIL. Anything else?

COL. D. Said she'd give the world if some happiness would come to you.

HAMIL. [Sound of derision.] One doesn't get that very often—doesn't matter! I shall take the makeshifts and get along, I daresay. Anything else?

COL. D. She told me—I think she must have meant me to say it to you, somehow—that now she couldn't marry anybody else—but Guy— she'd known him always——

HAMIL. [A little cynically.] That's it—depend upon it she cares for him more than she imagines. Thank God she does.

COL. D. Callender told me the boy had always been devoted to her. It seems he started for Japan directly he heard she was going to marry you, started back the moment he heard she wasn't.

HAMIL. Nothing like promptness in these matters.

COL. D. [*Looking round.*] Why, you have got an evening paper—there's a paragraph—the announcement——

HAMIL. [*Makes a quick involuntary movement forward, then back.*] Plenty of time—I'll look at it presently.

COL. D. I must be going. [*Gets up.*] Only looked in to make sure you were here.

HAMIL. [*Hesitatingly.*] Have you seen or heard anything of—of—Juliet?

COL. D. Only what Callender told me.

HAMIL. Callender?

COL. D. It seems he went round the next morning. He admired her and wanted to say something kind, I believe. He's a soft-hearted old man—she had vanished—completely. The school is sold—a man called Johnson runs it now.

HAMIL. I knew that.

COL. D. [*Half afraid, and with a touch of tenderness.*] She was a wonderful creature, I shall never forget her—[*Stops abruptly.*]

HAMIL. I wish you'd come up the Nile with me.

Col. D. Wish I could, my dear fellow, but there's no chance of it. Perhaps I'll meet you on the way back in April—I must be off. Shall we dine together to-morrow?

Hamil. Should like it.

Col. D. Good. United Service at eight.

Hamil. [*Fidgeting with a cigarette, and trying not to look eager.*] Do you know when the marriage is to be?

Col. D. In a fortnight.

Hamil. Ah! I shan't be here.

Col. D. Off so soon?

Hamil. [*Nods.*] I can't stand this climate, and a wandering life suits me.

Col. D. Well—to-morrow. [*Exit.*

Hamilton *goes with him, returns in a moment, shuts the door, seizes the paper, searches for paragraph.*

Enter Becker.

Hamil. [*Sits down at writing-table.*] Oh, did I ring, I did so inadvertently, but since you are here you may as well know—that I am going away even sooner than I had intended—the end of next week at latest.

Becker. Yes, sir. That lady I told you about has called again, sir.

Hamil. Tell her the house is sold—I am sorry—if she wanted it.

Enter very softly, behind Becker, Madame Bun-

SEN. HAMILTON's *back is turned. He is busy with his letters, etc.*

BECKER. [*Embarrassed, but making the best of it.*] Mrs. Enfield would like to see you, sir.

[MADAME BUNSEN *signs to* BECKER *to go.*

HAMIL. I can't see her Becker—or any one. Say I am sorry the house is sold.

[*But* BECKER *has gone, the door is shut.*
MADAME BUNSEN *is standing a few feet inside the door.*   [*Pause.*

MADAME B. Maur—ice.

[HAMILTON *gives a start, looks round and rises quickly.*

HAMIL. You!

MADAME B. Yes, I.

HAMIL. How did you get here?

MADAME B. I called myself, Mrs. Enfield, and followed the servant in. I had to see you. I *must* speak to you.

[*While she speaks, he retreats a little to the other side of the fireplace and stands where* COLONEL DEMPSTER *had sat.*

HAMIL. I have no wish to see you—or to speak to you.

MADAME B. [*Entreating, but firm.*] But I must—I must speak——

HAMIL. You will be good enough to go. [*Puts out his hand to ring the bell which is on the left.*]

[*As he does so, she springs forward.*

MADAME B. No! Not yet!

[*He, as if to escape her touch, retreats a
    little to the right with a shrinking
    movement.*

There is fair play for every one—even for me,
and you must let me speak. You won't let me
write to you. I went to the lawyers, the letters
are there unopened.

HAMIL.   There is nothing to write about. It
is no good trying to varnish over the facts. You
have destroyed my chances of happiness twice
over, there is nothing to be said—about anything.

MADAME B. If I have destroyed it *three* times,
it is no reason for my being treated with in-
justice. I want you to listen—are you afraid?

HAMIL.   Afraid?

MADAME B. [*Scornfully.*] Yes, afraid—you
must be—if you will neither open my letters nor
hear what I have to say.

HAMIL.   If you have anything to say, put it
into three words—and then be good enough to
go.

MADAME B. You say I destroyed your happiness twice——

HAMIL.   We needn't go into the first occasion;
on the second you destroyed all that, after years
of isolation and bitterness, seemed to be in
sight.

MADAME B. [*Amazed.*] You think I went to her on purpose?

HAMIL. You went [*with a shrug*] and the result you know, of course.

MADAME B. [*Breathlessly.*] I went, but—Maurice—I had no idea—I did not dream—of—what was going on. I did not even know you were in London—or in England—I did not know where you were.

HAMIL. You could easily have discovered—this is nonsense.

MADAME B. [*Scornfully.*] You are insulting —as one would expect a man to be who will neither hear one—nor read one's letters. Listen! I never came across your name. I know now that it was printed often, in connection with political things, but I never read political things. I knew nothing—nothing—about you. Two years ago, when I came back to England, I tried to find out where you were. I went to Worcester —and stayed at the little inn near your sister's house.

HAMIL. The Forester—yes.

MADAME B. I heard that you were in South America—I thought London was safe to me— that probably you were never coming back. I started the riding-school—it was the only thing I could do, and called myself "Madame Bunsen." I knew no one—made no acquaintance—I

spoke with the pupils, but that was all. I liked
that fair girl—something drew me to her—I think
she liked me—because I took pains with her riding, perhaps. One day she brought me some
flowers from her garden—her mother sent them.

HAMIL. [*Cynically.*] Her mother!—I remember.

MADAME B. Her father came sometimes to
look on at her. And Mr. Armitage with his sister—they were all friends together——

HAMIL. This has nothing to do with it. Why
did you discover yourself to Miss Callender? I
should have had to tell her—but——

MADAME B. [*Not allowing him to finish.*] I
went about a mare—that one of the pupils wanted
to sell—a girl who was going away—she had telegraphed. Miss Callender told me she had given
up the riding lessons because she was going to
be married. I congratulated her, thinking that it
was Mr. Armitage. She said, " No, it was Mr.
Maurice Hamilton." I had not heard the name
spoken except by my own lips for years—it went
to my heart like a sword. It forced a cry from
me—I betrayed myself. And then you entered
—I remember nothing more. Oh! [*With a passionate shudder of pain.*]

HAMIL. Thank you for explaining it—I am
glad to know. [*Goes towards the bell.*]

MADAME B. Stop, Maurice—once more. We

shall never meet again, I will take care of that; there is no occasion to be brutal.

HAMIL. I have no wish to be brutal.

MADAME B. I want you to know that I wouldn't have done it had I known, I would rather have died. I *have* nearly died since, I think, with the misery, the madness, the knowledge that I had again destroyed your life. I must have been sent into the world to do it—twice over—and each time not knowing it.

HAMIL. [*Bitterly.*] You must have known the first time pretty well.

MADAME B. [*Impetuously.*] Oh, that's because you don't understand—men cry out when women do this or that, but they never see how they have helped——

HAMIL. Helped! [*Sound of impatience.*] What you did needed little understanding to make it plain.

MADAME B. [*Bitterly.*] And even that you hadn't—you were always dense—you are now—you never had much passion in you—you never set your love for me above all else in life—or things would not have happened as they did.

HAMIL. This is rather a strange charge and the last I should have thought you could bring against me—remembering how I was carried away by my love for you——

MADAME B. And yet you couldn't make it

strong enough to hold me. When you married me, I was nineteen—I had known you one month —not a month. How was I to know your ways— or the manner in which you expressed yourself? My father was my mother's lover till the hour he died—he lived at her feet—she had lovers always, all her life—I grew up among them, and to be a woman and not loved—not loved enough— seemed terrible!

HAMIL. Not loved enough! [*Amazed.*] Why, from the moment I saw you first—I adored you.

MADAME B. For a month, the month before we were married, you lived for me; you brought me flowers and jewels and sweets, and the first days of marriage you loved me—you loved me. [*Passionately.*] I felt it. But before we were at the end of the voyage you had changed a little.

HAMIL. I had not changed—I was going out to my post—there were things I had to think of —I had my work, you were too young to be interested in it.

MADAME B. I know, but I didn't want you to think of anything but me, I wanted you to be my lover always. I will tell you something— I did not love you very much when you married me—I'd known you but a little while—but it was natural to be married, and I was flattered and pleased. Three months afterwards I could have died for love of you. There came suspicion and

jealousy—my father's Italian blood, perhaps, that
rose and mastered me——

HAMIL. Suspicious and jealous of *me?*

MADAME B. Yes. Jealous of everything that
took you from me—suspicious of your absences.
You expected me to take your love for granted,
it maddened me that you could bear me out of
your sight—that you sent me away from you.

HAMIL. You mean that I sent you up to Simla?
It was impossible to keep you down in the heat.

MADAME B. But I would have borne the heat
—wanted you only to think of *me*—of having
me with you—with you though it killed me—that
is what a woman likes. And when you came you
were not impatient enough—not jealous of all the
men who hung about me—and I wanted you to
be. Out of your sight no one had a word or
look from me. But when you came I was desperate and wanted to make you see that you must
love me—guard me—think of me—but you didn't
care, you didn't care enough.

HAMIL. I never dreamt of all this. Why
didn't you tell Mrs. Sinclair?—she would have
told you——

MADAME B. I was too proud. I was so young
and undisciplined, and it's her heart that governs
such a girl as I was. Why didn't you know—
then you would have held me? Why did you
trust me so?

HAMIL. Is a man not to trust the woman who is his wife?

MADAME B. Not a girl of my temperament. You took an exotic and sent it to a place where all the sights and sounds nourished it. And you were so calm—oh! that calmness drove me mad— so certain you were safe. It didn't occur to you to assure yourself that you were, or to make me swear every day that I was the same. When one is young as I was, nothing in the world matters but love—I thought that nothing else should exist —I thought that if I made you jealous it would rouse you—that was how it all began. Archie Farence was reckless, and loved me, I wanted you to see that he did—but you were blind and saw nothing. He told me that you didn't care—that you couldn't—*couldn't*——

HAMIL. This is amazing—this state of mind— it never entered my head—I thought you knew that I was devoted to you—I worked chiefly to give you the things that would make you happy —and I trusted you.

MADAME B. Yes, you trusted me—too much— nineteen—and half Southern. . . . Do you remember the last time you came to Simla? You were so preoccupied you forgot to bring the neck- lace you had taken away to have mended, before the dance at the Whartons'—it was another proof

of how little you thought of me while you were
absent. I don't know how it came about—I
swear I don't, Maurice. It seemed as if taunting
fiends gathered about me that night—and you
were so cold and preoccupied, you sat at your
table writing, sheet after sheet—I longed to tear
them into strips——

HAMIL. There had been two cases of cholera,
and I was anxious about you—didn't want you
to know how anxious——

MADAME B. [*With a cry.*] Oh! If I had
guessed—how could I? But you said——

HAMIL. Well?

MADAME B. You said you would come on to
the Whartons' and you didn't. Farence was there
adoring me. There was one moment in the garden, after a dance, when he stooped and kissed
the ground I had stood on. [*Turns away.*] The
end of it was that I went off with him. It was
half done from longing to make you jealous, to
make you suffer. Oh! If I could make you feel
for a single minute the storm that raged in my
heart. The man who was with me was intoxi-
cated with passion, was jealous if he suspected
I was thinking of you. He told me he would
strangle me if I even looked at another man—*that*
seemed to me to be the real thing—but I only took
it from *him* because *you* had not given it me.

HAMIL.   And you mean that you did not even leave me for a man you loved better?

MADAME B.   As God lives, no, Maurice, I left you on an impulse, an hour's desperate reign of one passion in a hurricane of many passions, and before the day came when as a matter of honour he married me, I was the most miserable woman in the world.

HAMIL.   He loved you after your own fashion at any rate.

MADAME B.   No, not even that.   There came an awful awakening, it made me shudder—it made me loathe him—long before he left me.

HAMIL.   He left you!

MADAME B.   I drove him away—I shrank from him—and oh, the peace of the day he went—and I was thankful for the beggary that came——

HAMIL.   Beggary?   That too!

MADAME B.   Yes.   And pain and misery of every sort.   But not vice, Maurice, I kept clear of that.   I have loved no man but you, and sinned only with that other.   As God in Heaven lives I swear that to you.

HAMIL.   Why didn't you take the money I tried to settle on you at the time of the divorce?

MADAME B.   That would have been the last depth of all.

HAMIL.   Did Farence do nothing for you?

MADAME M.   [*With a shudder.*]   I sent it back

—I was only an incident—that was part of my degradation. His friends forgave him—men are often forgiven—women never——

HAMIL. It must be so. It may be cruel, but it has to be. We put them so high—that when a woman sins it is the betrayal of a Christ—and even the man who is the Judas can't forgive her.

MADAME B. I know—I know.

HAMIL. Where were you when Farence died?

MADAME B. In Australia. I never saw him again. He died in England.

HAMIL. And what did you do all those years?

MADAME B. I nearly starved at first. I was ill—broken [*shuddering*] and in the Melbourne hospital for months. There was a horse-dealer's wife in the bed next to mine—when I was better, she made her husband hire me to ride the horses he wanted to sell. It was the only thing I could do and I liked it. The quick movement—the long gallops into the bush—the mystery I was to them, for they knew nothing. That was how the years went by. At last I could bear it no longer—I had saved some money, it brought me to England. I crept to the inn at Worcester and asked for you, as I told you. My mother had died—refusing to forgive me—but she left me what she had—little enough—I saw an advertisement of a riding-school and bought it, and suddenly prosperity came.

HAMIL. [*Gently.*] I'm glad to have heard this —and I am sorry for all you have suffered. [*Takes a step as if going forward to the bell.*] I wish we had both been different.

MADAME B. [*Despairingly, going between him and the bell.*] Once more—not yet. Oh! Maurice, these minutes are the last we shall ever have together.

HAMIL. Why did you come to-day, and why have you been trying to see me all these months?

MADAME B. I couldn't bear it any longer— I felt I must see you—just once more. I knew all that you had thought me—I wanted to make it plain—to show you how it had been, to—to make you hate me less——

HAMIL. I don't hate you—you poor child. . . The crooked deed always sows pain and misery. You have reaped it and I have not escaped. Probably *you* thought as *I* did that peace had come, till the day we met—in that room that looked over the garden.

MADAME B. I would have given worlds not to have gone. I should have died if you had married her, but I wouldn't have prevented it——

HAMIL. *You* died, if I had married *her!*

MADAME B. Yes—died—died, I think. For all these years, even in the first mad one in which I left you, I've loved you—that has been my pun-

ishment, my harvest—to see your figure clear and
distinct in the distance before me, and to know
I should never reach it, to know that some day
you would give all that I had left—to another
woman. I knew it must come, and I have tor-
tured myself imagining her—fair and good, and
all that I was not—I have seen your face turned
towards her and heard your whispers without being able to catch the words, and I've killed her in
my thoughts—and put *my* face against yours and
my arms where hers had been, and love for me—
not for *her*—but for *me*—into your heart again.
A maddening dream of joy—I have clenched my
hands and locked my teeth to keep the cry of misery from my lips when it was over—[*Change of
manner.*]   I didn't mean to betray all this but
I am glad I have said it—it has come. You shall
never see me again—or hear—or know. [*Takes
up a wrap which she had left on chair.*]

HAMIL. [*Who is carried away by her passion.*]
Juliet! Is all that you have said the truth?

[*Goes towards her as she turns to go.*

MADAME B. I've never lied to you, Maurice;
even I have not done that.

HAMIL.   You mean that you have loved *me*
all these years?

MADAME B. [*In a low, tragic voice.*]   All these
years and every day of them. You cannot say
that you have loved me—as I would you if you

had left me. You went to the fair girl—and loved her——

HAMIL. Yes—I loved her.

MADAME B. I know—I saw her and felt it.

HAMIL. She was the expression to me of all that once I had imagined you would be when you were a little older.

MADAME B. No—no——

HAMIL. And from deep down in my heart, buried in bitterness and misery, often your face—as I saw it first—looked up at me.

MADAME B. Oh—no—no.

HAMIL. *She's* going to marry another man.

MADAME B. And you—are miserable.

HAMIL. No, I'm not miserable—it is over—it seems to have vanished—and all the other memories have come rushing back. Juliet! My poor whirlwind—my little lover—I used to call you that in the first month—I wish things had been different—with all my heart I wish it.

MADAME B. I would give my life—my every hope of heaven to have them so—or if you had left me, for then I would have forgiven you, and loved you more—because of the days I didn't dare remember. Ah! let me go——

HAMIL. No—no——

MADAME B. I can't bear it any longer.

HAMIL. [*Springing forward.*] You shall never go if I can help it. I am longing to take you back.

MADAME B. [*Bewildered.*] You forgive me?

HAMIL. Forgive you? It's *your* forgiveness I want, for my blindness, my seeming coldness—give it me—give it me—shall we put it all behind us, and start out across a new world? How could you think I didn't love you enough—you were so beautiful. Could you bear with me again? Shall we have another marriage-day, and begin life once more together?

MADAME B. Oh! no, no—I could bear the misery, the shame even—but such joy as that would kill me——

HAMIL. You shall live for it in my arms. [*Puts them round her.*] There is a harvest from suffering too—a harvest of peace.

MADAME B. [*Looking up at him dazed.*] For the dead—only for the dead——

HAMIL. For the living sometimes. Juliet—Juliet!

CURTAIN.

THOMAS AND THE PRINCESS

A PLAY IN FOUR ACTS

DRAMATIS PERSONÆ

THOMAS LOBB, *a boy* (*afterwards Robert Vallide*)
ROBERT VALLIDE (*formerly Thomas Lobb*)
ROBERT VALLIDE, SENR., *his uncle*
EARL OF BARNSTAPLE, *past middle age*
GEOFF, LORD STRATTON (*in the Guards*), *his son*
SIR JAMES CAXTON
COLONEL ENDSLEIGH, *Indian Staff Corps*
SIR GEORGE FISON, *a famous doctor*

LADY SARAH STRATTON, *Lord Barnstaple's sister*
LADY IDA, *his daughter*
LADY CAXTON (JULIA), *his niece*
THE HON. MRS. MURISON, *another niece*
MAY MURISON, *her daughter* (*a little girl of six
at first, not seen then*)
SERVANTS, &c.

ACT I., ENGLAND.
TIME: Seventeen years ago.
SCENE: (Interior) A drawing-room in Harford
      Terrace, Regent's Park.

ACT II., ITALY.
TIME: Present day. Afternoon.
SCENE: (Interior) Sitting-room in Lord Barn-
      staple's Villa at Alassio on the Italian
      Riviera.

ACT III., ITALY.
TIME: Ten days later. Late afternoon.
SCENE: (Exterior) Garden of the Villa.

ACT IV., ENGLAND.
TIME: Three weeks later.
SCENE: (Interior) A sitting-room on Campden
      Hill, W.

ACT I

TIME.—Seventeen years ago, about noon, on a spring day.

SCENE.—Interior. MRS. MURISON's house in Harford Terrace, Regent's Pàrk. Drawing-room well furnished, refined. Windows at back (not down to the ground) showing tops of trees, so as to suggest that the room is on the first floor. Fireplace on R.; door on L.

When Curtain draws up LADY SARAH is discovered on chair R. near the fire. She is middle-aged, handsome, and distinguished-looking, rather mannered.

Near centre of stage, MRS. MURISON, about twenty-six, a pretty, graceful woman, with a sweet but rather stiff manner, is talking with SIR GEORGE FISON, a celebrated doctor: they are both standing.

MRS. M. I can never thank you enough, Sir George.

SIR G. My dear lady, I am delighted to think the results have not disappointed us—I know what the child is to you——

MRS. M. Just my life——

LADY S. [*Sharply.*] More than either of the other two children; and then, you know, Doctor —I keep forgetting, I mean Sir George—I did congratulate you?

SIR G. You did, thank you very much——

LADY S. And then it's her first child.

SIR G. I know. And the father away, fighting for his country. [*To* MRS. M.] I hope you've good news?

MRS. M. None at all for the last few days; but he was safe then.

SIR G. Letters, of course, are difficult— though the War Office does all it can.

MRS. M. We owed so much to Gordon. And he wants to help to carry out his work in Egypt.

SIR G. Well, we are doing great things there . . . You must hope for the best. . . . Keep the child out of doors as much as possible.

MRS. M. I told nurse to wrap her up well.

SIR G. Quite right. You are fortunate in having this park at your front door.

MRS. M. I stand at the window and watch them half a mile away sometimes.

SIR G. Ah! [*Smiling.*] It's lucky for children that they have mothers.

> [*While they are speaking* THOMAS *enters with a scuttleful of coals, which he puts down by the fireplace. He is about ten, dressed in tidy but poor clothes, wears*

*a working apron, and has a refined, deli-
cate little face.* SIR GEORGE *looks at
him as he passes.* THOMAS *touches his
forelock. Exit.*

SIR G. [*About to go.*] Nice face that boy has.
Does not look very strong though. [*Shakes
hands.*] Glad to have seen you again, Lady
Sarah. I hope Lady Barnstaple is better?

LADY S. I've not seen her lately; I've been
staying at Hampton Court with my sister.

SIR G. Oh, yes—Lady Caroline Lismore.
[*To* MRS. M.] Your mother. I remember that
she went there after her husband died. I hope
she is not quite alone?

LADY S. Oh, no; she has a niece, poor Claude's
child—Julia—who is eighteen now. Perhaps you
don't remember her?

SIR G. Dear me, yes, I do. Her parents died
in India.   .   .   .   Well, good-bye. [*Turns
back.*] By the way, you didn't tell me how Lady
Barnstaple was?

LADY S. Not at all well. My brother has
bought a villa at Alassio, on the Italian Riviera,
for her.

SIR G. Humph! I'm sorry . . . The
children are well, I hope—Geoffrey and Ida,
isn't it? . . . Lord Barnstaple is making a
great name in the political world. [*To* MRS. M.]
Send for me if anything goes wrong.

MRS. M. I will—and thank you—thank you for all your kindness.

SIR G. Not at all.

[*Exit* SIR GEORGE. MRS. M. *rings the bell.*

LADY S. Well, Evelyn, that anxiety is over.

MRS. M. I hope so. [*Rings again.*] Thomas must be told not to come in when there are visitors here.

Enter SERVANT.

[*To* SERVANT.] Send Thomas to me—as soon as he has filled the scuttles. [*Exit* SERVANT.

MRS. M. [*To* LADY S.] He is the son of those poor people who had charge of the empty house next door; do you remember?

LADY S. Oh, yes, you made Turner cut off a great many slices of roast mutton for them when I was here six months ago, and had them sent, too before you ate your own.

MRS. M. Poor things, they were hungry—and needed a great many. Father and mother, and Thomas and Polly, and the poor skinny baby that died.

LADY S. A good thing it did, my dear, if it was skinny—it wouldn't always have had you to send it roast mutton. [*Evidently anxious to dismiss the subject.*] They were country people, you said——

MRS. M. The father was a Cornish man. He had been a carpenter, I think. I saw him one night warming his thin hands by the fire, and the next day when I went to see him he was dead—I put the flowers I had taken at his feet.

LADY S. [*Indifferently.*] Poor man! Better off, no doubt. And has the widow found another empty house to take care of?

MRS. M. No, she does a little charing, and we bought her a mangle; Polly goes to a board school, and Thomas carries out newspapers for the stationer round the corner, but as that's over at eight in the morning, and I wanted a boy to clean knives and boots, and carry up coals——

LADY S. You sent for Thomas.

MRS. M. He is such a good boy and he adores May——

LADY S. [*Impatiently.*] Of course he does . . . but I want to speak to you about your mother. I have hurried up to town because I have no patience with her—I never had much without her perhaps you will say.

MRS. M. Dear Aunt Sarah, I wouldn't be so rude; besides I love your impatience.

Enter THOMAS. *He touches his forelock and stands by the door.*

LADY S. [*Evidently angry at the interruption.*] Oh——

MRS. M. Come in, Thomas. . . . What is that bulging in your pocket—why it moves!

THOMAS. [*Pleased and important.*] It's some

white mice, M'm, for Miss May. Her brown one died just before she was took ill. . . . I got these a week ago and thought perhaps you'd let me give 'em to her to-day.

Mrs. M. Are they loose in your pocket?

Thomas. Tied up in a handkerchief. But I've mended the catch of the cage. I am glad to hear she's to go out, M'm.

Mrs. M. How did you know?

Thomas. I went up and asked nurse, directly after the doctor'd gone down. I thought he'd gone, M'm, or I wouldn't have come in with the coals just now.

Mrs. M. Oh, that was it—I wondered. Why didn't you give Miss May the mice when you went up?

Thomas. Didn't like to do that, M'm, till I'd asked you if you didn't mind——

Mrs. M. Oh—how nice of you.

Thomas. Thank you, M'm. It's a good thing [*with a different sound in his voice*] she's well, isn't it, M'm? [Mrs. Murison *nods.*] We were scared that night, all of us.

Mrs. M. We were indeed, Thomas. . . . Well, go up and give her the mice.

Thomas. [*With a little triumphant smile.*] They're as white as milk.

[*Touches his forelock to* Lady S. *and* Mrs. M.

[*Exit.*

LADY S. Nice boy; knows his place, and a little more human than most children of that class.

MRS. M. Human? Oh, Thomas is human enough. I shall never forget the night we thought May was going to die. I believe he sat on the steps all through it. The servants found him outside the area door at daylight half dead. They dragged him in, and when they told him that the crisis was over and she might live, he put his head down on the kitchen table and sobbed—the relief was too much. I shall always remember him when I think of that night. . . . [*Change of manner.*] Well, what has been happening at Hampton Court? You've been staying with mother, I hear.

LADY S. My dear Evelyn, your mother is driving me out of my mind. She is my sister, so I have a right to say what I think of her, even to you.

MRS. M. [*Amused.*] Yes, of course you have, Aunt Sarah—go on.

LADY S. She is a most worldly woman.

MRS. M. But why suddenly?

LADY S. Young Endsleigh has gone to India, as you probably know, without speaking to Julia——

MRS. M. I am certain they care for each other.

LADY S. Then he's an idiot not to have told her so. And Julia—a girl in love is always like an ostrich with his head in the sand—has been breaking her heart and thinks nobody knows it.

MRS. M. Mother couldn't help his not speaking.

LADY S. I believe she prevented him—any one could see that he was fond of Julia—at any rate he has gone, as she intended him to go, without declaring himself. And last night the poor child accepted Sir James Caxton, that stupid man who has just got in for Fieldborough.

MRS. M. Oh, no, Aunt Sarah—not Sir James? He's the dullest man in the world.

LADY S. He's an owl, but he's very rich and has no near relations.

MRS. M. He must be forty.

LADY S. I daresay. And depend upon it he'll live to be eighty.

MRS. M. How did it happen?

LADY S. Well, it has been quite evident that something was in the man's mind, for he went down five times in a fortnight, mooned about, and said nothing, stared at Julia, and went away as inarticulate as he came. It's a miracle to me how such an idea as marriage got into his head.

MRS. M. I can't think why he was returned for Fieldborough.

LADY S. Bribery, of course.

Mrs. M. Julia might marry any one, and at eighteen there's no hurry.

Lady S. Sir James is very rich and that appeals to your mother.

Mrs. M. [*Thoughtfully.*] And it's an excellent family of course. . . . Do you think he's in love?

Lady S. My dear, an owl doesn't fall in love. He wants to arrange himself in life, and is doing the best he can—from an owl's point of view. She'll run away in a year if Frank Endsleigh comes back, and then there'll be a pretty scandal.

Mrs. M. But why did she accept him?

Lady S. Your mother has been telling her that if anything happened to her, she would have to go out as a governess, or some nonsense, for of course, the dear Queen only gave those rooms at Hampton Court to your father's widow.

Mrs. M. I know.

Lady S. So she persuaded Julia that it was her duty to accept Sir James, and Julia is so miserable that she would marry anybody, or throw herself down a well, or do anything else she was told. I was extremely angry and came away the first thing this morning. At the station I telegraphed to Sir James to come and see me here at twelve o'clock.

Mrs. M. Here? Aunt Sarah! What are you going to do?

LADY S. I shall not mince matters: but it's twelve o'clock now; so perhaps he won't come— he is probably afraid, for my manner was not pleasant last night—I made it unpleasant.

MRS. M. That clock is five minutes fast. I can't think why mother hasn't written to me.

LADY S. She's coming up this afternoon, with Julia—coming here, to surprise you; that's why I did a really desperate thing, and wired to the man.

MRS. M. I am so amazed at your courage.

LADY S. I'm amazed, my dear Evelyn, that you don't appear to be shocked at your mother's conduct.

MRS. M. Poor mother, the money has dazzled her.

LADY S. And she has forgotten her own youth —it's extraordinary to me that women do. I'm fifty, but I know what it feels like to be in love as well as if I were twenty.

MRS. M. Many girls marry for money and are content. Think of Mary Wallingford, and that vulgar millionaire last year, do you remember?

LADY S. Of course I do—Mr. Ruddock—the ready-made clothing man—but he was clever at any rate. Sir James is so dull.

MRS. M. [*With a shudder.*] Yes; but it was

worse than this— When May grows up if she were to marry a man like Mr. Ruddock——

Enter THOMAS *with a telegram on a tray; he stands unnoticed for a minute and listens with wide open eyes at the mention of* MAY'S *name.*

LADY S. Or like Sir James?

MRS. M. I would rather see her married to a dull man like Sir James, than to some new-made millionaire who had been a tinker or a tailor, perhaps; and who, at the back of one's head, one knew ought to be sitting with the servants.

THOMAS [*Touching his forelock.*] Telegram, M'm.

MRS. M. Oh, I didn't see you, Thomas, you should speak. Wait—perhaps there's an answer. [*Takes up two telegrams from the tray.*] One for you, Aunt Sarah. [*Hands it to* LADY S.] [*To* THOMAS.] Why didn't Turner bring them in?

THOMAS. I told her I would, M'm, 'cause mother's here and wants to know if you can see her for a minute.

LADY S. [*Reading her telegram.*] "With you at 12.15." He's coming!

MRS. M. [*Reading her telegram.*] Mother has telegraphed that she and Julia will be here at four. [*To* THOMAS.] No answer. . . . . I can't see your mother this morning.

[THOMAS *touches his forelock and is about
to go when she says*

Wait a minute. Ask her to go into the dining-room and wait.

[THOMAS *touches his forelock. Exit.*

LADY S. [*With a grunt.*] H'm; the man's coming.

MRS. M. [*Amused.*] You shall have that interview alone.

LADY S. Yes, I had better see him alone. I shall speak with the greatest plainness—but come back after a few minutes.

MRS. M. What do you think Julia really feels about it?

LADY S. [*After a pause.*] I don't want to betray the child's confidence, but she is crushed and miserable and doesn't care what becomes of her. I went to her room last night; she threw herself into my arms. She is broken-hearted about the Endsleigh boy. The young idiot is too poor to marry yet.

MRS. M. Yes, of course.

LADY S. But he's not too poor to be engaged, and they are both so young they could wait.

Enter SERVANT; *announcing*

SERVANT. Sir James Caxton.

Enter SIR JAMES, *almost middle-aged, a dull, heavy-looking man.*

MRS. M. How do you do, Sir James?

SIR J. How do you do? How do again, Lady Sarah? [*Nodding to her.*] [*To* MRS. MURISON.] Heard the news, I suppose?

MRS. M. Yes—I was very much surprised——

SIR J. Thought you would be . . . How's the child? Been ill, hasn't she?

MRS. M. She is better, thank you.

SIR J. That's right—I suppose you know that your mother and Julia—you, cousin, isn't she, yes, of course—are coming up this afternoon?

MRS. M. I have just heard from them.

SIR J. That's all right then—Lady Sarah, you were good enough to telegraph for me, so I'm here.

LADY S. I want to talk to you.

MRS. M. And there is some one waiting to see me in the drawing-room.

SIR J. You haven't congratulated me yet—I suppose you forgot—it doesn't matter; it's only a form.

MRS. M. [*Going towards the door.*] Yes, it's only a form.

SIR J. Allow me. [*Opens door.*]

[*Exit* MRS. MURISON.

SIR J. [*Going awkwardly towards* LADY SARAH.] Well what's the telegram about?

LADY S. Sit down, Sir James, I want to speak to you. I mean to speak plainly.

SIR J. Quite right. We are both plain people.

LADY S. I took my courage into my two hands, and telegraphed.

SIR J. I thought you probably took a pencil.

LADY S. What do you mean?

SIR J. [*Sheepishly.*] Only a little joke. Courage is an excellent thing, but no good by itself for writing a telegram. [*She makes an impatient gesture.*] Well, what is it?

LADY S. Why did you propose to my niece, Julia?

SIR J. Because I want to marry her—excellent reason——

LADY S. She's not in love with you—not a bit—you must know that.

SIR J. Sorry for it. I don't believe in young women being in love before they're married—time enough afterwards.

LADY S. My sister made her accept you because you have twenty thousand a year. I speak plainly, for there is no one else to do it. You are a good and worthy man, but you were not made to marry a beautiful girl like Julia.

SIR J. Perhaps not, but I don't see that anything is gained by saying it now.

LADY S. Sir James, that girl is breaking her heart for a boy who went to India the other day, without speaking, because my sister, who is a very worldly woman, prevented him.

SIR J. I'm sorry; I'll take her about and she'll forget him.

LADY S. Don't marry her—the engagement is not announced yet, no one knows about it except ourselves—back out of it—be generous; be kind. Julia dared not refuse you, she is miserable at the thought of marrying you.

SIR J. Well, but she needn't be—I'll do what I can——

LADY S. Don't marry her. Give her up. Don't make a tragedy of that young thing's life.

SIR J. I won't if I can help it, but I mean to marry her. The boy who went to India was a fool;—didn't know how to use his chance; she'll forget him soon; [*gets up to go*] I will do my best to please her.

LADY S. I thought you would be generous— I thought you would see the whole thing.

SIR J. I'm going to be generous. I won't tell any one of this conversation.

LADY S. But why do you want to marry her after what I have told you?

SIR J. I'm very dull.

LADY S. [*Almost losing her temper.*] You are dreadfully dull.

SIR J. That's why I want to marry. I shan't say you told me about the boy. . . .

But I shall keep my eyes open—and I can take care of my own.

LADY S. [*Indignant, with a note of feeling in her voice.*] I am a foolish old woman, I've done more harm than good. I thought perhaps you would understand.

SIR J. I quite understand, but you see the woman who doesn't get the man she wants is unlucky and can't help it—has to put up with it; but the man who doesn't get the woman he wants is an ass. I always think you should take what you want if you can get it—I want her.

LADY S. I feel as if I'd made a fool of myself—and done no good.

SIR J. I like a woman who makes a fool of herself. She's generally a nice woman, there's where you get the pull of us. I rather like fools, though they bore me if they're men. Good-bye.

LADY S. [*Looking at him wonderingly.*] I believe you'll be kind——

SIR J. I'm not up to much, but I'll try.

Enter MRS. MURISON.

MRS. M. Are you going, Sir James?

SIR J. Just going. Hope to come this afternoon, if you will allow me—meet Lady Caroline and Julia.

MRS. M. You are coming to meet them?

[*Rings.*

SIR J. Yes, *au revoir.* [*Exit* SIR JAMES.

MRS. M. What happened, Aunt Sarah?

LADY S. [*Snappishly.*] Nothing. The man's stupid. [*Evidently quite reluctant to acknowledge her defeat.*] I wish I hadn't sent for him.

MRS. M. What did he say?

LADY S. I can't tell you now, I am too angry. Did you see Thomas's mother?

MRS. M. Mrs. Lobb—Oh, yes—Thomas is going to Canada——

LADY S. [*Evidently not in the least interested.*] Good thing for him, perhaps.

MRS. M. Yes, I suppose it is. Mrs. Lobb comes from Cornwall, and when she was a girl her brother went to Canada; but he has always been poor till lately because he was so set on education, she says.

LADY S. Wasted his time, of course, on learning things of no use to him instead of doing his work—served him right.

MRS. M. [*Amused.*] He is beginning to do better and has sent for Thomas. The Captain of the trading ship who promised to take him back only found Mrs. Lobb this morning—and his ship sails to-morrow. Thomas goes with him at four o'clock from Euston to-day.

LADY S. What does the uncle do besides being set on education?

Mrs. M.   Oh—something with railways.   Poor woman, she was miserable at losing her boy. . . . But I want to talk about Julia and Sir James.

Lady S.   I would rather not own it, but that man thoroughly worsted me, and——

Mrs. M.   [*Evidently listening for some movement outside the house.*]   Wait till the children have gone—they are just ready—we shall hear them go by.   [*Goes to the window and opens it.*]   The air is lovely, so soft—and the sunshine will do May a deal of good.

> Thomas *enters while she is speaking. He has taken off his apron, evidently washed his face and brushed his hair. Stands, cap in hand.*

Thomas.   [*Touching his forelock.*]   Please M'm, I've come to say good-bye.

Mrs. M.   Yes, I know—come in.   [*He is standing by the door.*   Your mother has told me all about it.

Thomas.   [*Going a few steps into the room.*]   She's very keen on my going, M'm, but I don't like leaving her and Polly. . . don't know how they'll manage.

Mrs. M.   Oh, but it's a splendid chance for you.

Thomas.   That's what she says, but it's come so sudden-like.   I believe chances always does, and

I don't suppose I should come to much carrying out the papers——

Mrs. M. [*With an encouraging smile.*] Or blacking our shoes.

Thomas. I like doing anything for you, M'm. [*Turns his head towards the window, and his face lights up.*] I thought I heard them. Miss May and the others are just going.

[*Sounds outside, as of wheels.*

May. [*Only her voice—a child's voice—is heard, she is not seen.*] Mother, dear—Mother, dear.

Mrs. M. [*Going towards the window.*] You must say good-bye to her.

Thomas. I did, M'm. I thought you wouldn't mind.

Lady S. [*Who has followed* Mrs. Murison *to the window.*] She looks much better.

Mrs. M. [*To the children, who are presumably beneath the window.*] Good-bye, dears. Don't let her get too tired, Nurse. I'm saying good-bye to Thomas, May darling.

May. [*Her voice is heard.*] Tell him to come back again.

Mrs. M. [*Turning to* Thomas.] She says you are to come back again, Thomas.

Thomas. [*Going towards window, but standing shyly a step away from it.*] I'll come back, Miss May, I'll be sure to come back.

MAY. When will you come?

MRS. M. [*Repeating.*] When will you come? she says.

THOMAS. [*To* MAY.] I don't know, but I'll be sure to come, Miss May; don't you fear.

MRS. M. Good-bye, darlings.

> [*The children evidently go on,* MRS. M. *kisses her hand to them, closes the window, and comes back into the room.*

MRS. M. [*To* THOMAS.] Have you seen your uncle's friend who is to take you to Canada?

THOMAS. No, M'm, but mother has. She says he is a very nice gentleman.

MRS. M. The voyage will do you good.

THOMAS. That's what he said. Mother told him I was delicate, and he said the sea might set me up and start me growing. But I don't like leaving her and Polly [*struggling to keep back emotion*] and I don't like leaving you and Miss May . . . I couldn't 'a' gone if she hadn't been better.

MRS. M. Thank God, she's well.

THOMAS. [*Going, then hesitating and speaking shyly.*] Please, M'm, I want to thank you for all your kindness to us . . . I don't know where we'd 'a' been without you. Father said you were our best friend—it's one of the last things he did say.

MRS. M. Thank you for telling me—I know you'll be a good boy, Thomas.

THOMAS. I'll try. Good-bye, M'm.

MRS. M. [*As* THOMAS *goes towards the door.*] Oh, but you must shake hands with me. [*Quickly taking something from her purse.*] There is a sovereign for your little pocket.

THOMAS. [*Half reluctant.*] Thank you, M'm, but I didn't want that to remember you by. [*Raises his head as he takes her hand and looks at her.*] I'll never forget you as long as I live.

MRS. M. I don't believe you will. Good-bye, dear Thomas, may you grow up strong and well, and be a brave man. [*Stoops and kisses his cheek.*

[THOMAS'S *head droops, as if to hide his tears, he touches his forelock, quite ignores* LADY S. *Exit without saying a word, closing the door softly.*

MRS. M. [*Looking after him.*] Ah——

LADY S. My dear Evelyn, how could you kiss the charwoman's son—the boy who blacks your shoes?

MRS. M. He looked so little to be going across the world alone, I couldn't bear to see his pale face and sad eyes. And I thought of how he had sobbed the morning he heard that May was better—and of his father as I saw him last, lying still, with the surprised smile on his face——

CURTAIN.

ACT II

Time.—*Present. Seventeen years later than last Act. An afternoon in April.*

Scene.—*Sitting-room in* Lord Barnstaple's *villa at Alassio, charmingly furnished. Wide doors at back leading on to loggia, with marble or stone balustrade, and steps in centre leading down to orange-garden. The orange-trees should be seen, bearing fruit and blossom. At the back mountains and olive-trees; on one side a bit of the blue Mediterranean.*

- *Seated on the right is* Julia (*now* Lady Caxton), *about 36, beautiful, pleasant, but distant in manner to any but her own people. She is reading some letters; the post has evidently just come in.*

At the grand piano on the left May Murison *is playing very softly. She is 23, girlish, fair, charming.*

By the window Sir James Caxton *is standing looking a good deal older than in the last Act.*

Far down stage Robert Vallide, Sen., *stands*

127

listening to the piano. He is a tall, shrewd, eager man of 55, keen, businesslike, and kindly.

VALLIDE. [*To* JULIA.] Do you know, Lady Caxton, I believe I have heard that tune before?

LADY C. [*Amused.*] May! Mr. Vallide says he knows that tune.

MAY. It is a very old one—it's Sullivan's "Distant Shore."

VALLIDE. I'd like it again. They used to play it at Montreal in old days. It always made me feel home-sick.

SIR J. [*To* VALLIDE.] Isn't it time you went to meet your nephew,

VALLIDE. [*Looking at watch.*] You are right, Sir James, it is. If that train's punctual he'll be here in a quarter of an hour. Thank you, Miss Murison.

[*Gets up and goes towards door.*

JULIA. Go through the garden—it's nearer.

VALLIDE. I will. [*Exit by garden. Looks back and says:*] Here's Lord Stratton coming.

[MAY *begins to play.*

VOICE. May! Are you there?

[*She evidently hears but goes on playing.*
LORD STRATTON, *25, a heavy, stupid-looking young man, is seen coming up the loggia.*

SIR J. [*To* MAY.] Geoff's calling you.

GEOFF. May! [*Entering the room.*] I say, do come out——

MAY. [*Stands up and nods her head at him.*] I don't want to come out.

GEOFF. Yes, you do. I want to talk to you.

MAY. [*Sits down and begins to play again.*] I don't want to be talked to.

GEOFF. Oh, all right.

[*Marches off into the garden. Evidently cross.*

JULIA. I must say you are a very cool young lady.

MAY. Dear Julia, why am I cool?

JULIA. Are you not engaged to Geoff?

MAY. No, not yet, though in a sort of way I have given in this morning—at least I said I'd *try* and marry him. Mother wants it so much, and he's Uncle Edward's son.

JULIA. It doesn't seem to strike you that Geoff is the only son of Lord Barnstaple, and one of the best *partis* in London.

MAY. Poor old Geoff!

JULIA. Most girls would jump at him.

MAY. Poor old Geoff!

Re-enter GEOFF.

GEOFF. [*To* JULIA.] I say, Julia, make her come for a walk.

MAY. I don't want to go for a walk—I want to see Mr. Robert Vallide. He'll be here directly; his uncle has gone to the station to meet him—he's frightfully pleased at the idea of his nephew getting into Parliament, and I want to see what he is like.

GEOFF. The blessed carpet-bagger.

MAY. He isn't a carpet-bagger.

GEOFF. Well, tub-thumper. Do come out.

MAY. I want to stay here.

GEOFF. You're awfully disagreeable this time. . . . The Pippins want me to go and stay with them in Paris.

MAY. [*Picking up a letter from the piano.*] Well—you like Miss Pippin. [*To* JULIA.] I've had a long letter from mother. She's so pleased with our new house on Campden Hill—she is getting it ready, working like a Trojan—how did Trojans work hard, Geoff?

GEOFF. Why—like Trojans. [*Looking round.*] I'm getting sick of this place, too much scenery about—there's no room for anything lively.

MAY. You'd better go to Paris.

GEOFF. I will if you worry me so.

Enter IDA, 24, *pretty and lively.*

MAY. Here's Ida. Is Aunt Sarah better?

[*Gets up and goes towards* IDA.

IDA. A little—but she's very cross.

JULIA. What have you been reading to her?

IDA. Jane Austen. She says all her people are tiresome, and all their aims trivial. And, she doesn't care how well they are done, she wouldn't have known them for the world, and doesn't want to hear about them.

JULIA. Is she coming down to tea?

IDA. I don't know. I told her Mr. Vallide's nephew was coming. She asked what he was like.

MAY. What did you say?

IDA. I told her that he had the New World vigour and the Old World politeness.

MAY. Why, Ida, you are quite eloquent.

IDA. [*With mock pathos.*] It doesn't matter, he likes some one else, as usual. He told me all about her one evening.

MAY. About whom?

IDA. [MAY *turns her head and listens.*] Some girl he remembers. He hasn't seen her for years, but he always wonders everywhere he goes if she will be there.

MAY. How sweet of him. [*To* GEOFF *as they saunter towards the loggia together.*] Very well, I'll come for a little while.

> [IDA *goes to the piano, makes business.*
> [SIR JAMES *watches* GEOFF *and* MAY *disappear.*
> [JULIA *takes up a letter in her lap and says to* IDA.

JULIA. Evelyn only just missed getting the old house in Regent's Park again.

IDA. Really! I didn't know May had this waltz. [*Looking at music.*

SIR J. What, the house where Lady Sarah abused me for proposing to you?

JULIA. It didn't make any difference.

SIR J. No, it didn't make any difference—in one way—good thing Evelyn's not going back to it.

JULIA. Why? [*Ida might play softly.*

SIR J. It was there that she heard that her husband was killed in Egypt.

JULIA. [*Nods.*] Seventeen years ago. How strange of you to think of that.

SIR J. I think of a good many things. [*Restlessly.*] I wish this young man would arrive——

IDA. [*At piano.*] Anxious to see your successor, cousin Jim?

SIR J. Want to get out of politics—but I want to get out of everything.

JULIA. Oh, Jim, we all do sometimes. Life could be such a wonderful thing—only it isn't.

SIR J. [*Sheepishly.*] Well, I bought you that ivory carving to-day, it's coming home when it's cleaned up——

Enter LORD BARNSTAPLE. *He is past middle age. Thorough Tory, a little stiff but kind, as all his people are; agreeable and pleasantly condescending in manner*]

SIR J. Well, Barnstaple?

JULIA. [*To* SIR J.] Oh! . . . [*To* LORD B.] Jim has bought that ivory for me, Uncle Edward.

LORD B. Awfully good of him, my dear. He is always finding pretty things for you. Where is Vallide?

JULIA. Gone to meet his nephew.

LORD B. Ah! [*Rings.*

Enter SERVANT.

[*To* SERVANT.] See that a room is ready for Mr. Robert Vallide—Mr. Vallide's nephew. He will arrive almost directly.

SERVANT. Yes, my lord. [*Exit* SERVANT.

JULIA. [*To* LORD B.] Uncle Edward, did you know that Mr. Vallide wasn't a Canadian?

LORD B. Of course. He's a West of England man. Went out young to make his way, I imagine.

SIR J. That's why he's so keen on education.

LORD B. He did a great deal for it in Canada.

SIR J. Felt that he didn't get enough of it himself, probably.

LORD B. He knows a good deal. I am never very keen on the people who have made what they call their pile and hail from—anywhere. But I like Vallide. When I was doing the Colonies—he was at Ottawa then—he took me all over the Canadian Pacific, so I saw a good deal of him. I hadn't seen him since till I met him at Monte Carlo the other day—doing Europe—and it was my turn to show civilities.

IDA. You knew his nephew first in Canada, didn't you, father?

LORD B. He came out after taking his degree.

JULIA. And then?—the nephew, I mean?

LORD B. Then—he turned up in London anxious to go into politics or something of that sort. Our Party had just got in, I wanted a Private Secretary, and he was good enough to come to me. But we were turned out after a few months.

JULIA. You were all such rabid Tories, what could you expect?

LORD B. I wish there were more of us; this country wasn't built for a democracy—or by one. And Socialism, if it comes, will pull it down and only leave chaos in its place. Young Vallide is a remarkable man and I shall be glad if he gets in for Fieldborough.

SIR J. Perhaps he'll wake them up. I never did.

LORD B. They're waking up of their own accord—that's the worst of it.

[LORD B. *crosses over to* SIR J.

IDA. [*Looking up from the piano.*] Geoff's

American friends the Pippins are in Paris, father. Colonel Endsleigh is going out to them for a few days and may come on here.

LORD B. Ah! A good fellow, Endsleigh.

LADY C. [*Looks up quickly at the mention of* ENDSLEIGH'S *name. To* IDA.] He's coming to Alassio?

SIR J. [*Sulkily, watching his wife.*] Why should he come here?

JULIA. Why shouldn't he? I knew him when I was a girl—before he went to India——

SIR J. Well, you don't now.

IDA. He's a great friend of mine, cousin James.

SIR J. Friend of yours—is he? Oh—if that's it! [*Pause.*

LORD B. Look here, Caxton, when young Vallide comes we had better get to business at once.
[*Goes to* SIR J. *on loggia.*

Re-enter GEOFF *and* MAY *together from garden, they pass* SIR J. *and* LORD B., *who look after them curiously.*

GEOFF. [*To* JULIA.] We are not getting on a bit.

MAY. Not a bit.

GEOFF. May used to be much nicer.

MAY. But I am deteriorating. I'm much nicer now than I shall be presently.

GEOFF. I shan't stand it.

MAY. [*Provokingly and laughing.*] Don't, dear Geoff, don't.

[SIR J. *and* LORD B. *get out of hearing.*

IDA. You are the strangest creatures.

GEOFF. May used to be a nice girl.

MAY. I'm not now.

GEOFF. No, you're not. I've half a mind to go to Paris.

MAY. There's a great deal going on there.

GEOFF. Yes, there is—and they want me.

MAY. [*Teasingly.*] I am sure they do. If you took the six o'clock train from here, to-day, you would be there to-morrow morning?

GEOFF. [*Savagely.*] Oh!

[*Goes off hurriedly through the loggia.*

IDA. [*Who, with* JULIA, *has been looking on at them half-amused.*] Really, May, you do worry him.

MAY. I can't help it. I'm very fond of him; he's a dear boy, but I don't want to marry him—that's the whole story—I—don't—want—to—marry—him.

IDA. I wonder where he's gone?

[*Goes out to loggia and looks after him; thus* JULIA *and* MAY *are left virtually alone.*

MAY. I can't bear telling Ida that I don't want Geoff—because he is her brother; but what can I do?

JULIA. There isn't any one else?

MAY. No. But it would be dreadfully slow to marry a cousin—not like being married at all; only like staying on a life-long visit to a relation.

JULIA. He has been fond of you so long now.

MAY. [*Nods.*] Ever since that summer in Switzerland—years ago—when I had a pig-tail —he pulled it when we quarrelled. But he killed all the wasps.

JULIA. It's splendid of Uncle Edward to want you to marry him.

MAY. Oh, yes, I know; and mother does, too. I *am* trying. But the Barnstaples are poor; Geoff ought to marry money—and I want to wait for the fairy prince.

JULIA. The fairy prince generally comes too soon or too late. . . . Don't marry Geoff if you don't love him! There's only one thing in a woman's life worth playing for, and, if she misses it, everything else is a makeshift.

MAY. [*Change of manner.*] I wonder—did you take makeshifts?

JULIA. I took the things I was told I couldn't do without. That's what many women do—[*In a low voice, with a glance towards* SIR JAMES] but—I have played the game fairly.

MAY. [*Gravely.*] Dear Julia——

[IDA *saunters in, and, as she does so,* MAY

takes up a white parasol that has been by the piano.

MAY. I'm going down to the Curiosity Shop —there are two old Savona pots that mother would like——

IDA. Take Geoff with you.

MAY. We should only quarrel. . . . It is warm enough for July.   [*Exit by loggia.*

IDA. May never seems to fall in love with any one, and *every* one does with her.

JULIA. I know.

IDA. I wish they did with me; but I am the kind of girl that men call a good sort and tell things to—that's all.

JULIA. I saw you sitting out for hours with Mr. Robert Vallide at the Benson Greys.

IDA. I daresay, and we talked about other people—people who care talk about themselves.

JULIA. [*Suddenly.*] Perhaps he'll fall in love with May—it wouldn't please her mother.

IDA. No, it wouldn't . . . Men are very strange. There was Teddy Haston—he used to ride with me every day, but he never said a word. . . . I believe he's dumb.

JULIA. I thought girls didn't want to be married nowadays.

IDA. I don't want to be married, but I should like to have a crowd of lovers following me— it must cheer one up so—as it is, no one has ever proposed to me at all, except Colonel Endsleigh.

JULIA. [*Quickly.*] Frank Endsleigh! Did *he?* When?

IDA. In January; and even he wasn't in love —told me he never had been since he first went to India. He cared for some girl then, but she married for money——

JULIA. [*Trying to keep her manner natural.*] Why didn't you accept him?

IDA. Why should I? A middle-aged man, not even in love with me?

JULIA. [*Ruefully.*] Yes, he's middle-aged——

Re-enter LORD B., SIR JAMES, *and* GEOFF, *not* MAY.

LORD B. [*Half-amused, half-vexed.*] Look here, Geoff and May have been squabbling again —he says you were both here, so you know about it——

GEOFF. And I'm tired of it, I shall go to Paris. Endsleigh's there, and the Pippins— Janetta Pippin is worth a dozen of May—I believe she'd——

LORD B. Nonsense, my boy—we don't want any Miss Janetta Pippins in our family. You have told us all a dozen times that your heart is set on marrying May.

GEOFF. It was—but it isn't now.

LORD B. She was just coming round.

GEOFF. I don't believe she'll ever come round. Look here, let me go for a week to Paris—she told me to go, and I should like to take her at her word——

LORD B. Suppose she asks you to stay—what then?

GEOFF. Why—Oh!—she won't—not she——

IDA. Father, let him go—it would be far better. [*Bell heard.*

JULIA. There's the front door bell, Mr. Vallide bringing in his nephew with proper formality, I suppose.

GEOFF. I'll get out of the way.

JULIA [*To* IDA.] And they don't want us.
　　[*Exeunt* JULIA, IDA, *and* GEOFF *by garden.*

　　　　　[*Stage left to* LORD B. *and* SIR JAMES.

　　　　　Enter SERVANT.

SERVANT. Mr. Vallide and Mr. Robert Vallide.

　　　　[*Enter* MR. VALLIDE *and* ROBERT VALLIDE. ROBERT *is about twenty-seven, good-looking, good manners, with an air of reserve and simplicity. He should have a distinctive personality as of a strong man able to hold his own.*

LORD B. [*Going forward to him.*] How do

you do, Vallide? Good of you to come. Not
very tired, after your journey?

ROBERT. Not at all, [*shaking hands*] and delighted to come.

LORD B. Do you know Sir James Caxton?

SIR J. How do you do? [*shaking hands.*]

LORD B. Well now! Are your things here——

ROBERT. I left them at the hotel on my way
up.

LORD B. Oh—but we expect you to stay with
us—plenty of room.

ROBERT. But——

LORD B. We want you—then we can talk
over things at leisure.

ROBERT. [*After a little pause.*] Thank you
very much—my uncle refuses to take me on to
Rome with him.

LORD B. Good: we are here for another ten
days, and my sister—Lady Sarah Stratton—she
has kept house for me since my wife died—is
expecting you. Now—shall we get to business?
Your uncle wants to go to-night, so there isn't
much time.

SIR J. I don't know whether I need stay?

LORD B. Yes—yes—we want you. [*To* ROB-
ERT.] No doubt you were surprised to get your
uncle's telegram.

ROBERT. [*With a smile.*] No. He was always prompt—and always telegraphs.

VALLIDE. Ah! the world I live in is a sturdy youngster, in a hurry to overtake the old one.

LORD B. Quite right—let's sit down. [*To* ROBERT.] Mr. Vallide, your uncle expects a great deal of you.

VALLIDE. I do. He must be Prime Minister some day.

ROBERT. Rather a large order, uncle Bob!

VALLIDE. It can be done—step by step. One gets to the top of a house by a ladder, not a jump.

LORD B. [*With a smile.*] There's generally a trap-door, and narrow stairs that lead to it. [*Turning to* ROBERT.] Is your interest in politics as keen as ever?

ROBERT. Quite.

LORD B. Good. Have you thought of going into Parliament?

ROBERT. Yes—but I didn't expect——

LORD B. Of course not, never expect anything. . . . Sir James intends to resign his seat for Fieldborough at the end of the Session. I happened to mention it to your uncle the other night, with the result that — well, the telegram.

ROBERT. You think——

LORD B. I can think of nobody better to suggest to the Party than yourself—my opinion is sure to be asked on account of my local influence

—and we shall be most fortunate if we can induce you to stand.

SIR J. It would bother you less than most places; there isn't much to subscribe to, and it's a good way from London . . . they can't bring you down for every bazaar or vestry meeting.

ROBERT. [*To* LORD B.] I should be delighted if I thought I had a chance.

LORD B. Chance—of course you'd have an excellent chance. It might be well to get some local standing, if you rented a place, for instance. I believe there'd be no difficulty. [*Looking towards old* VALLIDE.]

VALLIDE. [*Quickly.*] None. He can have as much money as he pleases, and half a million the day I see M. P. written after his name. There'll be another half-million when I die.

ROBERT. This won't do. [*Putting his hand on his uncle's shoulder.*] You mustn't take any notice of him, Lord Barnstaple.

VALLIDE. You are *my* boy. I haven't any one else.

ROBERT. Yes, uncle Bob, I'm your boy, but too old to be tipped any longer.

LORD B. Well, we shall be at Fieldborough at Whitsuntide, perhaps you'll come down and see a little of the neighbourhood.

ROBERT. Thank you very much. You have

taken me by surprise. But it is what I would like immensely.

VALLIDE. You can spend money like water.

ROBERT. No! Uncle Bob. It's difficult to disappoint you, but you gave me the weapons to fight my own battle, and you must let me do it. I don't want to spend money like water, and I'm not going to take that half-million—while you live at any rate. You may want to alter your mind about it, before you die.

LORD B. There'll be expenses.

ROBERT. They needn't be extravagant—and [*looking at his uncle*] I can meet them. I am modern enough to want only the money I've worked for.

LORD B. Humph—I hope your views are sound—some of us, you see, can't help having money without working for it.

ROBERT. An inheritance—excellent. It gives people a chance to do all sorts of things for the world that would never get done at all if everybody had to work for a living. Don't think I imagine that the working class consists only of those who earn money—some of the best work in the whole world has been done by men who never earned a penny in the technical sense—they wouldn't have been able to do it if they had been poor.

LORD B. Good. And on other points?

ROBERT. On all points I am, politically, precisely what I was when I had the honour of being your Private Secretary.

LORD B. That's right.

ROBERT. But I should like to try for Fieldborough without taking a place, or trying to dazzle the electors. If there's a fight all the better, but I don't want a money one.

SIR J. Quite right. Money's overrated. I never got anything out of it, and if people can get it out of you they never want anything else; it's generally a most degrading element in human life.

VALLIDE. Well—it's only a man with a comfortable income who can afford to say that.

SIR J. [*To* OLD VALLIDE.] I daresay—I don't think you want me any more just now—I shall be happy to be of use to your nephew if I can.

[*Exit* SIR JAMES *by loggia.*

LORD B. [*Turning to* ROBERT.] You are a pretty good speaker, I believe?

ROBERT. I haven't had much opportunity, except at the Union—at Oxford; which doesn't count for much.

LORD B. Well, but you helped Fuller with his election?

ROBERT. I did a little. [*Modestly.*]

[SIR JAMES, *at end of loggia, signs to*

LORD B., *as if he wanted to speak to him.*

LORD B. [*Evidently pleased with* ROBERT's *modesty.*] Ah! I think we shall get on. [*To the* UNCLE VALLIDE] He is quite right.

VALLIDE. I'm delighted to hear you say it, my lord.

LORD B. And don't be disappointed. Some day he will marry, then you can settle that half-million on his wife, or his heirs, he'll want it as a background for his career, though he refuses it as a foundation.

VALLIDE. [*Good-naturedly.*] I'm very angry with him, but I rather like him for it——

LORD B. One moment—I think Caxton wants to speak to me.

[*Exit* LORD B. *to loggia, where he stands well out of hearing, talking to* SIR J.

ROBERT. Thank you for that, Uncle Bob. [*Then with a change of manner.*] And look here, it was splendid of you to telegraph me, and Barnstaple's a brick. I'll fight Fieldborough with all my might, if I get the chance. He said I was ambitious—he's right—I am. Don't be afraid, Uncle Bob, no trap-doors or back staircases, but look up to the topmost rung, I'll make for it. Probably I shall come down crash like the Master-Builder, but never mind.

VALLIDE. I'll make the fall soft for you if

you do. [ROBERT *shakes his head.*] And Lord Barnstaple gave me a tip just now by which I'll cheat the death-due monger of a good deal all the same——

ROBERT. You immoral old scoundrel!

VALLIDE. [*Delighted.*] So you'd better set about collecting them.

ROBERT. Collecting what?

VALLIDE. Belongings. A wife, to begin with——

ROBERT. No, thank you——

VALLIDE. I think Lady Ida's sweet on you.

ROBERT. Nonsense. She's a good sort, but not that kind of girl. I say—[*change of manner*]—It's awfully kind of Lord Barnstaple to ask me to stay here, but I wish you'd let me go on to Rome with you to-morrow.

VALLIDE. [*Firmly.*] No, my boy, it would bother me. It's always been my way to see what I've got, then to put it aside. Do you remember when you came out to Canada first? Why, after a couple of days I wondered what I was going to do with you. Luckily, you had to be educated, that took you off. Just the same when you came back. I couldn't sleep the night before you arrived, but once I'd seen you again I didn't want you to stay very long. When a man's lived his life alone he has to be left to himself to the end. . . . Perhaps we mayn't get another word together this journey, but think over the hint I've given you. When you marry, I want to be proud of your wife——

ROBERT. [*Gaily.*] You shall——

VALLIDE. She'll be proud enough of you—you are made of the real stuff——

ROBERT. Don't say that or I shall have a weird future.

VALLIDE. Pure gold——

ROBERT. Pure gold is too soft for the wear and tear of this world, Uncle Bob—besides you make me feel like the good young man who died.

VALLIDE. Who was he?

ROBERT. He painted beautifully in water colours, and of such is the Kingdom of Heaven. Not my sort, Uncle Bob—I want to live, to live! I'm not the puny, half-starved boy any more—you nourished me, and the fresh life of the New World—where it is still morning time and the strength of the day is before it—stirs my pulses sometimes till I feel as if I could carry the universe in a bag swung over my shoulders.

VALLIDE. That's what I want you to do—that's what I want—[*lower tone.*] They're coming.

Enter JULIA and IDA by loggia.

IDA. How do you do, Mr. Vallide? [*Shakes hands.*] You know my cousin, Lady Caxton? [IDA *rings the bell.*]

JULIA. [*To Robert.*] How do you do? We all know *you*.

Re-enter SIR JAMES *and* LORD B., *talking; they hang back at first.*

SERVANTS *come in and lay tea. Right.*

[IDA *crosses stage with* ROBERT VALLIDE. *He and she stand first, then sit on sofa L., grand piano behind them.*

IDA. [*Turning to* ROBERT.] I'm so glad you were able to come.

ROBERT. So am I.

IDA. [*Looking round and speaking to* LADY CAXTON.] Julia, I wonder if you would make tea—I want to talk to Mr. Vallide.

JULIA. Of course. [*Sits down to table, with* SIR J. *and* LORD B. *near her.*]

IDA. [*Turning again to* ROBERT.] Father tells me that he has asked you to come to us at Court Acres—Fieldborough, you know.

ROBERT. I shall look forward to it.

IDA. It's very dull—Sir James was horribly bored—but they are waking up—that's what Father is so afraid of, for then they'll want to go away—there isn't enough work for them there.

ROBERT. It must be found! Every place should have its own industry—its own workers— work that can be done under a clear sky and in pure air. We want to grow strong men, not anæmics cooped up in cities——

IDA. Tell them so! Sir James wouldn't talk to them.

ROBERT. He *sees* things——

IDA. [*Quickly.*] I think that, too. Perhaps a spell has been put upon him and he has to be silent.

ROBERT. Perhaps. [*Looking round.*] This place is like a dream, and a spell sounds the most natural thing in the world. [*Looks round at the tea-table. Change of manner.*] Some tea?

IDA. Please. [*They go together to the tea-table at which* JULIA *is presiding, but remain standing.*

ROBERT [*To Ida.*] By the way, I met a friend of yours at dinner the other night—Colonel Endsleigh. [JULIA *looks up.*

IDA. [*Demurely.*] Oh.

ROBERT. He said he was coming to Paris and Monte Carlo, and going back by Genoa.

SIR J. [*Grumpily.*] When is he going back to India?

ROBERT. In October——

SIR J. [*Who has been listening.*] Ah!

ROBERT. [*To Ida.*] Now—bread and butter! [*Hands some to* IDA *who retreats towards sofa again with her tea.* ROBERT *puts the plate back on table and turns to rejoin* IDA—*looks towards garden, gives a little start, hesitates, and says in a different tone.*] Who is that coming up the garden by the orange-trees?

    [IDA *turns her head as* MAY MURISON *comes up the steps to the loggia.*

IDA Oh, it's my cousin. [ROBERT *stands stock still staring at her.* IDA *looking at him in surprise, after a pause.*] Do you know her?

ROBERT. [*Without moving his eyes from* MAY.] No.

    Enter MAY. ROBERT *stands hesitating. He and she look at each other.*

JULIA. [*To* MAY.] Did you get your pots?

MAY. I did.

LORD B. [*Gets up.*] Pots—what pots?

MAY. Two blue and white pots, old Sevona. I wanted them for mother.

LORD B. Where's Geoff?

MAY. I don't know.

LORD B. Oh. Well, let me introduce you to the future member for Fieldborough. [*To* ROBERT.] Vallide, this is my niece, Miss May Murison.

MAY. How do you do? [*She holds out her hand.*]

ROBERT. How do you do? [*He takes it as if in a dream.*]

    [IDA *gets up from the sofa, as if she knew that he wouldn't come back to her. Goes over to the tea-table and joins the group there.*

JULIA. [*From tea-table.*] Some tea, May?

MAY. Please.

[JULIA *pours out and gives it to* ROBERT.

[MAY *half-unconsciously retreats a step towards the sofa on L. where* IDA *had been sitting. Takes the tea from* ROBERT—*sits down. He first stands and then sits down beside her while they talk.*

JULIA. [*At tea-table to* IDA.] We must go over to Monte Carlo, Mr. Vallide has been telling us of a system.

VALLIDE. It only works for a time.

JULIA. I might get some money for frocks, in Paris on our way home. [*Laughter.*]

MAY. [*To* ROBERT.] Oh, yes. We've been quite excited since the telegram went. What did you think it meant?

ROBERT. I thought it was one of my uncle's sudden inspirations, but I was glad to come to Italy.

MAY. You will love this place, it's so little— and so still. No fashionable people or promenade, or Kursaal, or anything of that sort, only the mountains and the Mediterranean, and the olives, and there are wonderful walks.

[*During this talk it seems almost as if an*

enchantment stole over ROBERT, *as if he were under a spell from which he is only roused by the interruption at the end of the Act.*

ROBERT. I should like to do them all.

MAY. Oh, but you will, of course. Uncle Edward said he should ask you to stay——

ROBERT. Have you been here long?

MAY. I came with Lady Caxton a week ago.

ROBERT. Lady Caxton is——?

MAY. My cousin.

ROBERT. [*As if remembering.*] Yes. And Lord Barnstaple?

MAY. Lord Barnstaple is my great-uncle— my mother's uncle.

ROBERT. [*Keenly interested but trying not to show it.*] Of course—and Lady Sarah Stratton? I heard she was here—she is your—great-aunt?

MAY. Yes; she is upstairs to-day, doing a little gout, unfortunately. She has kept house for Uncle Edward since his wife died. She always takes care of some one——

ROBERT. Did she take care of you?

MAY. Oh yes, of us all,—my father went back to Egypt some time after Gordon died—and—— [*stops*]

ROBERT. [*Showing that he understands what she means.*] I know— That must have been?

MAY. Seventeen years ago, when I was a little girl.

ROBERT. [*Keenly interested, but trying not to show it.*] And then you went abroad?

MAY. Yes, with Aunt Sarah and lived in Switzerland for years.

ROBERT. And now?

MAY. Now we have come back—oh, but (*wonderingly*) it is only two minutes since we met, and I am suddenly telling you my family history —you seemed so interested—I suppose it was Gordon's name—an Englishman always thrills to it!

ROBERT. Always. . . . Did you like living in Switzerland?

MAY. Yes, but we were glad to come back. We are settling down now—on Campden Hill. Mother just missed getting our old house in Harford Terrace again by a few hours.

ROBERT. I saw some furniture going in last week.

MAY. But you didn't know it was *our* house, or that we had lived there.

ROBERT. I saw some furniture going into an empty house in Harford Terrace, I happened to be passing.

MAY. I dare say it was the one we lived in.

[*A burst of laughter comes from the tea-table.*

LORD B. No, that wouldn't do at all.

VALLIDE. You see, after a point the bank steps in and sweeps it all off.

JULIA. Well, I was told that if you followed the colour it was a very safe lead.

ROBERT. [*To* MAY.] Those gamblers are still discussing Monte Carlo.

MAY. It seems wicked to talk of money in this place, doesn't it? The valleys are choked with violets, and you can't think what the narcissus and the jonquils are like.

ROBERT. There's a little red Roman road— some one told me of it——

MAY. Through the olive woods; it goes to Santa Croce. At night, when the moonlight comes through the trees, it's like an enchantment.

ROBERT. [*Dreamily.*] It's like an enchantment here. What is the ruin on that top of the mountain over the way?

MAY. It's the princess's church.

ROBERT. What princess?

MAY. Hundreds of years ago there was a princess who loved some one who wasn't—anybody at all, and the king wouldn't let her marry him——*

ROBERT. So she built a church to be married in?

MAY. No, she married him first, in spite of all things.

* This is a well-known legend of Alassio.

ROBERT. I like that princess.

MAY. So do I.

ROBERT. And then?

MAY. And then they hid themselves away in a little châlet on the mountain, and were very happy for a long time.

ROBERT. Just those two together?

MAY. Just those two together. One day, by chance, the king came upon them. She was washing clothes, and singing while she did it, and the king was so struck with her happiness that he forgave them, and they went back to court. But sometimes, long afterwards, when he had been made a noble, they used to steal away to the little mountain home——

ROBERT. And then?

MAY. The princess said she would build a church to its memory. It was finished while he was at the war, and the night he was coming home she had it lighted up and waited for him. But he never came—he never, never came back. They light it up still once a year, and say a mass for his soul—up there in the ruins. So, you see, the story is not forgotten.

ROBERT. It will never be forgotten. It has the seed of immortality in it.

MAY. [Dreamily.] Among the high weeds, perhaps, growing close against its walls. [With *a little start.*] What a strange talk this is, Mr. Vallide!

ROBERT. It's only five minutes ago now——

[LORD B. *and old* VALLIDE *come forward talking together. There is a movement among the rest of the group.* MAY *and* ROBERT *get up.*

VALLIDE. I'm very much obliged to you for everything, Lord Barnstaple; I'm delighted to think that he's going to stay with you, and if Lady Ida takes him in hand a bit, why he'll be all right.

IDA. [*Looks round with a little laugh, and says to* VALLIDE.] I'll do my best——

MAY. [ROBERT *takes up a photograph from the piano behind the sofa.*] That's my cousin, Geoff —Lord Barnstaple's son, you know. He is here with us.

ROBERT. Oh, yes, Lord Stratton. [*Puts it down.*]

MAY. You knew him——

ROBERT. No. I never saw him. I was only Lord Barnstaple's political secretary for a few weeks. [LORD BARNSTAPLE *comes forward.*

[MAY *and* IDA *saunter towards the window with* VALLIDE *so as to be out of hearing.*

LORD B. [*To* ROBERT.] I saw you looking at my son's portrait.

ROBERT. Miss Murison has just been telling me——

LORD B. [*His face lighting up.*] Has she? She is a very interesting person to him, and—I'm speaking as if you were my confidential secretary again—I think—I hope—she is going to make him happy. Oh, there he is.

> [GEOFF *has appeared on the loggia, look-ing determined. He has chánged his clothes.*
>
> [LORD B. *leaves* ROBERT, *who has been aghast at his last speech, and goes to-wards his son.*
>
> [VALLIDE *and* SIR JAMES *come up to* ROB-ERT *and speak to him, but he stands watching* MAY *and the group on the other side of the room, though presum-ably he doesn't hear what they say.*

LORD B. [*To* GEOFF.] Where are you going?

GEOFF. [*To his father.*] I am tired of this place—can't think what you can see in it. Monte Carlo is good enough for me—or Paris—and I'm off there, unless—[*Looks towards* MAY.]

LORD B. [*To* MAY *anxiously.*] Ask him to stay, my dear.

MAY. To stay? [*Looks up, unconsciously, gives a glance towards* ROBERT.] Oh—I can't.

CURTAIN.

ACT III

TIME.—*Ten days later. Late afternoon.*

SCENE.—*Garden of the Villa. On* L. *a deep loggia with doorway into the house—which should be seen above it. The windows of the house should have green jalousie blinds. Rest of Stage taken up with garden—seats conveniently placed, &c. At back (a cloth) mountain with olives, and on top ruin of a church (with ruined windows). Bushes, flowers, &c., picturesque garden.*

On the L., *near doorway, sitting on a low chair* LADY SARAH STRATTON *looking much older than in the First Act, she wears a shawl, a walking-stick is against her chair. She has evidently been suffering, but her manner is as vigorous as ever.* JULIA *is sitting by her with an open book on her lap. To the* R., *lower down almost hidden from them by bushes or trees on a seat as if waiting,* ROBERT *and* MAY *are sitting together, but* LADY S. *does not know they are there.*

Farther back, centre of Stage SIR JAMES *is leaning against side of loggia looking sulkily ahead. Presently he smokes.*

LADY S. No, thank you, I don't want to hear any more. What did you say was the name of the woman who wrote it?

JULIA. [*Turning to the title-page.*] Eliza St. John Blake.

[MAY *and* ROBERT *amused, lean forward and listen.*

SIR J. What is the matter with her?

LADY S. She's vulgar. There isn't a creature in her book who hasn't a title.

JULIA. It's rather funny, you know. She alway speaks of " the Marquis " and " the Earl."

LADY S. Just as if they'd never been christened—or were illegitimate. It's extraordinary how many novelists are afraid to write of their own class of which at any rate they know something. They always want to gather up their skirts in a slum or to trail them through a palace—though they belong to neither, and very soon betray it.

JULIA. The middle-class is rather dull, you know, Aunt Sarah, they want to look outside it.

LADY S. Dull? Not at all; it's so enterprising and very often intellectual. Besides people are not made more interesting or less vulgar by being given handles to their names; it's a great pity the wrong people take them—they only look ridiculous; and plain misters have done most for the world. Look at the politicians, they do their best work in Lower House, when they are past it and stupid they are sent to the Upper one.

JULIA. How about Uncle Edward?

LADY S. [*With a certain amount of unconscious pride.*] My dear, he was born there; that makes a difference. I was very much amused a year ago at Montreux, there were some pushing people and Evelyn Murison who has a stiff neck——

MAY. Aunt Sarah!

LADY S. [*Disconcerted.*] Yes, my dear, your Mother has an exceedingly stiff neck, always had. . . . I didn't know you two were there—what are you doing—why don't you go for a walk?

MAY. Mr. Vallide is waiting for Uncle Edward, who wanted a talk with him.

LADY S. [*To* ROBERT.] Why are you going away to-morrow morning? My brother asked you to stay until the end of the week, didn't he?

ROBERT. I have had a delightful visit; but I'm afraid I must get back.

LADY S. Oh—Why—Who is this?

Enter from door under loggia on L. COL. ENDS-
LEIGH. *He is about 38 or 40, a distinguished,
soldierly-looking man. A little grave and
slow in manner.* ROBERT *and* MAY *go forward as they see him.*

JULIA. [*Evidently taken by surprise.*] Frank
—Colonel Endsleigh, when did you come?

[*Sir James comes forward.*

ENDSLEIGH. An hour ago. I have been having a talk with Lord Barnstaple and Lady Ida. How do you do, Lady Sarah? The old enemy? [*Pointing to the stick against her chair.*]

LADY S. My only lover, you should say—it is as troublesome as your sex and as constant as mine.

ENDSLEIGH. How do you do, Sir James? [*Shaking hands.*]

SIR J. [*Sulkily.*] How do? Is Geoff with you? We have been expecting him here.

ENDSLEIGH. No. I have come for him. [*Looking towards* MAY.]

JULIA. That is Evelyn's girl——

ENDSLEIGH. I knew her mother a good many years ago. [*Shaking hands with* MAY.] [*To* ROBERT, *nodding.*] You were just off when I saw you last.

ROBERT. I was. Have you come from Paris?

ENDSLEIGH. Yes.

SIR J. How long are you going to stay at Alassio?

ENDSLEIGH. An hour or two. The train for Genoa stops here at 7:30—I go by it.

Enter IDA *from loggia door on* L., *stands waiting a moment, then she stoops and speaks to* LADY S.

SIR J. [*Evidently satisfied.*] Why hasn't Geoff come?

ENDSLEIGH. He couldn't very well——

LADY S. [*To* IDA *who has been leaning down to her.*] Wants me? Is anything the matter. [*Tries to get up.*]

ENDSLEIGH. Let me. [*Goes forward and helps her with her stick, &c.*]

LADY S. I suppose I shall know soon enough. [*Exit with* ENDSLEIGH *into the house.*

IDA. [*To* JULIA.] Father wants you, and cousin James, too.

SIR J. [*Stirring himself with a grunt.*] What is it all about, I wonder?

JULIA. [*Lingers behind a minute with* IDA *and asks in a low voice.*] Has Frank Endsleigh come for you? Is that it?

IDA. No. He has been sent to explain why Geoff is not coming back. [*Exit with* JULIA.

[ROBERT *and* MAY *left alone on stage.*

MAY. [*Who has overheard.*] To explain why he is not coming back!

ROBERT. You have been expecting him?

MAY. I didn't know—I thought perhaps he would come. Uncle Edward wanted him. [*Looks up at the ruin on the mountain.*] This is the night they illuminate the church. I was afraid you wouldn't see it——

ROBERT. The Princess's lover never saw it. [*Checks himself. All through this interview he should keep himself well in hand.*] I wish we could have gone to Santa Croce again.

MAY. I wish it, too.

ROBERT. [*Pause.*] I wonder if we shall ever know each other again?

MAY. Know each other again—of course we shall—why we have been friends—friends—these last ten days. We have so many things in common.

ROBERT. [*Impatiently.*] Books and pictures and music—and the same Heaven or Hell to go to when we die. But for the rest our ways in this world lie apart.

MAY. Are we never to meet any more?

ROBERT. Meet? Of course we shall meet. We shall come across each other at evening parties, or nod from the stalls of a theatre. If I get in for Fieldborough and you are in London perhaps you will ask me to a Sunday luncheon, or if you are at—what is the Barnstaples' place called—Court Acres—for a Saturday to Monday.

MAY. I shall never be at Court Acres.

ROBERT. But that won't be knowing each other. And yet there will be always be behind us this ten days' dream at Alassio.

MAY. I wish we could take things out of dreams and carry them away.

ROBERT. The roots of most things lie in them——

MAY. And this time here——

ROBERT. Will help our conjectures in the future.—We have had some good days?

MAY. Such happy ones. [*Hurriedly, as if she were afraid of betraying too much.*] I simply love this place—and all the paths up the mountains.

ROBERT. Do you remember the charcoal burner's shed—where you told me about your mother, and little Dora studying art in Dresden?

MAY. She's taller than I am——

ROBERT. And Jack, who went up to Sandhurst last October?

MAY. [*Puzzled.*] I always feel as if you knew us.

ROBERT. I do—in my thoughts. I know exactly what your mother looks like.

MAY. [*Shyly.*] Would you care to come and see her?

ROBERT. No! [*Quickly.*] I will wait—till I have done more. Perhaps I imagine her younger than she is now—as she was when your father died.

MAY. I don't think she has altered very much.

ROBERT. Do you remember that time?

MAY. Oh, yes—so well, though I was very little. Aunt Sarah was such an angel to us. I shall never forget how she consoled me on my journey to Switzerland when I lost one of my white mice—— [*He gives a little start.*

ROBERT. One of your white mice?

MAY. They were in a cage—and I carried them all the way. Once at a station buffet, a waiter opened the cage door and didn't fasten it properly perhaps—it had been broken and mended.

ROBERT. Of course—— [*Stops abruptly.*

MAY. [*Looking up at him quickly for a minute, then going on unsuspiciously.*] One of them got out and I never saw it again. A little boy gave them to me who went to Australia. [*Robert turns his head.*] No, it was Canada—your country. . . . I imagine that mouse sometimes wandering about the world alone just as he may be doing.

ROBERT. Do you think the mouse has lived so long, or that he is as little as you remember him?

MAY. Don't be cynical—I like to imagine that the world is a fairy story; so let me be sentimental about my white mouse and Thomas.

ROBERT. Thomas?

MAY. That was the little boy's name.

LADY S. [*Heard off.*] I am going out again.

ROBERT. [*Quickly.*] Couldn't we go round the garden?

MAY. Not now. [*Half to herself.*] I must see Colonel Endsleigh. [*Then quickly.*] I think he brings me a message from Geoff. I wrote to him the other day, that is why I told you I should never be at Court Acres—I mean living there.

Enter LADY S., *and* LORD B., *and then* JULIA, *from door under loggia.*

LORD B. Well, May?

MAY. Where is Colonel Endsleigh?

LORD B. In the drawing-room. I wish you would go to him, my dear.

[*Exit* MAY *quickly into the house.*

[ROBERT *looks after her for a moment, then turns towards the garden and exit* R.

LADY S. Give me your arm, Edward, I should like to try and walk a little. [*They go on a few steps; she is evidently in pain.*] No, I can't do it. [*Sits down on seat* R.] Ah! [*With relief.*] This is very surprising news!

LORD B. Astounding!

LADY S. [*Drily.*] Evelyn won't be pleased.

LORD B. Neither am I.

LADY S. The money will be useful—Court Acres could absorb a good deal.

Lord B. We have never done that sort of thing, and—[*as* Sir J. *enters*]—I agree with Caxton, money is overrated.

Sir J. Everything is overrated, except the right things.

Lord B. It's probably a sudden infatuation —'pon my word, I shall be ashamed to tell May.

Julia. She won't break her heart, Uncle Edward.

Sir J. [*Meaningly.*] I think she finds Mr. Robert Vallide very agreeable.

Lord B. Vallide? Oh no, that's absurd. [*Pause.*] But she has talked to him a good deal now I think of it.

Sir J. Why shouldn't she?

Lady S. [*Drily.*] I don't think her mother would like it. As I said an hour ago, unfortunately in the young man's hearing—she is a very stiff-necked woman.

Julia. We don't know any one belonging to him—except his uncle, of course—but he's very clever.

Lord B. Oh, yes, clever enough to be Prime Minister one day, and as for money—still, you know——

Lady S. Evelyn is a difficult woman to cope with. There were some people at Montreux one winter—rich, and only occasionally vulgar, they had a house in Park Lane——

LORD B. Of course——

LADY S. I believe it has become rather a low neighbourhood?

LORD B. [*Humouring her.*] A combination of Houndsditch and Throgmorton Street.

LADY S. Well, it's gone down. But nothing would induce Evelyn to call upon them, she said they were upstarts.

LORD B. Quite right. She has her own views and sticks to them.

LADY S. And she would no more let her daughter marry young Vallide than she could fly.

LORD B. No—I expect not.

SIR J. Humph! he's not a fool, might do worse; where is Endsleigh?

JULIA. Talking to May. I think he has a message from Geoff.

Enter ROBERT *from garden* R. *crosses stage to go into the house.*

LORD B. [*To* ROBERT.] Oh, Vallide! I wanted you—we might have a few minutes. You start early to-morrow and——

[LADY S. *makes a movement as if in pain.* What's the matter—a twinge?

LADY S. A horrible twinge. [*Gets up from seat.*] I'll go to that chair.

ROBERT. Let me help you.

[ROBERT *takes her to chair on loggia,* JULIA *helps.*

JULIA. I am afraid you are in horrid pain.

LADY S. I'm in damnable pain.

LORD B. My dear Sarah—tut—tut—tut——

LADY S. My dear Edward, I'm making a plain statement to describe a fact.

ROBERT. And I'm sure it gives you some relief, Lady Sarah.

LADY S. Of course it does. You are a very sensible young man, and my brother says you will be Prime Minister one day.

ROBERT. Lord Barnstaple is much too kind.

JULIA. [*To* LADY S.] You had much better come in and take your dose. [*Turning to* SIR J.] Will you help her, James? Uncle Edward wants to talk to Mr. Vallide.

SIR J. Lean on me—there you are.

[*Exit* LADY SARAH *into house with* JULIA. SIR J., ROBERT, *and* LORD B. *left alone on stage.*

LORD B. I wanted to tell you, Vallide, that I had a letter from headquarters to-day and the Carlton highly approves. In fact, everything is before you; you have only to reach out your hand.

ROBERT. I can never thank you enough.

LORD B. [*Kind, but firm.*] My dear fellow, I am very glad if I've been of any use to you. [*Pause.*] By the way, there's—er—something else I want to say—a personal matter—it seems to me that you have had a good many talks with my niece since you came.

ROBERT. [*Surprised and a little stiffly.*] Miss Murison has delightful views about—the things in which most people are interested.

LORD B. Quite so. Shakespeare and the musical glasses—I believe young people discuss them still—but under different names. She is a charming girl and no doubt she will make a great marriage. Her mother—who is a very ambitious woman—would never consent to anything else, she expects it in fact.

ROBERT. I quite understand.

LORD B. When you came I told you that I hoped some day she and my dear boy Geoff would be everything to each other——

ROBERT. I beg you to believe that I have taken care never to forget it——

LORD B. I'm sure of it. As a matter of fact he asked her to marry him, but—they're cousins, which prevents things from being so romantic as they ought to be—at least that's *her* idea—and —to cut it short he is engaged to an American girl—pretty, Endsleigh says, very much in love with him, and an immense fortune which will be useful of course—useful—and—well it can't be helped.

ROBERT. [*Brimming over with delight but trying to conceal it.*] I congratulate you, she is certain to be delightful.

LORD B. You're very kind—but how do you know?

ROBERT. Americans are always delightful. Depend upon it, she's charming.

[*Holds out his hand unconsciously.* LORD B. *shakes it heartily.*

LORD B. I hope you're right. . . . And you don't think she has mistaken him for a duke? One must make that little joke since she's an American.

ROBERT. [*Enthusiastically.*] She takes him for what he is—a gallant young soldier and the only son of a distinguished statesman.

LORD B. Thank you, Vallide. By the way, it's no secret—[*looking at his watch*]—Endsleigh is going on to Genoa at 7:30, he won't let us make dinner any earlier for him—says he would rather dine in the train.

[*Turns to go, his back is to* ROBERT, *who stands stock still with his chin in his hand.* IDA *comes to door under loggia but he doesn't see her. With a sudden start he throws his hat into the air.*

IDA. [*Running out.*] Mr. Vallide, what is the matter?

ROBERT. [*Holding out his hands to her.*] Hurrah!

IDA. [*Laughing, and taking them.*] Yes, but why?

> [*While they are laughing,* MAY *comes out on to the loggia followed by* SIR J., *but he hangs back and is not noticed.* LORD B. *stops to talk to* MAY. SIR J. *joins them.*]

ROBERT. [*To* IDA.] Ah!

IDA. Do tell me—what it is. Are you Prime Minister already?

ROBERT. Not yet. [*Confidentially.*] But —Lord Stratton is going to be married.

[*She stares at him, then evidently comprehends.*]

IDA. But you told me at the Benson Greys there was some one—you used to know——

ROBERT. I have dreamt of her all my life, but now——

IDA. Now?

ROBERT. Now I am awake.

IDA. [*Puzzled.*] What will happen?

ROBERT. I shall know when I have been in London twenty-four hours.

IDA. Oh, you are a riddle.

ROBERT. Of which I long to know the answer.

> [LORD B. *draws back as if he were speaking confidentially to* JULIA, *who has*

*just re-entered and joined the group
at the loggia.* SIR JAMES *and* MAY *saunter out into the garden.*

ROBERT. [*To* IDA *significantly looking towards*
SIR J.] Take him away.

[*She nods, evidently understanding.*

IDA. [*To* SIR J.] Cousin Jim, I have been
trying to get hold of you. Let us go down the
garden. The pepper-trees and the laburnums
are so lovely in the twilight.

SIR J. [*Looks round, sees that* JULIA *and*
LORD B. *are together. Hesitates.*] Oh—don't
know that I care for pepper-trees and laburnums——

IDA. And the little banksia roses are coming
out on the wall by the sea. We might go for five
minutes while Colonel Endsleigh is finishing his
talk with Aunt Sarah—she won't let me get a
word with him——

[*This evidently reassures* SIR J. *Exit
with* IDA *on* R. *down garden.*

LORD B. [*To* JULIA.] I'll show it to you if
you like.

[*Exit* LORD B. *by loggia into house, followed by* JULIA.

[ROBERT *and* MAY *left alone on stage.*

ROBERT. [*The twilight is evidently coming.*]
It seems as if an enchantment had fallen again
—just as it did the first evening——

[*He stops and they look at each other em-*
barrassed.

MAY. [*Half hesitating.*] You know Geoff is
going to be married?

ROBERT. I know—it is splendid——

MAY. Why are *you* so glad?

ROBERT. [*His restraint has vanished.*] Because—because I'm devoted to Miss Pippin.

MAY. To Miss Pippin! You are altogether
different—quite suddenly.

ROBERT. The world is altogether different—
quite suddenly. The door of Heaven isn't open;
but it's creaking on its hinges.

MAY. Is it because of the letter Uncle Edward had from Downing Street?

ROBERT. No.

MAY. He thinks you'll do all manner of things.

ROBERT. I'll attempt them—I'll make for
them—for the sake of—her at whose feet they
will be laid.

MAY. [*Slowly.*] Who is she—mayn't I know?
I've told *you* so many things——

ROBERT. I want to tell you—everything. But
not yet. Sometimes I feel as if you understood
without any telling. . . . I long to speak,
but I mustn't—I can't. It isn't lack of courage
—it is something better than courage that holds
me back. There is an obstacle——

MAY. An obstacle!

ROBERT. Yes—but in England——
MAY. In England?
ROBERT. It may be swept away.—I don't know—I only know that I long to see you always—I keep breaking my resolutions—these little hands draw me on in spite of myself. I daren't say any more—but I am going to-morrow on my life's quest. If we never meet again, I shall think of you—dream of you——
MAY. [*In a low voice.*] And I of you.
ROBERT. [*Hesitates, then with an evident determination to control himself.*] Let us go and look for the others.

> [*They turn towards the path* R. *down the garden, stop for an instant and look up at the ruined church on the mountain. With an irresistible impulse,* ROBERT *turns to* MAY, *takes her hands, and says in a low passionate voice*

My princess—*my* princess—as long as I live—remember that.

> [ROBERT *and* MAY *disappear. The stage is empty.* LORD B., ENDSLEIGH, *and* JULIA *come through the loggia door into the garden.*

LORD B. [*Looking round.*] Where have they all gone?
JULIA. They're all in the garden. I saw May's white dress disappearing. [*Looks* R.

LORD B. I want to see Ida for a moment. I'll go after them.

[*Exit by the way the others went.*

[JULIA *and* ENDSLEIGH *left alone on the stage.*

JULIA. [*To Endsleigh.*] Why does he want to see Ida?

ENDS. I don't know—something about Geoff, I suppose.

[*They sit down and look at each other for a moment on seat* L. *centre by loggia.*

JULIA. This is the first time we've had a word alone since you came from India.

ENDS. I know—and I've been home three months. Your husband's a good chap, but he stalks you in such a sportsmanlike manner—when I'm near, at any rate—that I can't get a word in.

JULIA. We were such friends in old days——

ENDS. I don't think he wants us to be friends now.

JULIA. Why shouldn't we be? I think you are rather fond of—of—Ida——

ENDS. I asked her to marry me, but she wouldn't—didn't think it good enough, I suppose.

JULIA. [*In a voice she can hardly make steady.*] You told her that you had cared for some one before—that you had cared for years.

ENDS. I don't know what made me tell her.

JULIA. You did care? I thought it couldn't be true——

ENDS. It is—though I don't like owning up to you.

JULIA. Why? I've always wondered——

ENDS. Well, you see, I was awfully fond of *you* once. I think you liked me a bit, too. Do you remember how we used to pull about on the river? And the walks up and down the walled garden at Hampden Court.

JULIA. Yes.

ENDS. You were awfully pretty—and it doesn't seem to me that you've altered much. There was a wet day at the end—when we looked at the pictures.

JULIA. And sat in the window seat.

ENDS. That's it. I believe I was fonder of you that day than of anything in the world. Lady Caroline was in the garden and saw our heads through the window. It was only four days before I went away . . . and she gave me a talking-to before I left that night.

JULIA. Aunt Caroline did?

ENDS. [*Nods.*] She said you didn't care for me in that way—that you were ambitious and I was a pauper——

JULIA. O—h!

ENDS. I can tell you I was pretty hard hit for the first few days on board. . . . There was a girl going out to Bombay, five years older than I was, and she took me in hand. It was about the only thing that could have cured me.

JULIA. And it did cure you?

ENDS. In ten days I was her abject slave. At Calcutta and Simla—by some extraordinary luck we were always at the same place—we spent weeks together. It was an infatuation, I suppose; but it overwhelmed me like a wave. I fancy it amused her a good deal. She married Galsted, that man who got a peerage the other day for giving a public park somewhere.

JULIA. Have you seen her since?

ENDS. Yes—she would have liked to fool me a little more, I think. She didn't mean any harm, but she is the sort of woman who likes to have a current of sentiment running through her life.

JULIA. [*Cynically.*] And you forgot me entirely?

ENDS. No; but I jammed you down and stamped on you whenever you tried to come up. When I met Ida, a few months ago, she had a look of you in the eyes which sent me raking over the old ground. And she's an awfully good chum.

JULIA. If you want to marry her, you must tell her that you love her.

ENDS. [*Slowly.*] I am not sure that I do; but it seemed—like taking up the old story.

JULIA. [*With a bitter laugh.*] Oh, you men are so incomprehensible. Long ago I thought you cared for me—I was certain you did—all those hours on the river, and in the garden, and the things you said——. I was certain—certain—certain that you cared.

ENDS. I did.

JULIA. And yet Aunt Caroline made you believe that I wanted money; and you went away without a word, and told a girl on board the boat about me.

ENDS. She saved me from blowing my brains out.

JULIA. And you've been infatuated with her more or less all your life. Now you want to marry Ida——

ENDS. Let me explain. I loved you honestly enough, but I was hot-headed. If I hadn't done something I might have gone headlong to the devil.

JULIA. So you made love to a woman five years older than yourself——

ENDS. Well, but after all you seem to have been happy enough——

JULIA. It isn't fair to a man when you bear his name to go about looking dissatisfied; I've tried to play fair——

ENDS. Caxton has twenty thousand a year. I couldn't have done you as well as that.

JULIA. [*Almost without knowing it.*] What is the good of gold when you want bread— [*Checking herself.*] Shall you ask Ida again?

ENDS. I couldn't to-day. [*with a change of voice*] the sight of you always pulls the strings of everything that is strongest in me.

> [*He stoops suddenly and kisses her hand which is resting on the back of the seat, his face is three-quarters towards garden, hers turned away from it.*

> [ROBERT *appears from garden right; the two men look at each other for one second and* ROBERT *retreats. A minute later his voice is heard as if advancing.*

ROBERT. All right, Sir James, Endsleigh is here.

> [JULIA *rises quickly, goes towards house, but stops as* SIR JAMES *appears. She and* ENDSLEIGH *stand facing him from different points.*

SIR J. [*Looking from one to the other.*] Eh —interrupted a talk?

ENDS. [*Rather stiffly.*] Lady Caxton and I are old, old friends.

SIR J. I am aware of it. Sorry to be in the way, but——

JULIA. [*Haughtily.*] You needn't apologise
—we had finished what we had to say.

Enter LORD B. *from the garden, evidently hur-*
ried.

LORD B. Oh, there you are, Endsleigh. You
have only ten minutes—barely that, unless you
stay till to-morrow?

ENDS. I fear not. Where are the young
ladies? I want to say good-bye to them.

LORD B. [*Looking round.*] I thought they
were here. But there's no time—I am going with
you to the station. [To ROBERT.] Come too?

[ROBERT *hesitates.*

ENDS. Yes do, Vallide.

ROBERT. I will, if you wish it.

ENDS. Good-bye, Lady Caxton. I don't know
if we shall meet again before I go back to
India. But if I am in London——

SIR J. [*Firmly.*] We shall probably be away.

JULIA. [*To* ENDSLEIGH.] And you will have
a great deal to do.

LORD B. Come—come—you'll lose that train.
It's nearer by the garden.

[*Turns towards extreme left.*

JULIA. Good-bye.

[*Shakes hands with* ENDSLEIGH *and turns*
away.

[*Exeunt* ROBERT, LORD B., *and* ENDSLEIGH
by garden.

[*Julia and Sir James alone.*

Sir J. What were you talking to Endsleigh about?

Julia. [*Defiantly.*] I shall not tell you.

Sir J. Oh!—well, I can take care of my own——

Julia. [*Bitterly.*] Take care of your own? You mean that you are always watching me—listening—spying upon me.

Sir J. That's rather a strong word.

Julia. Yes, too strong, perhaps, but you seem to be always suspecting me—and the everlasting togetherness of marriage, as you interpret it, is terrible.

Sir J. What do you mean?

Julia. I mean that I want to be free, to be trusted, not to be perpetually stalked. . . . Can't you understand that every human being longs to be alone sometimes. Oh, the luxury of it!

Sir J. You weren't alone just now.

Julia. That has nothing to do with it. [*Softening.*] I don't mean to be brutal, but I am distracted—go away now, James. [*Holding out her hand, half entreating.*] Let me be by myself. [*Turns towards house and half hesitates, then goes back towards middle of stage.*] And I want to go back to England, I can't bear this any longer——

Sir J. I'll take you back to-morrow.

Julia. *Take* me back—oh, of course! Go in and leave me—now at any rate.

> [*He turns towards the house, and stops as* Lady S. *hobbles out on to the loggia, making business with her stick, &c.* Sir J. *helps to seat her in her chair, gives a sort of grunt, looks back at* Julia, *then exit.*

Lady S. Thank you.

> [Julia, *standing in the middle of the stage, looks in the direction* Endsleigh *has gone, and gives a sigh of relief.*
> [Lady S. *pretends not to see her for a moment.*
> *Enter* Servant *with a telegram.*

Servant. [*To* Lady S.] It's a telegram for Mr. Vallide, my lady.

Lady S. [*Crossly.*] Well, you must find him —where is he?

Julia. [*With a start, going towards* Lady S.] He has gone to see Colonel Endsleigh off. [*To* Servant.] He can only be at the turn of the road. [*Looking left.*] You might run after him, perhaps it's important—then he can answer it from the station.

> [*Exit* Servant. Julia, *with a quick passionate movement, throws herself*

on her knees beside the chair, and puts her arms round LADY SARAH.

JULIA. Aunt Sarah, I want you, I want you so.

LADY S. He hasn't been making love to you?

JULIA. No, he *never* cared, and Aunt Caroline spoke to him—before he went to India.

LADY S. I knew she had——

JULIA. He told a girl on board the boat about me, and fell in love with *her*. He has been infatuated with *her* more or less all his life till lately. With her—not with me—with her. [*A sort of hysterical laugh.*] Oh, Aunt Sarah, what fools women are, and yet he was good and honest—at least *that*.

LADY S. I have no patience with good men, they are always stupid. My dear—[*soothing* JULIA]—I knew she'd spoken to him that night; he was a young idiot. [*Pause.*

JULIA. [*In a whisper.*] I'm frightened for May.

LADY S. For May?

JULIA. It may be the same story over again.

LADY S. [*Stifling a twinge of gout which makes her wince.*] What do you mean?

JULIA. She has been falling in love with Mr. Vallide; I've seen it, and Evelyn would never hear of it, you know——

LADY S. Never!

JULIA. Besides——

LADY S. Besides what?

JULIA. There's some one else—he told Ida about her—some one he has thought of all his life.

LADY S. [*Thoughtfully.*] I believe he cares for May—I saw his face—I am old, but I know the signs.

JULIA. It may be just the glamour of Italy and the Spring, as it was the glamour of the river and the walled garden at Hampden Court that I mistook. Frank didn't care—and look at Geoff, he thought he cared about May, for years —and now this American girl.

LADY S. Young men ought to be hanged, in rows. As for May, as you say, her mother would never hear of it. The young man might as well care for the moon, as far as she is concerned.

[IDA *and* MAY *appear from end of garden on* R.

JULIA. Hush, here she is.

[JULIA *stands up quickly in the shadow under the loggia by* LADY S.'s *chair with her back to the house.* IDA *goes forward towards loggia.* MAY *remains in centre of stage, looking up at the ruined church on the mountain. Then sits,* R. *The twilight deepens.*

IDA. [*To* JULIA, *laughing.*] They've gone, haven't they? I didn't want to say good-bye to Colonel Endsleigh.

LADY S. [*Sharply.*] Oh—why not, pray?

JULIA. Why not?

IDA. [*In a low tone to* JULIA.] If dumb men can't talk, they can sometimes write. I've had a letter from one this evening.

MAY. Isn't it splendid that they light up the church to-night? Mr. Vallide will see it.

JULIA. [*Going towards her.*] The Princess lighted it up, and waited for her lover; but he never came.

MAY. [*Dreamily.*] Perhaps their spirits are stealing back to it now, through and through the shadows——

JULIA. What does it matter? They are not human any more.

> [LORD B. *appears at door of loggia evi-*
> *dently rather excited, and speaking*
> *presumably to a servant behind him.*

LORD B. Send them all on at once. [*To every one.*] I've got some news for you.

IDA. News!

LORD B. Vallide has gone. Had a telegram just as we started.

MAY. [*Getting up quickly.*] Gone!

LORD B. Gone on with Endsleigh to catch the express for Rome. Uncle there down with

fever—wants his nephew to take him back to
Canada—sails from Genoa early next week.

MAY. To Canada?

LORD B. It's the deuce. Vallide feels he
ought to go. I was to tell you, and say good-bye
to you all. The worst of it is that he has no
idea when he will be back. The uncle may be ill
for a long time, and keep him over there. I'd
made all sorts of plans with him for next week
in London—very tiresome.

LADY S. [*Drops her stick; he picks it up and
gives it to her.*] Humph!

MAY. To Canada!

LORD B. Awkward, isn't it? You see [*To
LADY S.*] if he goes—— What is it, another
twinge?   [*Arranges her cushions, &c.*

JULIA [*Going closer to* MAY.] Did he tell
you he loved you?

MAY. [*In a whisper.*] No—but he does. I
know he does.

JULIA. There is some one else?

MAY. No! there is *no* one else. . . . I
can't believe that he is gone——

JULIA. [*Almost in a whisper.*] He'll never
come back. It is always the same story. He
will never, never come back.

LADY S. [*To* LORD B.] What did he say?
Was he upset?

LORD B. Yes, a good deal, but—I say! Look

at the ruin! [*They all look up at the ruined church on the mountain, which is illuminated.*] Pity Vallide isn't here. He spoke of it the last thing. He wanted to see it.

MAY. [*Almost staggering.*] The Princess's lover never saw it—he never saw it lighted up.

JULIA. He never came back. [*Soft music.*] Listen. They are chanting a ghostly mass— a mass for the dead. [*A soft mass is heard in the distance—very faintly. Whispers.*] He never came back!

MAY. Julia! [*Staggers towards seat.*]

CURTAIN.

ACT IV

TIME.—*Three weeks later.*

SCENE.—*A sitting-room in* MRS. MURISON'S *house on Campden Hill. A pretty room with chintzes, &c., (obviously on first not ground-floor), fireplace* R., *with door same side lower down, Door* L.: *At the back facing the stage two mullioned windows, square paned and pretty. When open they show trees in blossom in the garden, laburnums, &c., between the windows there is a little white bookshelf.*

When the Curtain draws up MRS. MURISON, LORD BARNSTAPLE, *and* LADY SARAH STRATTON *are discovered.*

LORD B. [*Looking round.*] I think you've done very well, Evelyn. It's an extremely pleasant house.

MRS. M. This is May's own little sitting-room.

LADY S. When she is married it will do for Dora—Edward, we ought to go.

MRS. M. Won't you wait and see Julia? She'll be down directly. James is coming for her at half-past three.

LORD B. I am glad to hear it. I don't know

191

what happened between them at Alassio—[*To*
MRS. M.] Do you?

LADY S. I can tell you, my dear Edward,
Julia wanted to get rid of him for a fortnight.
All women want to get rid of men sometimes—
but we can't make them believe it.

LORD B. She could have stayed quietly in
Eaton Square, he hasn't been in London.

LADY S. But she wanted to get away not only
from James Caxton, but from everything that
was his—to think out things and set her life
straight.

LORD B. Well, I give it up—something went
wrong, Julia insisted on bringing May back to
her mother—pretended she wanted her. Caxton came as far as Dover with them, then went
off to Fieldborough and sulked.

MRS. M. He has written to her—they are going home together. . . . You've not told me
anything about Ida—and Frank Endsleigh.

LADY S. He has gone to Sicily—till he goes
back to India.

LORD B. There's no idea of anything between
them. He's too old. Teddy Haston is always
about the house now—the youth has merit.

MRS. M. His people are extremely nice. [*To*
LORD B.] You will be very lonely if she marries
too, Uncle Edward.

LORD B. Well—no doubt we shall see a great

deal of Geoff and his American young lady—
who has charming manners.

LADY S. But her mother is tiresome—I knew
she would be.

LORD B. She'll go back to America; and the
turbulence of the Atlantic settles many difficulties.

LADY S. The girl's pretty——

MRS. M. I hear she's lovely.

LORD B. Well, you'll be able to judge for
yourself this afternoon. They are coming to see
you—but he told me to say he was afraid they
could not get here till half-past five. . . .

Enter MAY.

MAY. Julia will be down in ten minutes——

LORD B. I don't think we can wait. . . .
We like your new house, May——

MAY. And my little sitting-room—[*Looking
round.*

LORD B. It's charming, my dear. But [*looking at her*] you don't look as well as you did at
Alassio—how's that?

MAY. It's only London. [*Goes over to the
book-shelf between the windows.*] Italy is an
enchanted land——

MRS. M. She has been so quiet since she came
back.

MAY. Do you like my book-shelf, Aunt Sarah?

LADY S. Book-shelf? Oh, yes, I notice that
that is one of the modern affectations. Girls must

have little book-shelves now—painted white—full of little books, nicely bound.

MAY. [*Laughing.*] Modern poets—precious essays—pocket editions of the classics, and sometimes we read them. [*With a twinkle in her eye.*]

LORD B. My dear, you are growing cynical. [*Looks at her curiously.*] Have you heard from Vallide?

MRS. M. Why should May hear from Mr. Vallide?

LORD B. I should say it's not unlikely—they were great friends.

MAY. Do you know where he is, Uncle Edward?—Is he coming back from Canada?

LORD B. He hasn't gone to Canada. His uncle is much better and sailed two days ago. Vallide arrived in London this morning.

MRS. M. [*Pleasantly.*] Who is this Mr. Vallide?

LORD B. The new candidate for Fieldborough; we all liked him very much at Alassio.

LADY S. I understand that he'll be Prime Minister some day.

LORD B. He's very well thought of, I can tell you——

MRS. M. Yes, but *who* is he?

LORD B. He is the nephew of a man I met in Canada—who did a great deal for education—and designed a few railways—a millionaire of course—the young man came over here and was my private secretary when I was in office.

LADY S. He's an Englishman—but we don't know who his people are—or whether he has any——

MRS. M. I see—pushing himself to the front with the help of his uncle's money—and careful to say nothing about his antecedents like those people at Montreux——

MAY. Mother, you mustn't say that! You can't think how delightful he is—how simple—and clever—and well-bred——

MRS. M. May! [*Surprised and as if she suddenly suspected.*]

LADY S. [*To* MAY.] I told you your mother's neck was stiff.

MRS. M. Think of the vulgarity of wealth in these days.

LADY S. Not at all. Think of the comfort of it. The vulgarity of many people who possess it is unfortunate of course——

MRS. M. All the money seems to go to the lower class now, it pushes them in everywhere.

LORD B. That's true—but the Chancellor of the Exchequer will tone things down—give him time, he doesn't need very much.

LADY S. Meanwhile we are expected to invite the postman to dinner and the sweep and his wife for a week-end. But you needn't agitate yourself,

my dear, there will always be a difference of
class, though the fences are broken that used to
separate them.

MRS. M. [*To* LORD B.] Is this Mr. Vallide an
educated man—I suppose he is as he was your
secretary?

LORD B. [*Grudgingly but with conviction.*]
He's a man we shall all be proud to know some
day.

MRS. M. [*Uneasily.*] I dislike new people—I
can't help it.

LADY S. They make an excellent variety show.

MAY. Oh, don't say that, dear Aunt Sarah.
The race started fair, with everybody equal. But
some had the best instincts, and made for the
right things, and kept them and were nourished
on them—and others had to take what was left.
I suppose that's how the difference of class came
about. And though the difference will always exist there must be new people added to the best,
or the best will die out. I haven't expressed it.
very well—but, perhaps you know what I mean.
The oldest, grandest house has to be propped up
with new material, and once it was a new house
too——

LORD B. May! I didn't know that you thought
about these things—you are quite eloquent.

MAY. Every one thinks.

LORD B. I wish they did, my dear, the world

would be better and less of a beer-garden. Come, Sarah, we won't wait for Julia.

LADY S. [*Going.*] We shall all meet in Bruton Street to-night.

LORD B. [*To* MAY.] I won't tell Vallide what you said about him, it might turn his head.

MRS. M. [*To* LADY S.] Good-bye, Aunt Sarah.

[MRS. MURISON *rings the bell, they all go towards the door.*

LORD B. [*Looking back at* MAY.] A very nice room indeed, my dear, good-bye.

[*Exeunt* LADY S. *and* LORD B.

[MRS. MURISON *and* MAY *return into the room.* MAY *stands by her book-shelf.* MRS. MURISON *by the fireplace.*

MAY. [*After a pause.*] I wish we had some flowers, mother—Geoff and Miss Pippin are coming—the drawing-room is very bare.

[*Goes to piano and begins to play.*

MRS. M. I'm afraid we can't send for any now. [*Business.*] What is that tune you are always playing——

MAY. " The Distant Shore."

Enter SERVANT, *with a note on tray, gives it to* MRS. MURISON.

[*Exit* SERVANT.

MRS. M. [*Opens the note, looks at signature, says to herself*]. Robert Vallide!

[*Reads it and stands silently thinking.*

[MAY *still playing very softly.—Pause.*

MRS. M. May, did you like this Mr. Vallide?

MAY. [*Gets up from the piano and stands by the book-case again looking at* MRS. M.] Yes, mother.

MRS. M. Uncle Edward seems to think a great deal of him.

MAY. Every one thinks a great deal of him.

MRS. M. Did you like him—very much? [*Tenderly.*] Won't you tell me, darling?

MAY. [*Passionately.*] How can I after what you said. [*Change of manner.*] Oh, but you've always been such a dear mother, why shouldn't I tell you—I never met any one like him. I don't believe there *is* any one like him in the world.

MRS. M. Do you think he cares for you?

MAY. Yes. [*Then doubtfully.*] I thought he did—but he hasn't written—he hasn't done anything. I think I know the reason of—of——

MRS. M. Of what?

MAY. Of his not speaking—but I thought he would have written—I've been miserable this last week. But I *know* he cares—and I can't tell you what he is—he isn't like any one else I have ever met. Ida said before he came that he had the new-world vigour and the old-world charm —he has—and he's so straight, so clever—I can't think why he should hold back. . . . Why he didn't tell me——   [*Pause.*

Mrs. M. Suppose you go for some flowers. [*Evidently this is a sudden thought.*] Wilson can go with you in a taxi—to Solomon's——

May. It would take so long—he arrived in England to-day uncle Edward said—if he came——

Mrs. M. It's too early yet, you will be back. Why didn't you tell me before? You have hardly mentioned his name.

May. I couldn't. Mother, what a dear you are. . . . He said he was coming to England on his life's quest—that at the end of twenty-four hours he would know . . . I can't think what he meant. And yet I feel that it had to do with me. . . . I think that—that—he isn't anybody—in the sense that is so much to you. He is just a new man; but there are great things before him—he is going to do them—to do them himself. Isn't it much better than if they were all behind—and the honours had been won already by his ancestors—and *he* did nothing— better than if he were living on the reward of deeds done long ago by others?

Mrs. M. Why, May!——

May. I know it's going to be very difficult for you, darling—at least I think it is—if he comes. If he *does,* I want you to remember that —that my happiness is at stake, that—that—I love him—I wouldn't own it to any one in the

wide world but you—and to him if he should
ever ask me. Oh, mother, dear——

Mrs. M. [*Tenderly and surprised.*] My darling, you must trust me . . . There's the bell!
It is Sir James, I expect . . . The drive will
do you good. Go and bring back some flowers
—and green boughs to deck your room—tell Wilson I said she was to go with you.

> [*Exit* May *quickly* L.
> [Servant *announces*]

Servant. Sir James Caxton!

> *Enter* Sir James.

Sir J. How d'ye do?

Mrs. M. Julia will be here directly, she's
quite ready.

Sir J. Oh! [*Looking round.*] Nice house
—cheerful.

Mrs. M. So glad you like it. You've been
at Fieldborough?

Sir J. At Fieldborough—shan't be there much
more. You know that?

Mrs. M. What do you think of your probable
successor?

Sir J. What, Vallide? Decent chap. Very
decent chap, indeed.

Mrs. M. You liked him?

Sir J. Yes; piece of luck for Fieldborough
if they get him.

Mrs. M. O—o—h! [*Thoughtfully.*] And

you thought—But here is Julia—and I didn't give May a cab fare.

Enter JULIA.

JULIA. [*To* SIR J.] I heard you come.

[*Exit* MRS. MURISON.

[SIR JAMES *and* JULIA *alone*.

SIR J. [*To* JULIA.] Well—better?

[*Holds out his hand*.

JULIA. Much better. And you?

SIR J. Pretty well. Ready to come home?

JULIA. Yes, if you want me.

SIR J. You can do as you like. It's dull alone, but it's dull anyway. I've never got much out of it—I thought I should—but I didn't.

JULIA. What do you mean?

SIR J. I don't know. Look here, Julia, you never pretended to care much about me—I'm old—and ugly—and dull, I suppose, but I want to know the truth. Was Endsleigh making love to you? Vallide slipped back to give you warning, but I saw you through the trees. He was the chap who were breaking your heart about when you were a girl. No one told me his name, but I knew.

JULIA. Yes, it was Frank Endsleigh.

SIR J. And it's because of him that you have always kept me at arm's length—given me my due to the letter, but nothing else.

JULIA. [*Half tragic.*] But nothing else, Jim, nothing else. I prided myself on playing fair, but I haven't done so.

SIR J. [*Suspiciously.*] Eh? What?

JULIA. In my heart, I mean. Outwardly I did—absolutely. I was talked into marrying you; but I never pretended to care. I know how good you've been to me, how many things you've given me . . . I counted my bangles only yesterday—wasn't it silly—with all the different stones, and looked at the sable cloak you gave me on my birthday last year. You always tried to win me with money and goods and chattels.

SIR J. Women generally like them. I was too old to make love. Besides, I thought you cared for the other chap——

JULIA. I did—all the years that I have been married to you—I never wrote—or sent a message—but at the bottom of my heart, at the back of my head, there he lived, and I thought he cared for me—that his life was just waiting—waiting——

SIR J. For me to die?

JULIA. [*Quickly.*] No, for some indefinite time when we should justify ourselves to each other and then go our separate ways. He only came back from India five months ago—why didn't you let me speak with him?

SIR J. I knew he was the man.

JULIA. Ten minutes talk would have cleared everything away. But I never had it till that day at Alassio.

SIR J. What did he say for himself?

JULIA. [*With a half-tragic, half-scornful laugh.*] He told me about a woman he had met on board the boat, and how he had loved her all his life. Her—not me! The whole thing has been a myth—a mistake, a farce. I've wasted all the good years of my life on a dream.

SIR J. So have I.

JULIA. You!

SIR J. Well, I never thought about anything but you, or wanted anything else——

JULIA. [*Almost pathetic.*] Why didn't you say so? You always grunted and hung about and said nothing.

SIR J. I thought you knew.

JULIA. Perhaps I did—but there are some things one doesn't choose to know—won't know —till they're put into words; and gifts are no good.

SIR J. I thought they'd make you come round —I've had a bad time—but you didn't know that.

JULIA. It has ended. And—there was nothing—nothing said at Alassio to make you unhappy. He kissed my hand and explained about the other woman. That was all.

SIR J. Why did you insist on coming to stay with Evelyn?

JULIA. Because the house had tumbled down in which for years I had put all my dreams. I wanted to be alone to think over its ruin. Every human being wants to be alone sometimes——

SIR J. [*Bitterly.*] And the everlasting togetherness of marriage is so terrible.

JULIA. [*He is standing by her; she is sitting down on the sofa.*] Oh, Jim, dear—forgive me —it shall be better. I am *glad* we are together.
[*Kisses his hand.*

SIR J. Don't do that—I can't bear it. Perhaps it's too late; but we have a fair field at last.

JULIA. It's not too late—it shan't be too late —I have been a fool.
[*Putting her cheek against his hand.*

SIR J. Of course, that's why I'm one——

JULIA. Why are you one?

SIR J. [*Tenderly.*] There is nothing like a woman who is a fool for getting at you—and making you another.

JULIA. Oh, Jim!

SIR J. But it hasn't been much of a show for either of us.

JULIA. [*Gets up.*] Let us go home—this very minute. Where's Evelyn? [*Goes to door on* R.] Evelyn. [*Calling.*] We are going. [*To* SIR J.] Is the carriage here?

SIR J. Yes—and there's a new rug in it—black bearskin.

JULIA. Oh, you! [*Laughing, and going towards the door—turns back and kisses him.*] I must go and get ready.

Enter MRS. MURISON.

JULIA. Couldn't you show him the drawing-room, Evelyn? [*To him.*] It's such a nice house, and a garden. . . . Did you see the laburnums and the lilacs? [*Goes to the windows at back of stage, pushes open the casement a little way, then draws back, and says*] Mr. Vallide is just coming in at the gate—he didn't see me.

MRS. M. [*Quickly. Rings.*] Wait——

Enter SERVANT.

MRS. M. [*To* SERVANT.] Show the gentleman who is at the front door into the drawing-room. [*Turns and looks at* SIR JAMES *and* JULIA, *obviously agitated, but trying to conceal it.*] I didn't think he would come so early.

JULIA. You knew he was coming?

MRS. M. Yes—I knew.

SIR J. Is that why you asked me about him?

MRS. M. He sent me a note just now—asking me to see him alone.

JULIA. I believe he has come to——

MRS. M. [*With a thrill of dismay.*] You mean?

JULIA. Yes—yes—for May.

MRS. M. [*Ruefully, and evidently knowing what is before her.*] I don't want to give her up—it was different with Geoff; that was a thing that had grown—besides *he* was one of *us*. I want to keep her a little longer.

JULIA. But if they love each other?

SIR J. [*With conviction.*] I believe he's a good chap.

MRS. M. But I don't want it to be Mr. Vallide —and yet if she cares——

JULIA. Let him have her—her young lover— her first lover—nothing else will ever be the same. Oh, Jim, forgive me. [*Quickly.*] I didn't mean to hurt *you;* but youth only comes once——

MRS. M. [*To* SIR J.] You like him, *you* like him?

SIR J. Have said so already, excellent chap, —fond of May—certain of it—a millionaire, or uncle a millionaire—same thing.

MRS. M. Oh, I hate money—I mean when the wrong people have it.

SIR J. He's the right person—he'll know what to do with it—was at Balliol—Fellow of his College—probably a prig when he left it—what more do you want?

MRS. M. It's a great deal, but—I must go to him.

JULIA. See him here, Evelyn—in May's room.

MRS. M. [*Helplessly.*] She is all the world to me.

JULIA. [*Who has gone towards the door with* SIR J.] I know. . . . [*Gratefully.*] Thank you for everything you have been to me. We'll go.

SIR J. [*Hesitating.*] Vallide is a good chap —he'll do more than any of *us*.

[*Exeunt* SIR JAMES *and* JULIA.

[MRS. MURISON *alone, makes business for a minute—rings.*

Enter SERVANT.

MRS. M. Ask Mr. Vallide if he will come here.

[*Exit* SERVANT.

Pause. Re-enter SERVANT.

SERVANT. Mr. Vallide.

Enter ROBERT.

MRS. M. How do you do?

[*Shakes hands—her manner is quite courteous, but cold.*

ROBERT. You don't know me, but——

MRS. M. But I have heard of you. You were in Alassio the other day—Lord Barnstaple and Lady Sarah were here just now.

ROBERT. Oh——

MRS. M. Won't you sit down? I think you left before they did?

ROBERT. I was hurrying back to London——

Mrs. M. But you have been in Rome since?

Robert. I had to go there suddenly, but I wanted to come back to England—it's so difficult to explain though I have come to do that.

Mrs. M. I don't understand. [*Then quickly, as if anxious to avoid explanation.*] You have known Lord Barnstaple a long time, I think?

Robert. A long time. In Canada first——

Mrs. M. And afterwards you were his private secretary, he told me to-day.

Robert. For two or three months only——

Mrs. M. [*Hurriedly.*] It was unlucky the Government went out so soon. And now you are going to put up for Fieldborough? Sir James Caxton has been its member for eighteen years. He was here, too, just now; he thinks you are sure to succeed him.

Robert. Perhaps—I don't know. It depends —on—the matter that has brought me here.

Mrs. M. [*Beginning to face it.*] On the matter that has brought you here?

Robert. At Alassio I met so many of your relations——

Mrs. M. Oh, yes, Lady Sarah Stratton, she is my Aunt—the Caxtons—and my daughter, of course.

Robert. And your daughter—is she back? She was going to Paris.

Mrs. M. Lady Caxton brought her home—

sooner than was intended—the day after you
left, I think——

ROBERT. And she is here?

MRS. M. She is here; but she is out just now.
[*Hesitating.*] She didn't know that you were
coming. . . . I thought I should prefer to
see you alone—you said you wanted to see *me.*

[*Evidently feeling bound to come to a point.*

ROBERT. Yes, it is you that I have come to
see. It was to see you that I was hurrying to
England, but the night before I was to start
a telegram came, saying that my uncle was down
with fever——

MRS. M. And naturally you went to him.

ROBERT. As soon as he was better we went
to Genoa. His ship sailed from there for Canada. I watched it out of sight two days ago,
then took the next train for England. Does all
this say anything to you—But it's impossible
that you should remember me.

MRS. M. Remember you? Have we met before?

ROBERT. Yes—we have met before—that is
why I have come—why I held back at Alassio——

MRS. M. I don't understand.

ROBERT. Do you remember Thomas——

MRS. M. Thomas?

ROBERT. Thomas Lobb?

MRS. M. [*Looking at him.*] Oh, yes, of course

—the little boy who went to Canada. Do you know anything about him or—do you know him? I should like to hear of him again.

ROBERT. I am Thomas.

MRS. M. You! Oh no——

ROBERT. It is so—I am Thomas.

MRS. M. It's too extraordinary! . . . You went to Canada—your uncle sent for you.

ROBERT. But I came back after two years.

MRS. M. We were abroad——

ROBERT. I know. I used to walk by the empty house, and look up at the window, closed and dusty, through which I had heard May's voice for the last time—[MRS. M. *gives a little backward movement as he says* MAY's *Christian name, and he corrects himself cynically.*]—your daughter's voice. . . . I didn't know where you had gone. I rang the bell and asked the caretaker once; but she could only tell me that you were in Switzerland.

MRS. M. [*A shade patronising, and just a little haughtily.*] I wish you had written, I should have been so—interested.

ROBERT. I didn't want you to know anything about me. I wanted to see you, but without your seeing *me*.

MRS. M. Why shouldn't you want us to see you?

ROBERT. Because I had learnt even then that

I couldn't meet you on the old footing, and I knew that you would not receive me on any other—there were stretches and gulfs between us.

MRS. M. You shouldn't say that.

ROBERT. [*Not noticing.*] All these years I have been trying to make a bridge across them —not with any definite end in view, but only that I might take some place in the world that was nearer yours. I knew all the prejudices——

MRS. M. I was born with them——

ROBERT. Oh yes, I know—forgive me. [*Suddenly.*] I have often thought of the day we saw you first—you came into the room where my father sat over he fire warming his hands; you had some flowers, you brought him some more the night he died, and put them at his feet— I remember just what you looked like—tender and sweet, but very proud; and even that remembrance has made me feel as if there were mountains not to be crossed.

MRS. M. [*Again evidently frightened at what she has to face.*] Why should they be crossed?

ROBERT. I didn't know till I saw May coming in from the orange garden at Alassio—and loved her—but I've loved her all my life, thought of her, dreamt of her, lived for her. In my thoughts everything has been laid before her, that is why I have come.

MRS. M. [*Drawing back a little.*] I can't discuss it—or listen to any more on this subject. Tell me about your mother—where is she?

ROBERT. She died five years ago. My uncle sent for her to Canada. She lived a life of ease and tried not to find it dull, [*cynically*] and wore dresses to which she had never been accustomed and tried not to feel awkward in them. But she was happy enough, thank God.

MRS. M. It's all so unbelievable. And Polly?

ROBERT. Polly calls herself Mary now—and is married to a sturdy Canadian who owns more territory than he can walk over in a week.

MRS. M. And you—you went away Thomas Lobb. Why have you come back Robert Vallide?

ROBERT. My second name was Robert and I liked being called by it—it was my father's—and my uncle is proud of his Cornish name. The Robert Vallides have never been of any consequence—fishermen or miners, or engineers—men who were near the earth or the sea and battled with it, but they can be counted a long way back—he didn't want the name to die out.

MRS. M. And you—what happened to you when you first went out?

ROBERT. I was sent to a school-marm for a couple of years, then back to England with a tutor. When I was licked into shape, and had travelled a little, I went to Oxford.

MRS. M. And are you a fellow of your College?

ROBERT. You knew?

MRS. M. Lady Caxton told me.

ROBERT. Ah!

MRS. M. And then?

ROBERT. Then I started out in the world—on my own; various things came my way that lead towards politics. Lord Barnstaple has proposed that I should offer myself as a candidate for Fieldborough.

MRS. M. It's so bewildering—I can't believe that you are Thomas.

ROBERT. But it's true, it's true. I used to carry out newspapers in the morning, and bring up coals into your drawing-room, and try not to let you see that I found them heavy—I want you to realise all that I was and used to do—you gave my mother a mangle.

MRS. M. Oh! [*Drawing back again.*] How clever you have been, how good! You will think me—so narrow, so vulgar——

ROBERT. No, I understand. . . . The last day I was in England while I stood by the door waiting with a telegram, I heard you say that when May grew up you would rather she married a beggar in her own class than a new-made millionaire. . . . I'm not a millionaire—yet at any rate—that at least is an extenuating circumstance—I know all that you feel about—about—I don't want to say upstarts. [*With a weary smile.*]

Mrs. M. I can't help it, I never have been able to stand the new people who come rushing through the world seizing the things of which they've no knowledge and for which they've no reverence —I don't mean this for you, of course—you'll think me full of snobbish prejudices——

Robert. I like them. It's the knowledge that for generations back, one behind the other, your people helped to safeguard the country and did great deeds for the world. But I am just as proud of *my* sturdy ancestors—my fisher-fathers and thrifty mothers—as you are of knowing that some of yours were Crusaders. Mine worked for their country, too, and gave me the instinct to work—in a different manner from theirs, but with as much determination—and I will, if this day goes well with me.

Mrs. M. Your mother must have looked so different. [*Evidently trying to make time.*]

Robert. She used to think herself a great lady, and was counted one in the colonies. She would never let me remember the old days, Mary quarrels with me if I even mention them, and wouldn't come to England for the world, lest any one she knew once—there isn't a soul to do it—should remember her.

Mrs. M. [*Looking at him, dazed.*] I can't believe it, even now. [*Pause.*

Robert. [*A little desperately.*] Do you remember the day I wished you good-bye—a little lad going off alone to the other side of the world —without a penny save the present you had given me. You kissed me, just as if I had been your own son—this last three weeks I have dreamed that perhaps I should be. If she cares for me, won't you let it come true? I love her— I love her—and I think she loves me back again.

Mrs. M. I can't——

Robert. Is it such a crime to have been poor —to have worked——

Mrs. M. No, no, it's wonderful. Oh, what can I say? I *want* to be different—if it had only been——

Robert. [*With an odd smile.*] If it had only been some one else's shoes I blacked.

Mrs. M. Yes, somehow it would seem quite different.

Robert. Or any one else's daughter that I wanted to marry——

Mrs. M. I know—I know. I should laugh at the objections—it's only experience that teaches. You didn't speak to her or tell her this? She doesn't know——

Robert. That I love her—she must know it,

though I didn't put it into actual words, I wouldn't till I'd seen you.

Mrs. M. That was like you. [*Looking up at him.*] Some men would have taken advantage —would have tried to win her without any scruple.

Robert. A man has a right to try and win the woman he loves if they are both free and he knows he can make the way smooth for her, but this is different—I couldn't win *her* against your will, I remember all you were, all you did, too well; and if you say it mustn't be I will go away and never see her again. I will make it my burnt sacrifice to your goodness in past years. But I am a man, strong and well—and ready to work. I love her—and will win all things for her—I think I could reach down the stars if she would take them from me.

Mrs. M. [*Evidently struggling.*] I can feel how much you care for her. It wrings my heart —I feel as if I'd no right—but I can't——

Robert. [*Following up his opportunity.*] Why not? Let me speak to her—give me my great chance of happiness—I will make a career worthy of her.

Mrs. M. [*Hesitates.*] What can I say? Oh, what can I do?

Robert. Does it matter so much that once we were starving and that——

Mrs. M. No—no. Kings have starved before now.

Robert. And beggars have been kings. And a king might black the shoes of a whole nation, but he would still be a king—why should it make so much difference to the beggar——

Mrs. M. You must think me hateful——

Robert. No——

Mrs. M. You must—I feel myself so and yet——

Robert. I think you proud and dear and sweet—as I have always thought you——

Mrs. M. [*Turning suddenly.*] I will be— I will be.

Robert. You will give me my great chance— you will trust me?

Mrs. M. Yes—I will do it.

Robert. I may see her—speak to her——

Mrs. M. [*Hardly able to speak.*] Yes—you shall speak to her. She shall decide.

Robert. I shall never be good enough for her —never. And perhaps it is all a mistake and she doesn't care. Yet I have dared to hope— do you think—do you know—if there is hope for me?

Mrs. M. She must tell you that herself.

> [*She is still reluctant and wonder-
> struck.*

Robert. Whichever way it goes, she is the

meaning of life to me. [*Crosses to her.*] Wish me luck when I ask her if she loves me.

Mrs. M. [*Quickly.*] I heard the gate click . . .

> [*She goes to the window, opens it, stands looking out for a moment, as in First Act.*

May. [*Voice heard.*] Mother, dear—mother, dear! [*Just as in First Act.*]

Mrs. M. [*To* May.] I want you, dear, some one is here—has come back.

> [Robert *stands with his face towards the window.*

Mrs. M. [*To* Robert.] She is coming. [*Comes from window, goes towards door, turns and puts her hands on his shoulders with real feeling.*] If *she* will—I give her to you—It is in her hands. [Robert *lifts her hands and kisses them.*] My son, Thomas, I wish you luck.

> [*Exit* Mrs. Murison.

> [Robert *alone for a minute, watching the door, then*

> *Enter* May.

> [*She stops; he goes forward; but seems for a moment unable to speak.*

May. I knew it was you—Uncle Edward told me that you had arrived.

Robert. And you know—you must know why I'm here—— [*Pause.*]

MAY. You said there was some obstacle——

ROBERT. It is swept away—the world is ours if *you* will . . . I couldn't speak to you at Alassio, there was something I had to come to England—to come here and explain——

MAY. [*Evidently understands now what the obstacle was.*] Ah, I see——

ROBERT. [*Not heeding.*] Something that you don't know, dear. I love you—you must know that I love you—all my heart and life are yours, but there was something else that had to be done —to be told before I could dare to ask if you cared for me—I must tell you what it is before you answer—wait——

MAY. But I know already.

ROBERT. You know?

MAY. Yes—that you are Thomas—you betrayed it that last day of all.

ROBERT. Betrayed it?

MAY. Yes, yes—by the catch of the mouse-cage—when I thought it over, I knew——

ROBERT. And it makes no difference?

MAY. Difference? It makes a world of difference—I shall be so proud of you.

ROBERT. My darling! [*Takes her hands and raises his head with a little, happy, triumphant laugh.*] I've come back, Miss May—I've come back—the Princess's lover has come back!

CURTAIN.

*THE MODERN WAY

A COMEDY IN THREE ACTS

*Adapted from a story that appeared in an American
magazine four years ago.

DRAMATIS PERSONÆ

LORD GAYSFORD (*Freddie; in the Guards*)

DUKE OF LEXHAM

ALGERNON WAKE (*nephew to Duke, cousin to Margaret*)

GERALD MASSINGTON

CYRIL TREMAYNE

SIR GEORGE SILCOT

BENSON, *an ex-butler*

RUCKER, *Lady Gaysford's butler*

LADY GAYSFORD (*mother to Freddie*)

HON. MRS. MASSINGTON (*sister to Freddie*)

LADY SILCOT

MRS. MERLIN

MRS. CALSON

JENNIE (*her daughter*)

SYBIL DOLWYN

MARGARET WAKE (*niece to Duke*)

Guests, Waiters, etc.

ACT I.
SCENE: *Drawing-room in Grosvenor Place.*
TIME: *Afternoon.*

ACT II.
SCENE: *Conservatory at Warringford House.*
TIME: *Same evening.*

ACT III.
SCENE: *Margaret's sitting-room in Pont Street.*
TIME: *Next afternoon.*

The action of the play takes place in twenty-four hours.

ACT I

SCENE.—*Drawing-room in Grosvenor Place. Fireplace on R., no fire. Chairs, couch, table, &c. Exit on L. Wide open windows at back of stage, showing balcony with red baize over the balustrade, cloth representing tops of trees in Buckingham Palace Garden over the way.*

SERVANT *on balcony arranging chairs, and making business about the room.*

LADY GAYSFORD *also moves about the room arranging various details.*

She is middle-aged and distinguished-looking. A little cold in manner, but kind, and devoted to her son.

LADY G. You needn't put many chairs on the balcony, Rucker; I expect very few people. Put an easy-chair—one or two.

RUCKER. Yes, my lady.

LADY G. And bring in tea the moment the King and Queen have passed.

RUCKER. Yes, my lady.

Enter GERALD *and the* HON. MRS. MASSINGTON.

She is 27 and fashionable-looking. Her husband is a rather tiresome little man about 85, precise in manner. [*Exit* RUCKER.

MRS. M. Well, mother. [*Kisses her.*] We have come.

LADY G. My dear Rhoda! I'm so glad you managed to get here.

RHODA. We were very late last night, and I have had neuralgia all the morning, but I insisted on coming. The streets are decorated, and——

GERALD. An awful crowd——

RHODA. It was impossible to drive. We pushed our way through, and Gerald grumbled horribly—but he always does, so it doesn't matter.

GERALD. [*Rather disagreeably.*] I think I've enough to grumble about.

RHODA. How many have you asked?

LADY G. Not more than half a dozen. I really didn't think of it till this morning.

RHODA. Oh! And that nice red cloth! [*Looking towards window.*] You might have done something for so many people you don't want at any other time——

GERALD. Who are not lively enough for dinners, eh?

LADY G. I have asked Sir George and Lady Silcot, and one or two others, and I sent a note round to Mrs. Merlin an hour ago; but perhaps she had gone out, or is afraid to face the crowd.

GERALD. Merlin? What a silly name. Who is she?

LADY G. You took her in the other night.

GERALD. Oh, the purring woman, Freddie's platonic friend.

LADY G. She's very sweet.

GERALD. Humph! Where does she live?

LADY G. At Albert Gate. She has a flat.

GERALD. She would.

RHODA. Gerald is horrid to-day. I think she is charming. People say she has an offer every day in the week and two on Sundays.

GERALD. What, of flats?

RHODA. Why, no—of marriage.

GERALD. I wouldn't marry her.

RHODA. Of course not—you couldn't; it would be bigamy. [*To* LADY GAYSFORD.] I don't think she'd mind the Duke.

LADY G. He'll never marry again. He was much too devoted to his wife. I've asked him this afternoon, and his nephew, Mr. Algernon Wake.

RHODA. I thought relations were rather strained between the Duke and Algy.

LADY G. I never take any notice of that sort of thing. One can't in London. Dear Mr. Wake is rather tiresome sometimes——

GERALD. A jackass.

RHODA. No, not exactly a jackass.

LADY G. But I rather like him. I asked them both on purpose, and shall pretend not to know there is any awkwardness.

RHODA. You see, Algy thinks he ought to have an allowance if the Duke is never going to marry again—there's only one other life between.

LADY G. Yes, Mr. Wake must succeed some day, of course.

RHODA. Meanwhile, the Duke thinks Algy ought to marry money—or work. People have such a mania about work nowadays. Of course he invited that pretty American girl and her mother to Lexham Castle on Algy's account.

LADY G. What, Miss Calson? I thought Mr. Wake was in love with Margaret—but every one is. Besides, he and Margaret are first cousins—it wouldn't even make a change of name.

GERALD. In China it isn't lawful to marry any one of the same name.

RHODA. Mother, do tell me about Freddie and Margaret. I saw them in the park yesterday sitting on two chairs under a conspicuous tree, talking for at least half an hour. They looked just as if they were engaged.

GERALD. Or each of them married to somebody else?

LADY G. It's only friendship—I am sorry to say.

GERALD. [*To* RHODA.] More platonics. Your mother doesn't approve of them—this is a degenerate age.

RHODA. Platonics are all very well for middle-aged frumps.

LADY G. Of course.

GERALD. It's a very ancient form of friendship.

RHODA. That's what I say, it's all very well for old people.

GERALD. Humph! [*Saunters towards the window.*

RHODA. [*Turns anxiously to* LADY GAYSFORD.] I thought you said Freddie was coming in, hasn't he a week's leave or something?

LADY G. Yes, he'll be here directly. He gets off when they have passed Westminster Abbey.

RHODA. You think he's *sure* to come?

LADY G. Certain, for he made me invite the Dolwyns.

GERALD. [*Looking round.*] What? The dolphin?

LADY G. The dolphin?

RHODA. They call Sybil the Dolphin.

LADY G. Oh, I thought they called her the corkscrew. The Dolwyns made their money out

of it, you know. Freddie is infatuated with her
—simply infatuated.

RHODA. And yet there's Margaret.

LADY G. I know [*impatiently*] and it would
be so much better, but it's only friendship. He
spends his whole time running after Miss Dolwyn.

RHODA. She's very handsome—and rolling in
money.

Enter SERVANT, *announcing.*

SERVANT. Miss Margaret Wake, the Duke of
Lexham.

> *Enter* MARGARET, *young, pretty, sympa-*
> *thetic, rather grave, and the* DUKE,
> *57, cynical but agreeable and distin-*
> *guished-looking.*

[*Exit* SERVANT.

LADY G. [*To the* DUKE.] How do you do.
. . . My dear Margaret. [*Kisses and evi-*
dently likes her.]

MARGARET. Uncle Edward brought me—it was
so amusing to see the crowd.

DUKE. How d'ye do, very good of you to
ask us. We got through very well. Ah, Massington, how do you do? [*Shakes hands with*
GERALD *and* RHODA.] What time do they go by?

LADY G. Very soon now——

DUKE. You were kind enough to say I might
bring on any one who was lunching with me so
I ventured to tell two charming American ladies,

Mrs. and Miss Calson, that I thought you would
give them room.

LADY G.   My dear Duke, I'm delighted—any
friends of yours.

DUKE.   Perhaps you know them by sight.
Miss Calson is a beautiful girl and her mother's
a very sensible woman, they will be charmed to
make your acquaintance.

LADY G.   Nice of them——

MARGARET.   [*Looking round.*]   Where is Freddie? He told me to be sure to come early——

LADY G.   [*Who evidently likes* MARGARET.]
I always like you to come early.

MARGARET.   He said he had something very
particular to say to me.

LADY G.   [*Eagerly.*]   Did he?   [*Her face
lighting up*] and something to say to *you*, dear?

MARGARET.   I think it's about [*lowering her
voice*] Sybil Dolwyn, you know—he said he had
told you.

LADY G.   [*Disappointed.*]   Oh!——

RHODA.   [*To* MARGARET.]   I hope he will
come—I want to talk to him [*confidentially*]—I
must. [*She and* MARGARET *get together at* L. *of
stage and sit down.*]   You weren't at the Daw-
sons' last night. I was, unluckily, and——

SERVANT.   [*Announcing.*]   Mr. Algernon Wake
—Sir George and Lady Silcot.

Enter ALGERNON WAKE, *rather fair, 25, weak*

looking . . . and the SILCOTS, *usual society types.*

LADY G. [*To* LADY SILCOT.] I'm so glad you
were able to come. Is Sir George quite well?

SIR GEORGE. Never better. [*Shaking hands.*]

WAKE. How d'ye do, Lady Gaysford? [*To
the* DUKE.] I saw Margaret towing you along,
Uncle Edward.

DUKE. [*Distantly.*] How do you do, sir?
[*To* LADY SILCOT.] Glad to see you—I heard
Silcot's speech the other night.

SIR G. It was too short, I'm afraid.

DUKE. Not at all——

WAKE. How do again, Margaret? Hullo,
Massington—you were rather late getting into
the Carlton last night.

RHODA. [*Looking up.*] What did you go to
the Carlton for, Gerald?

GERALD. Supper, of course—what does one
go for?

WAKE. [*Looking rather silly.*] I never understood two men going to the Carlton myself
—however it may be your idea——

RHODA. Oh! [*Laughing.*] That's so like
Gerald.

WAKE. [*Aside to* MASSINGTON.] I didn't say
that it was——

GERALD. [*Falling in with the joke.*] I was
with an old friend.

WAKE. Ah! looked old. I went on to Mrs. Dawson's bridge-party. Mrs. Massington was losing fivers without turning a hair——

RHODA. Don't tell tales of us all—[*with a nervous laugh.*]

GERALD. [*To* RHODA.] You told me you only lost twenty-five shillings.

WAKE. —And winning 'em all back like anything.

[*Winks at* RHODA.]

GERALD. More than she did last time.

LADY G. Don't you think you had better go to the balcony, there are always things to see.

Enter SERVANT, *announcing.*

SERVANT. Mrs. and Miss Calson.

They enter, fashionably dressed. Mrs. Calson is middle-aged, very talkative. Jennie, 26, is pretty and charming. They are both much interested in everything that is English.

MRS. C. Lady Gaysford?

LADY G. Yes—I'm very glad to see you.

MRS. C. [*American accent.*] Our friend, the Duke of Lexham, said you would be so kind as to let us see your King and Queen go by—and as we've been wishing so much to make your acquaintance, we took courage and seized this opportunity——

LADY G. So kind of you.

MRS. C. Well, the kindness is the other way.

This is my daughter Jennie. She and I are in England for the first time, and—why, Duke, there you are again. [*Turning to* LADY GAYS-FORD.] You English people are very good to us Americans; we've had a lovely time.

JENNIE. Just splendid I call it.

MRS. C. We were longing to have a good look at them to-day, but it didn't occur to us to take places till it was too late. And one of the things we have come over for, of course, is to see them. Your King is really a King, you know, and as for the Queen, why she's just lovely.

DUKE. Ah—we all think that.

MRS. C. We were presented last week, but we were so nervous about our trains, we didn't know what we were about. Whatever you wear them for I can't think. Just when you want to have all your courage about you, you put on a thing four yards long to take it off. Why, here's Miss Wake again; we saw her just now at the Duke's.

GERALD. [*Aside to* ALGY.] Does she always talk as much as this?

WAKE. Never leaves off while she's awake. When she's asleep probably snores. [*Goes towards her.*] How d'ye do, Mrs. Calson? Hope you don't forget me—was at Lexham, you know.

MRS. C. Why, it's Mr. Wake. Of course I

don't forget. I saw you walking about in the Park with Miss Dolwyn this morning. I think her the most beautiful girl I ever set eyes on.

WAKE. So do I. [*With a foolish laugh.*] Oh, there's Miss Calson—I didn't mean that—I meant, you know, she was too——

JENNIE. Well, she's just lovely, anyway. I could look at her all day.

WAKE. So could I—I mean half a day.

MRS. C. [*To* LADY G.] These houses are in the most splendid position. It's such a privilege having Buckingham Palace Gardens opposite. I expect you see them all walking about —do they enjoy taking exercise?

[*The* DUKE *and* ALGY *get together.*

LADY G. Well, I'm afraid I can't tell you; we don't look for them—they mightn't like it. I think you have met my daughter, Mrs. Massington?

[*Looking towards* RHODA *who is talking to the* SILCOTS.

RHODA. [*Getting up reluctantly, evidently bored.*] How do you do?

[*She goes back* L., *and* MARGARET *and the* SILCOTS *group.*

[GERALD MASSINGTON *goes towards balcony.*

MRS. C. Why, yes, we have met several times. I understand, too, that you have a most delightful son—in the Guards. We hope to make his acquaintance.

JENNIE. Guardsmen must have a lovely time —I expect he is longing to be a hero.

Enter FREDDIE, LORD GAYSFORD, *in uniform, any regiment of Guards.* *Twenty-four, and boyish.*

LADY G. You must ask him that question, I think. Here he is. [*To* FREDDIE.] My darling —I have been hoping for you.

FREDDIE. [*Going up to his mother and kissing her quite simply.*] I was afraid I shouldn't get here after all, Mum. Is your head better? How do you do, Duke? [*To* WAKE, *with rather a disagreeable nod.*] There you are.

WAKE. [*With a silly smile.*] Saw you this morning. Wondered if you saw me.

FREDDIE. I saw you. [*Goes over to* MARGARET, *who is still talking to* RHODA; *she gets up, and they look at each other in rather an intense manner.*] Margaret! this *is* good.

[*Puts his hand on* RHODA's *shoulder by way of greeting.*

MARGARET. [*To* FREDDIE.] How late you are. [*Half aside.*] I have so many things to say to you.

RHODA. Why don't you and Margaret shake hands? Have you seen each other before to-day?

MARGARET. No.

FREDDIE. We never shake hands—that's part of it.

RHODA. Part of what?

MARGARET. [*Gravely to* FREDDIE.] They don't understand.

> [MARGARET *and* FREDDIE *look as if they were going to talk together, when* LADY GAYSFORD *comes forward with* MRS. CALSON *and* JENNIE CALSON.

LADY G. Freddie, dear, the Duke has kindly brought two American friends. I want to introduce you to them—Mrs. Calson—and Miss Jennie Calson.

FREDDIE. [*Whose manners should be quite unaffected.*] How do you do? Kind of you to come.   [*Shakes hands.*

MRS. C. It's a great privilege to meet any one wearing that beautiful uniform. My niece, Anna, over in New York, says, after the King and Queen, she longs most to see the Guardsmen in England. Only she's quite sure she'd lose her heart to them all.

FREDDIE. They would like that.

JENNIE. [*To* FREDDIE.] Miss Margaret Wake told us a great deal about you to-day—we met her at her uncle's, the Duke of Lexham—that's why we hoped to meet you.

FREDDIE. I dare say she was much too kind. [*With the grave simplicity with which he always speaks of* MARGARET.] She is my friend. Won't you come out to the balcony? They'll be here directly.

RHODA. You've seen them already, Freddie; how do they look?

FREDDIE. Why, they look—well, just as they always do, you know.

JENNIE. Do you hear that, mother? Isn't it splendid? I suppose you don't know what the Queen wore now, Lord Gaysford? My Cousin Anna in New York will want to know—she'll want to know everything.

GERALD. [*Aside to* WAKE.] Does she always bring in Anna of New York?

WAKE. Always.

FREDDIE. [*To* JENNIE CALSON.] She wore —it was something—well, you know it was the sort of thing she always wears—awfully nice.

JENNIE. Don't you know what colour it was?

FREDDIE. It was blue, I think—no, it was mauve. I think it was mauve, it was *some* colour, I know. Let me take you to the balcony— then you will see directly that I'm right.

[*Gets rid of the* CALSONS *into the balcony.*]

RHODA. [*Still talking with* MARGARET.] Yes, I know, but what is one to do? Everything else is played out.

[RHODA *and* MARGARET *saunter towards*

balcony, but stop inside drawing-room.
RHODA *meets* FREDDIE *on his way back*
from the balcony.

RHODA. [*To* FREDDIE.] I do so want a talk with you.

FREDDIE. I'll come directly I've spoken to Lady Silcot.

[*Goes over to* LADY SILCOT, *who has been*
trying to waylay him.

[*The* DUKE *and* WAKE *still talking on* R.

DUKE. I'll do what I can for you, sir, if you behave yourself [*speaks significantly*] but I've no intention of allowing you a large income. You must do something for a living—the Radicals will be down on you if you don't—or you must marry money.

[*Looks significantly towards* MISS CALSON.

WAKE. It takes a woman——

DUKE. I invited Mrs. Calson and her daughter to Lexham solely on your account—to let her see you had family connections. Miss Calson is a charming girl, and she has £42,000 a year. Why didn't you ask her to marry you? If she didn't particularly care for you, she might have liked the place.

WAKE. I did—no go.

DUKE. I am not surprised. What did she say?

WAKE. Said her country wanted ageing.

Likes older men—that sort of thing—they've got young men over there.

DUKE. Dear me. She's a very remarkable girl.

WAKE. I've asked Margaret to marry me two or three times, but she won't either—cousins, you know—it would be so dull. I'm on to Miss Dolwyn now—the girl who drives the piebald ponies round the park.

DUKE.. Dolwyn? Let me see, *who* is she?

WAKE. Nobody. People made their money by a patent corkscrew.

DUKE. [*Makes a sign of slight disgust.*] I remember, of course—not the sort of thing I care for; but it is an excellent corkscrew—works easily—and sells largely, no doubt?

WAKE. Tons of it. They go everywhere—live in Park Lane.

DUKE. Of course. They are very rich?

WAKE. Rolling.

DUKE. Handsome girl, isn't she?

WAKE. Rather! Going to see her at the Warringfords' to-night.

DUKE. Humph! I'll drop in for half an hour, and look at her—might be as well——

SERVANT. [*Announcing.*] Mr. Tremayne.

FREDDIE. [*Coming forward, glad to escape from* LADY SILCOT.] My dear chap, I was hoping you'd turn up.

DUKE. [*To* TREMAYNE.] I thought you were off to Constantinople?

TREMAYNE. I start for Paris at nine to-night . . . go on to Constantinople in the morning.

LADY G. How do you do, Mr. Tremayne? Many congratulations on your appointment. [*To the* DUKE.] They'll be here soon. Won't you come to the window, and see that Miss Calson has a good place?

> [*The* DUKE *and* ALGY *go together towards the balcony, where the* CALSONS *make room for them.*
>
> [FREDDIE *detains* TREMAYNE *for a moment.*

FREDDIE. [*To* TREMAYNE.] Look here, I must speak to you presently.

TREMAYNE. Right. I'll come back in a minute.

> [*Nods significantly and goes and speaks to* RHODA.
>
> [FREDDIE *turns to* LADY GAYSFORD.

FREDDIE. Mum, dear, do come to me for a minute; they are all right there. [*Nodding towards balcony.*] I shan't see you again to-day. I am going back in an hour.

LADY G. Yes, dear. I have been longing to see you. I forget where you're dining.

FREDDIE. At Lady Bilson's—she's taking us all on to the Warringfords. I wanted to tell

you—[*They sit down together* R. *for a moment*]
—I've been thinking things over—making up my
mind. I mean—to risk it.

LADY G. You mean?

FREDDIE. That's it—I mean to ask Sybil Dolwyn. Margaret feels sure it's all right, and she
always knows everything.

LADY G. I wish it were Margaret.

FREDDIE. But *she* is my friend. . . . You
don't know Sybil.

LADY G. [*Reluctantly.*] She's very handsome,
of course.

FREDDIE. She's wonderful; she looks like a
young Empress, like a goddess, by Jove! Why,
every one looks after her even in the street.
I can't believe it's any good, but I mean to
risk it.

LADY G. I thought you said she was coming
to-day. I asked her and her mother, as you
wished it.

FREDDIE. She told me she was, then she said
she didn't think she could manage it. I telegraphed to know if I might fetch them, and
she answered, " Awfully sorry; can't come." I
was so glad she said *awfully*.

LADY. G. You are very fond of her?

FREDDIE. I love her—she *is* ripping.

LADY G. [*Trying to take it well.*] And you
are really going to ask her to marry you?

FREDDIE. To-night if I get the chance. Wish me luck, mother—wish me luck.

LADY G. I do, I do, Freddie, dear. I'll try and love her because you do—I *will*.

FREDDIE. [*Touching her hand.*] Mum dear!

RHODA. [*Coming up to them with* TREMAYNE. *To* LADY GAYSFORD.] Do let me have Freddie for a little while. I do so want him.

LADY G. [*A little emotioned, but trying to hide it.*] Yes, of course. Shall we see what is going on, Mr. Tremayne?

[*She turns to* TREMAYNE; *they go towards balcony.*

[FREDDIE *sits down by* RHODA.

RHODA. I do so want to speak to you, Freddie. I am up another tree.

FREDDIE. Oh—you are always getting up a tree, dear.

RHODA. But this is a dreadful one, and you know what Gerald's temper is.

FREDDIE. Well, no, I don't; but, of course, you do.

RHODA. I believe that Dawson woman keeps a gambling house, or something like it. Last night I lost £160, and I haven't £20 in the world without telling Gerald.

FREDDIE. [*Kindly but firmly.*] Look here, you shouldn't do it. You know you shouldn't.

RHODA. Well, but——

FREDDIE. It's a horrid trick—in a woman, losing money; if she wants to get rid of it, I think she should spend it on finery—that's all right, you know. If I had a wife, and she lost a lot of money gambling, I should be awfully angry. And I would never let her go again to the house where she had lost it.

RHODA. [*Astonished.*] Freddie! I never thought *you* would say that sort of thing.

FREDDIE. I didn't either. But I've been thinking about life and all sorts of serious things lately.

RHODA. You mustn't, you'll end up as a curate if you do. . . . I'm sorry I told you. But I'm in an awful fix and I thought perhaps you'd help me. I didn't sleep all night, I've had neuralgia all the morning, I didn't eat any luncheon—I believe I could die and not mind it—I could do anything except tell Gerald. Oh, Freddie, do help me.

FREDDIE. Of course I'll help you; what are brothers for—only don't do it again, there's a dear girl. When do you want it?

RHODA. I must have it to-morrow morning and notes, not a cheque.

FREDDIE. All right, I'll give it to you at the Warringfords to-night, will that do?

RHODA. Oh, Freddie dear!

FREDDIE. I want you to try and say Fred, Freddie sounds like some one who doesn't think of serious things you know.

RHODA. [*Astonished.*] What *is* the matter with you? You are so different since you became friends with Mrs. Merlin and Margaret Wake.

FREDDIE. I know, Tremayne used to be my only chum. But it isn't that—it's something awfully good. [*Reaches out his hand for a moment and draws it back.*] I'm going to ask Sybil Dolwyn if she'll marry me, I'm awfully in love with her—taken a regular header. I mean to risk it to-night.

RHODA. Oh. . . . I can't think why you didn't fall in love with Margaret. You seem so fond of each other.

FREDDIE. Of course we are, but we are *friends* —it is quite different, you know.

RHODA. You have been inseparable for such a long time. Do you mean to say it is all platonics?

FREDDIE. Poor dear Rhoda, you don't understand.

RHODA. No, I don't.

    [TREMAYNE *and* MARGARET *come towards them.*

FREDDIE. [*Looks up and says quite simply.*]

Rhoda doesn't understand a bit about our friendship, do tell her about it. It was when we were both staying at the Stickindales, wasn't it?

MARGARET. Two years ago. The weather was dreadful and it was a horrid middle-aged house-party—quite old in fact.

FREDDIE. Not a creature under forty, you know.

MARGARET. I was bored to death. Suddenly Freddie arrived——

FREDDIE. We knew directly we should like each other. She made me do a lot of things.

RHODA. What sort of things?

FREDDIE. Well, read books.

MARGARET. Learn some Omar Khayyam by heart.

RHODA. [*Looks up inquiringly.*] What's that?

TREMAYNE. Persian beggar, you know, lived in a tent or made tents or something. Knew a lot about flowers and wine and heaps of things.

RHODA. Think I've heard of him. Dead, isn't he?

FREDDIE. Oh, yes, quite dead.

RHODA. What else?

MARGARET. Go to the Queen's Hall concerts.

RHODA. Oh, *that's* why!——

MARGARET. Go to the Stage Society plays and read some books on Philosophy.

FREDDIE. I drew the line at the philosophy —after a bit, you know; but I went to a Bernard Shaw play—they talked a great deal, and made jokes I think; and people laughed, but there wasn't any love-making.

RHODA. [*Laughing and puzzled.*] I think you are too ridiculous. Oh, Margaret, I want to ask you——

[*Saunters away with* MARGARET.

[TREMAYNE *and* FREDDIE *together on* L.

FREDDIE. It's an awful bore, you're going away, old man.

TREMAYNE. Nine o'clock at Victoria to-night and good-bye to England.

FREDDIE. I shall miss you awfully.

TREMAYNE. You must come out and see me next time you get leave. Might have come with me, but I think you said your time was up next Monday.

FREDDIE. Besides, I couldn't just now. I should like to come and see you off, but I'm dining out, and going on to Warringford House. I want you to know, old chap—I've made up my mind to risk it——

TREMAYNE. [*Looking round slowly.*] The dolphin?

FREDDIE. That's it, but we won't call her that any more.

TREMAYNE. Sounds fishy, doesn't it?

FREDDIE.   Awfully fishy, but—er—but what do you think of it?

TREMAYNE.   Beautiful girl—no end of go.

FREDDIE.   Any amount—I hope it'll be all right.

TREMAYNE.   Sure to.   You're a nice chap——

FREDDIE.   Heaps of 'em about.

TREMAYNE.   A title——

FREDDIE.   They're awfully cheap just now.

TREMAYNE.   Pretty well protected though—only thing that is at present. . . . except the working class——

FREDDIE.   Don't joke, Tremayne—it's the wrong time. . . . Wish I could feel it's all right.

TREMAYNE.   Why, of course it's all right. You've been as thick as thieves for the last five weeks.   I saw Algernon Wake look as if he'd like to murder you on Thursday——

FREDDIE.   Poor beggar!   I'm awfully sorry for him—it's the second time he's been hit.   He's always on her track—makes himself into my shadow.

TREMAYNE.   Never mind, you're the substance.

FREDDIE.   [*Uneasily.*]   Wish I could be sure of that, you know.   Wake has been hanging round a good deal lately.

TREMAYNE.   He always hangs about——

FREDDIE.   Perhaps it's all right.   She let me

hold her hand for ten minutes the night before last. Should have spoken then but I broke her fan——

TREMAYNE. Did she swear?

FREDDIE. Not a bit. Awfully sweet about it—that's why I think it must be all right—she *would* have sworn if she hadn't cared. . . . Went to the play last night, her people took a box, a big one, family party. Awfully significant their asking me you know? On the way back motor broke down, she let me take her on in a hansom.

TREMAYNE. Well, she couldn't walk.

FREDDIE. Might have gone on with some one else—we all had to go on in hansoms or taxis or something. . . . I asked for two dances to-night on purpose—I feel awfully nervous—I suppose one always does. Can't believe she'll play up, when I think of what a stunner she is.

TREMAYNE. Wait till after supper if you can, it helps to get one's courage up.

FREDDIE. I will—but I wish you weren't going away. Look here, I'll send you a wire to Paris in the morning, telling you if it's all right. You'll be at the Bristol I suppose?

TREMAYNE. Only for an hour or two. I start again at nine or some unearthly time of that sort. Write to Constantinople, but it's sure to be all right.

FREDDIE. I shall blow my brains out if it isn't.

TREMAYNE. Nonsense, old chap, besides you haven't any. . . . But I say you are pretty far gone?

FREDDIE. Rather—never saw any one like her, sweeps you off your feet, you know. This time to-morrow I shall be the happiest man alive or——
[*Puts his hand to his head as if holding a pistol.*

TREMAYNE. [*Looking at him doubtfully.*] Nonsense!

FREDDIE. It isn't nonsense. I mean it.
[RHODA *and* MARGARET *on* L. *laughing.*

TREMAYNE. [*As* FREDDIE *goes towards them.*] Oh, no, you don't, old chap; but you are hard hit—[*when he is out of hearing*] and quite capable of making an ass of yourself.

FREDDIE. I say, Rhoda, you have had Margaret long enough now, she and I haven't had a word together.

SERVANT. [*Announcing.*] Mrs. Merlin.
[LADY GAYSFORD *comes from balcony and greets her.* MRS. MERLIN *is 34 or 35, very soft and purring in her manner, wears trailing rather artistic things.*

MRS. M. [*Takes* LADY GAYSFORD'S *hand in both hers.*] It was dear of you to send for me.

LADY G. I was afraid you weren't coming.

MRS. M. I thought I should never get here.

That dear Sir Charles Bassett brought me—no driving, of course; we had to walk.

LADY G. Let us have some tea, we shall be sure to hear the cheers when they are in sight, you must be so exhausted.

MRS. M. [*To* FREDDIE.] I am so glad to see you and dear Margaret—you two are always together.

MARGARET. [*Simply and gravely.*] We are great, great friends.

MRS. M. I know. He is my friend too, you mustn't think he doesn't love *me,* I know he does.

FREDDIE. Of course I do, ever so much.

GERALD. [*Turning his head.*] Oh, I say, there is tea going on.

[*Everybody comes in from balcony, F. and M. sit left.*

FREDDIE. [*To* MARGARET.] We shall meet tonight? [*They get to seat on* L.] You must keep four dances for me—we'll sit out two.

MARGARET. I'm not going—isn't it provoking? Mother will insist on our going to that party at Wimbledon, it's a coming of age thing, and they are old friends of hers.

FREDDIE. Oh, I say, it's awfully hard luck. I thought of course you were going to the Warringfords—I want you. Couldn't you come early for half an hour?

MARGARET. I fear not. We are to drive to

Wimbledon after the Marsden Lees dinner—I
can't help hoping that mother may be too tired.
She's been selling things all day at the Albert
Hall and is going there again to-morrow. Now
we've got a chance do tell me what you are going
to do. It seems years since we had a talk.

FREDDIE. I know—we've not met since yesterday morning. . . . Margaret, I've made
up my mind to ask her.

MARGARET. [*Clasping her hands, she seems
thrilled, but not pleased.*] Oh, Freddie!

FREDDIE. Try and say Fred: responsibilities
of life and that sort of thing coming on, you know
it sounds better.

MARGARET. [*Tenderly.*] I will, Freddie, dear.

FREDDIE. [*Puts his hand on hers and draws
it away saying half to himself and half to her.*]
Mustn't do that, must I? Comrades don't.

MARGARET. No, but we are real comrades,
Freddie—Fred, dear—I'm very glad [*with a
sigh.*] Oh! I do hope she'll make you very, very
happy.

FREDDIE. It's splendid of you to be so anxious.
You think it is all right, don't you? You see
that idiot Algernon Wake is always hanging about.

MARGARET. But she couldn't care for him.
Why, his ears stick out! [*Looking towards* WAKE.

FREDDIE. Still he'll be a duke one day, some-

times girls care for that sort of thing. I've got
money, of course, but that isn't any good to her
—she has pots of her own.

MARGARET. You've got yourself.

FREDDIE. That isn't much.

MARGARET. Yes, it is. [*Pause.*] I do so hope
that you really—really—love her? It would be
dreadful, if you married her and didn't love
her *enough*.

FREDDIE. I'm awfully gone on her, swear I
am. Look here, I shall try and get through after
supper. Think of me——

MARGARET. We shall be driving to Wimbledon.

FREDDIE. I'll come and tell you all about it
in the morning if I may?

MARGARET. I'm going to sleep at Wimbledon.
You might telegraph to me there "Lancaster
Lodge, Wimbledon Common," and come to Pont
Street at three—no, at four, to-morrow. I shall
be back by then. You must tell me everything
she says—we have been such great chums, you
know.

FREDDIE. Of course we have, and it isn't going to make any difference is it? I don't think
I could get on without you—in fact, I couldn't.

MARGARET. Oh, yes, you could. I wish——
          [*Stops, puts her hand to her throat.*

FREDDIE. I say, is there anything I could do

to please you? You look as if you'd gone down
a ladder, you know.

MARGARET. [*Half sadly.*] I want you to take
it seriously, Freddie, dear. I think if you read
some Rossetti before you started, or Browning;
I'm not sure that Browning wouldn't be better
if—but it won't. Some people would say Swin-
burne, you know; but I think he should be taken
later, when one is in the depths—there's no one
like him for bitter despair.

FREDDIE. I'll read the whole lot of them if
you like, and there's time. You always give one
the straight tip. [*Noticing* MISS CALSON, *who has
come to the tea-table.*] Can I get you anything?

JENNIE. Well, I was just looking for a little
milk, you seem to only have cream here, you're
that luxurious in England——

FREDDIE. Oh, well now, just think of New
York.

JENNIE. I don't see why I should think of a
place I don't come from.

FREDDIE. I thought you lived there—that
Americans always had town-houses there anyhow——

JENNIE. Well, now, isn't that like people who
don't know? Why, I've only been there once in
my life, and I don't think I'll go many times.
I am a Westerner; I daresay you don't know
what that means now, Lord Gaysford?

FREDDIE. I suppose it means the—well, the West.

JENNIE. That isn't a bad shot.

FREDDIE. I've heard a lot about it—it's a great big country, isn't it?

JENNIE. There isn't much of it left now but there's some—perhaps that'll be allowed to stay as it is. God knew what He was about when He made the world, and when man takes to improving it, I don't think he's much of a success, do you? Have you ever talked on this subject with any of the great thinkers? I mean about the world and what's done to it.

FREDDIE. How do you mean? . . . I think I know—but in London people only talk of themselves or of each other—always playing up, or playing off or something—and the world gets a bit battered.

JENNIE. Well, you see, out there in the West there are the mountains and the great forests and the rivers and all the things designed up in Heaven; and life among them is just simple and natural. . . . In New York and over here in Europe, you've just carted away nature as much as you could and set up towns and all the things that I suppose you call art—how in wonder you live the lives you do I can't imagine.

FREDDIE. It sounds splendid—out in the West, I mean—but what do you do all day?

JENNIE. Well, now, I'll tell you. You get up
at five, for one thing, in the summer anyway—
you see the sun rise——

FREDDIE. We often do that here. We wait
up for it, so it would be all right.

MRS. M. [*Coming forward.*] How do you
do, Miss Calson? Are you two making friends?
I'm so glad. [*To* MISS CALSON.] But you must
let him come and talk to me for a little while,
dear. I call him my boy, and I've not seen him
for such a long time.

JENNIE. Why, of course—I mustn't keep him
from you—besides, I think we *must* be going, if
these royalties don't come by—we've things to
do—[*gets up*]—at least——

FREDDIE. They'll be here directly—don't go,
I want you to tell me some more about the West
—I often think a good deal of the way we go
on is rot—we do it over and over again,
and it doesn't matter a bit if we're bored.

MRS. M. [*Intensely.*] That's *so* true!
                              [*No one notices her.*

JENNIE. [*To* FREDDIE.] I'll tell you anything you like—perhaps you are going to Lady
Warringford's ball to-night, and we'll meet
there. But you've got to talk to Mrs. Merlin
now——

FREDDIE. She'll like talking to you better——

MRS. C. [*From balcony.*] Jennie, you really

must come; it's quite wonderful to look out—it is just what we say it is at home.

Mrs. M. [*Sitting down and motioning* Freddie *to sit beside her, while* Miss Calson *goes to balcony.*] I thought I should never get a moment with you, but I know how many things you have to do.

Freddie. [*Gratefully.*] You always understand.

Mrs. M. I feel as if you'd something to tell me.

Freddie. [*Nodding an affirmative.*] But we can't talk here. Are you ging to Warringford House to-night?

Mrs. M. I can't. They expect royalties; it will be such a dreadful crush. I'm so afraid of crushes now. [*Pulls her chiffon scarf up closer round her neck.*] Let us sit down here, no one will hear what we are saying. [*Very confidentially.*] Now tell me, is Sybil going to-night?

Freddie. Yes, she's going. [*Pause.*] And I mean to risk it—if I get a chance. I believe they've covered in the gardens—or done something, anyway.

Mrs. M. She's a beautiful creature. I'm not sure that she's quite—quite good enough for you, dear.

Freddie. [*Rather hurt.*] You are not thinking of the corkscrews?

Mrs. M. [*In an anxious voice.*] No. I'm not thinking of the corkscrew. That sort of thing doesn't matter nowadays.

Freddie. Besides, she looks like an Empress. Her people must be somebodies.

Mrs. M. Perhaps they've come down in the world.

Freddie. And are climbing up again by the corkscrew——

Mrs M. And they are very rich . . . She's a lucky girl—if you love her——

Freddie. Perhaps she won't have me.

[*Nervously.*

Mrs. M. Oh, yes, she will. Algernon Wake has been hanging about her a good deal.

Freddie. I know. But I don't think she would have him—Margaret is certain she wouldn't.

Mrs. M. He'll be a duke some day—but she mayn't know that—and she'll have you——

[*Touches his hand and smiles.*

Freddie. I shall go under if she doesn't.

Mrs. M. No, you won't, dear. You'll face it like a man—but it'll be all right. Isn't she two years older than you are?

Freddie. Yes, but that doesn't matter a bit. I asked her the other night if she thought it mattered. I never saw a girl like her—I'm awfully gone on her.

Mrs. M. [*Gives him a fatuous smile. Puts*

out her hand.] Poor boy! Of course she's *very* handsome——

FREDDIE. She's splendid.

MRS. M. I always thought you'd end by marrying Margaret.

FREDDIE. She's my friend.

MRS. M. It would have been a much better connection, you know. You must come to-morrow and tell me everything. . . . I shall go away directly they have gone by. [*Looking towards the balcony.*] I have to dine at the Cramptons; one of their long dull dinners, I suppose—I couldn't get through without a little rest first, but I felt that I must see you. That's why I came.

FREDDIE. It *was* good of you. I wish you were going to-night.

MRS. M. [*Getting up.*] You must tell me everything to-morrow. [*In a thrilling voice.*] Don't be nervous; and give her a long, long kiss that you'll both remember all your lives.

FREDDIE. I say, you do know.

MRS. M. [*Half closing her eyes and taking his hands.*] We've all been through it, and——

    [*Excitement in the balcony—distant shouts.*

DUKE. Mrs. Merlin, where are you?

        [WAKE *and* RHODA, MRS. MERLIN, *all in the room go towards the balcony. Excited exclamations.*

Mrs. M. [*As she turns towards balcony with* Freddie.] You must tell me everything to-morrow. [*Exit to balcony.*

[Freddie *nods and looks towards* Margaret.

Margaret. [*In a low voice—almost sad.*] Freddie!

> [*It should be quite evident that she cares for him.*

Freddie. Margaret! You don't want to look out?

> [*They stand together centre of room. She shakes her head.*

All. [*In balcony.*] They are coming! They're really coming! Yes, it is!

> [Margaret *and* Freddie *seem to hear nothing.*

> [*Shouts grow louder, band in distance plays "God Save the King," cheers heard in the distance as the curtain falls.*

CURTAIN.

ACT II

Time.—Eleven o'clock the same night.

Scene.—Conservatory at Warringford House. Trees, flowers, seats, &c. Exits R. *and* L. *at back (or at centre), evidently leading to ball-room. Dance music heard faintly all through the Act. An Exit on* L. *half way down the stage, presumably leading to garden. Door on* R., *with curtains, leading to supper-room. Two or three small tables are placed just inside the conservatory, near the curtains, as if for overflow guests. In* C. *group of palms with settee beneath them. The whole scene should be picturesque, with sitting-out corners for dancers, &c. Guests stroll in and out.*

When the curtain rises BENSON *is discovered. He is fat, middle-aged, and consequential. Looks round as if puzzled, goes to curtained door on* R., *beckons.*

Enter MAN-SERVANT.

BENSON. That supper-room won't anything like take them all.

SERVANT. There's the library, Mr. Benson—but that's only for their Royal Highnesses.

BENSON. We could put half a dozen tables here.

SERVANT. Her ladyship said we could put them anywhere.

BENSON. Two could go here—[*indicating place*]—and one here—and——

[*Sound of laughter.*

ALGERNON WAKE *and* SYBIL DOLWYN *enter from ball-room at back.*

[SYBIL DOLWYN *must be handsome, beautifully dressed and insolent in manner.*

[BENSON *and* SERVANT *retreat hastily into supper-room.*

ALGY. [*Looking inane but devoted.*] Oh, I say, but you don't mean that, do you?

SYBIL. Yes I do. If you don't want it, of course we'll consider it off.

ALGY. But I want anything you want—you know I like 'em, don't you, Sybil—so glad to drop the Miss Dolwyn.

SYBIL. Very well, then. We'll consider it on for the present.

ALGY. Rather wish they weren't piebald—makes 'em look so got up.

SYBIL. I like them to look got up—it's smart—don't want any others.

ALGY. You're smart. There isn't one of 'em can touch you. Thought so this afternoon when I saw you behind the little beasts—much better than going to Grosvenor Place—only just got away in time to have a look at you.

SYBIL. I drove them round three times yesterday. Lady Barstock looked furious. That's the best of their being piebald, you can't help looking at them specially when you drive them tandem.

ALGY. I was there—saw you—nearly raised a cheer.

SYBIL. Rather amusing, wasn't it?

ALGY. Awfully. Told Uncle Edward about it this afternoon. Says he wants to see you.

SYBIL. What for?

ALGY. [*With a silly little gesture.*] Oh, well, you know. . . . He's heard about you. . . . You see, some day I shall be where he is——

SYBIL. You mean you'll be the Duke?

ALGY. That's it—awful bore in some ways.

SYBIL. There are compensations still, I suppose; when you have got through the poor relations and the death dues—but I expect he'll live as long as he can and only die when he can't help himself.

ALGY. Can't blame him for that. I don't believe in dying myself, do you? Nothing else to do when you've done it, so far as we know. [*She*

gets up.] I say, what's the matter? It's awfully nice here.

SYBIL. I want to go back. We're missing
everything out here, and I expect the Royalties
won't stay long—I rather like the Prince—the
Princess isn't a bad sort either—she was rather
amusing the other day.

ALGY. Quite right. I say, what do you think
of the Archbishop of Canterbury?

SYBIL. Never troubled my head about him—
should say he would be rather dull.

ALGY. Or the German Emperor—skittish, you
know, but not a bad sort and toning down on the
whole, sorry for it, rather like his skitting.

Enter from ball-room MARGARET *and* DUKE
OF LEXHAM *talking.*

MARGARET. Oh, no—dear Uncle Edward—of
course not—oh! [*Perceiving* SYBIL *and going
forward.*] Miss Dolwyn. [*To* SYBIL.] I
thought I should meet you here. Have you seen
Lord Gaysford? I know he was coming.

[ALGY *goes up to the* DUKE, *talks to him
aside, while* MARGARET *and* SYBIL *are
talking.*

SYBIL. [*Rather insolently.*] He's here, hanging round as usual—I saw him just now.

MARGARET. I wanted to see you too so much
—but I'm not going to stay—I must go directly
in fact—couldn't you sit down for two minutes?

It would be so nice to know each other a little better.

SYBIL. [*Rather unwillingly.*] Well? [*Sits down on settee with* MARGARET.] Why are you going away so soon?

MARGARET. Mother is waiting for me in the motor outside, we are on our way to a dance at Wimbledon.

SYBIL. Wimbledon! You wouldn't catch me going to a dance at Wimbledon—there won't be a soul worth speaking to there. Why do you go?

MARGARET. [*Choked off a little by her manner, and with an unconscious hauteur.*] They are old friends of my mother's, and——

SYBIL. Oh, I know—as bad as relations; aren't they? Always expecting you to go and see them or something—selfish, I call it.

MARGARET. Oh, no!

SYBIL. Yes, it is, what's the good of pretending it isn't? I never take any notice of them —just let them clamour. What did you want to see me for?

MARGARET. I wanted to talk to you, for Lord Gaysford and I are friends [*with the note that always comes into her voice when she says the word*] and he told me so much about you to-day.

SYBIL. [*Rather flattered.*] He's a silly boy. Did he tell you he smashed my fan the other night?

MARGARET. He was very unhappy about it.

SYBIL. So was I—mending it will cost twelve and sixpence.

MARGARET. He would love to give you another, I know.

SYBIL. He can if he likes—I'm rather fond of him—in a way—nice-looking, isn't he?

MARGARET. [*Cheering up.*] I'm glad you say that—he's so good, you know.

SYBIL. [*With a funny little laugh.*] That's against him—I think good people are slow, don't you? So little variety in them, nothing unexpected. [*Evidently bored with the conversation, she looks towards* ALGY, *who is talking with the* DUKE; *he takes the hint and comes toward her.*] I get bored——

MARGARET. Oh, don't say that! [*Seeing that the interview is coming to an end and anxious to make the most of it.*] I wonder if you would come and see me—in Pont Street—you would always find me after five.·

SYBIL. I'll try. [*With an anxious eye towards* ALGY *and the* DUKE.] Can't promise. I'm pretty full up just now. Freddie Gaysford told me you were very nice.

MARGARET. Did he?—but he is my friend, you know.

SYBIL. How much?

MARGARET. Much? I don't understand.

ALGY. [*To* SYBIL.] I say, I believe this is our dance and we are losing it all—and—er—my uncle wants to be introduced to you—heard lots about you——

SYBIL. [*To the* DUKE, *rather insolently, putting back her head.*] How d'ye do? Heard of you, too. [*Puts out her hand.*

DUKE. [*Bending over it.*] I am honoured —from whom?

SYBIL. Oh, your nephew just now . . . Saw you in the ball-room.

DUKE. [*Gallantly.*] I've been looking at you from a distance.

SYBIL. Very good of you, I'm sure. Hope the enchantment it lent to the view hasn't vanished. Daresay we shall meet again——

[*Turns to* ALGY.

ALGY. Meet often, I hope.

[*Exit* SYBIL, *rather hurriedly, with* ALGY.

DUKE. [*Puts up his pince-nez and looks after her. To* MARGARET.] Well, I don't think much of it.

MARGARET. Of what, Uncle Edward?

DUKE. [*Nodding in the direction that* SYBIL *and* ALGY *have gone.*] That! I suppose she can't help it, corkscrew has turned her head.

MARGARET. [*Anxiously.*] Then it's not her fault, is it? Don't you think a bad manner is sometimes only nervousness? She'll be different in time——

DUKE. H'm! I dislike these people myself, and a precious havoc they are making of the world; but we've got to put up with them, it's no good pretending anything else, we've got to put up with them—and if she'll marry Algy she'll do me a service.

MARGARET. [*Surprised.*] Oh, but she won't, Uncle Edward, I assure you. Freddie Gaysford is in love with her, and I think—I think she likes him.

DUKE. Freddie Gaysford in love with her! . . . Why, I thought Algy was certain of her, he said so. Well, I don't think Freddie's mother would like the corkscrew any better than I do, but something *must* be done or Lexham will be a ruin . . . Upon my life, I don't believe any one will take Algy off my hands, but we shall see. I wonder if those two nice American women are here yet—I know they're coming.

MARGARET. I like Miss Calson.

DUKE. [*With some emphasis.*] She's a charming girl, has forty-two thousand a year, and not a bit spoilt by it. I suppose they made it by cattle or something of that sort, and it works better than a corkscrew. She has told me a great

deal about the Western States of America; they
seem to have some nature left there still, as she
puts it, and she has come straight here without
being spoiled by the vagaries of New York.

MARGARET. You seem to like her, Uncle Edward.

DUKE. Yes, I do.

MARGARET. You had her to stay at Lexham
with that rather dreadful mother.

DUKE. I don't think the mother is dreadful,
my dear; she is only curious, as we all are about
new things and conditions. I had a little plot
to marry her daughter to Algy, but the young
lady wouldn't have anything to say to him—I
suppose I ought to go and look after them——

MARGARET. [*Eagerly.*] Oh, *do* send Freddie
to me if you can. I telegraphed to him saying
I would be here at 11:15 punctually for five minutes. I shall have to go at twenty past.

DUKE. [*Looking at watch.*] It's eighteen
minutes past now.

MARGARET. And he is generally so punctual.

Enter FREDDIE *with* MRS. CALSON.

Oh, here he is. [*To* FREDDIE, *who comes towards her.*] I was just telling Uncle Edward
that you are generally so punctual.

DUKE. [*Going towards* MRS. CALSON.] My
dear lady, I was going to look for you. I hope
your charming daughter is with you?

Mrs. C. Why yes, you may be sure I wouldn't come without her. We've been most anxious to find you. You'll tell us who every one is, and that's just what we want to know—at least I do—you see Jennie only cares for what she calls " a general impression," that's why——

Duke. Couldn't we go and look for her?

[*Exit with* Mrs. Calson.

[Freddie *and* Margaret *alone.*

Freddie. But it's splendid of you to be here, how did you manage it?

Margaret. [*Breathlessly.*] I told mother that we *must* have the motor for Wimbledon, and then I persuaded her to let me come in for five minutes on the way—she's outside waiting. I expect she'll be dreadfully cross, for you know how she hates motors, and it's grunting and groaning to-night; it simply whistled all the way down Piccadilly.

Freddie. They always do when anything's up—it's rather nice of them. Have you seen Sybil?

Margaret. She was here just now with Algy.

[*They sit on settee* c.

Freddie. He's been hanging about her all night, I expect he does it on purpose—however we've got a dance coming on and I'm going to take her in to supper. She's just ripping, isn't she? Every one looks at her, you know. That's what makes me feel that she can't care for such a duffer as I am. The Prince talked to her for five minutes as soon as he arrived.

MARGARET. [*Drawing a chiffon round her, &c.*] I wish it was over—I want you to be happy so much—you don't know——

FREDDIE. Dear Margaret! There isn't any one like you—I say must you really go? I'm awfully nervous——

MARGARET. [*Nodding.*] But you mustn't be nervous, Freddie, dear; remember you are a soldier.

FREDDIE. Oh, I don't mind gunpowder a bit, that's a trifle to this.

MARGARET. Did you do all I told you?

FREDDIE. Hadn't much time, but I did what I could—hunted everywhere, and couldn't find 'em, perhaps I threw them at something. I bought another lot—at least I got selections from Browning—I thought selections would do—and I bought all the other chap's stuff, but I couldn't manage to get more than twenty minutes at them. They know an awful lot of course——

MARGARET. Even twenty minutes would help to put you into a right frame of mind.

FREDDIE. If she refuses me I shall go under. She's such an awful stunner, I should owe it to her—there wouldn't be any one left to do it for if one didn't for a girl like that——

MARGARET. [*Staring at him.*] Do you care
so much?   [*They get up.*

FREDDIE. [*Nodding.*] An awful lot, there
isn't any one like her, and if she doesn't catch
on there won't be anything left to do except——
[*Shrugs his shoulders.*] I told Tremayne so to-
day. He said I'd taken it badly, but he's never
been through it himself.

MARGARET. [*Vehemently.*] I can't believe
that she doesn't care for you.

FREDDIE. Mrs. Merlin said she thought it
would be all right. But—I don't know how it
is—somehow I never can get at her—really I
mean—you see every one hangs about her. Why
only the other day at Hurlingham——

Enter RHODA *and* GERALD MASSINGTON.

RHODA. Oh, here he is. [*To* FREDDIE.] We've
been looking for you all round the place, I must
have a talk with you, Freddie.

                [GERALD *is speaking to* MARGARET.

MARGARET. [*To* RHODA.] Do you mind if he
sees me off first? I'm going to Wimbledon, to
a dance, with mother; she's waiting in the motor
outside and must be furious by this time.

RHODA. Gerald will take you. [*To* GERALD.]
Take Margaret down to the carriage—the motor
—or whatever it is—[*evidently agitated.*] Freddie wants to talk to me.

                [GERALD *goes towards her.*

MARGARET. [*To* FREDDIE.] You'll telegraph in the morning Lancaster Lodge, Wimbledon Common—I shall be there till twelve I daresay—and come to Pont Street in the afternoon—my new sitting-room is ready.

FREDDIE. [*Nodding.*] All right. [*As she is about to go, with a rush of feeling in his voice.*] I say, let's be very commonplace and shake hands this time——

RHODA. Why—I thought you never did?

FREDDIE. [*Explanatory.*] In case the motor stands on its head.

MARGARET. Or tramples us underfoot on Wimbledon Common.

FREDDIE. Oh, I say, Margaret! [*She and* FREDDIE *clasp hands for a moment, with a note of real feeling in his voice he says*] Good-night.

MARGARET. Courage, dear friend. [*In a low voice.*] . . . Good-night, Rhoda.

[*Exeunt* MARGARET *and* GERALD.

RHODA. Now perhaps we shall get a minute or two [*as she and* FREDDIE *are left alone*].

Enter WAITER *or* SERVANT *followed by* BENSON, *from between supper-room curtains on* R.

[*With a sign of impatience.*] Oh——

FREDDIE. Why, here's Benson—how do you do? [*Goes up and shakes hands with him.*] I didn't know you were back again. Are you with Lady Warringford?

BENSON. No, my Lord, only for the evening.
I'm back in England for good. I hope her ladyship is well? [*To* RHODA.] And you, Ma'am?

RHODA. Yes, thank you. I thought you left
mother to go and live in Paris.

BENSON. I hoped I was doing a new thing,
ma'am; so did her ladyship.

RHODA. What was it? I forget.

FREDDIE. He started a training-school for
turning French waiters into English butlers.

BENSON. The idea was an excellent one, but
the material over there was disappointing.

FREDDIE. Too thin?

BENSON. Too finicky, my lord, and they
haven't the manner. They may do for waiters,
but they'll never make good butlers.

RHODA. [*Impatiently, evidently anxious to be
alone with* FREDDIE.] And you've given up the
idea?

> [*While this talk is going on, the Servant
> brings in two small tables and puts
> them on* L., *and one or two more and
> puts them by palm-trees in isolated
> position.*

BENSON. [*Evidently perceiving* RHODA's *impatience.*] Yes, ma'am. When the season is
over, I hope to get settled again—it's too late
now. I know her ladyship is suited, unfortunately
for me——

RHODA. [*Still impatient.*] Yes.

BENSON. Meanwhile, dinner-parties, or balls, or anything that wants managing, I shall be happy to attend. [*Then as* RHODA *turns away to talk with* FREDDIE, *he says haughtily to the* WAITER.] That will do. You needn't do any more, Charles; we can't take any more tables from the supper-room.

[*Exit* SERVANT.

[BENSON *looks round, and turns as if to go.*

FREDDIE. [*With a sudden idea, going up to him and speaking confidentially.*] Look here, Benson, I shall come in presently with a lady for supper. You might manage to give us a table in a quiet corner.

BENSON. [*Evidently understanding.*] It shall be done, my lord. I'll put one just here. [*Indicates* L.C. *by palm.*] [*Exit* BENSON.

[FREDDIE *and* RHODA *alone.*

RHODA. Oh, do come and sit down for a moment. I *am* so anxious about that money—it *must* be paid to-night—and I'm dreadfully afraid of Gerald twigging there's something up.

FREDDIE. I've got it somewhere. [*Business with his pockets.*] Don't know what I did with it, though—oh, yes, it's all right. There it is. [*Handing her a roll of notes, which she quickly hides in the bosom of her dress.*] Promise me you won't do it again, there's a good girl.

RHODA. Oh, I can't promise that; you see, people won't have you if you don't play fairly high nowadays.

FREDDIE. Yes they will. You're awfully nice, you know, and there isn't any occasion for nice girls to do the things the other ones must.

RHODA. Do you think I'm nice? Brothers seldom worry about their sisters.

FREDDIE. Of course you're nice, and I am very fond of you. That's why——

RHODA. You are a dear.

FREDDIE. I wish every one thought me one.

RHODA. Doesn't Margaret?

FREDDIE. That's different, she's my friend, as I told you to-day.

RHODA. And are you really going to propose to Sybil Dolwyn?

FREDDIE. [Nodding.] I'm going to risk it.

RHODA. You'll get tons of money with her—that's something.

FREDDIE. I don't want them; I only want her. P'raps she won't have me.

RHODA. Oh—h—h! [Contemptuously.] She'll jump at you. Why, you're one of the best *parti*s in London. I wish she wouldn't—I don't care for her.

FREDDIE. If she refuses me I shall be done for.

RHODA. Nonsense, she won't; she knows bet-

ter. Of course we're not going to let other people say it if you marry her; but she's an outsider
—she knows it herself.

FREDDIE. [*Quickly.*] Look here, Rhoda, I
wish you wouldn't say that kind of thing. It isn't
—well, it isn't sportsmanlike, you know. You
see, you don't understand Sybil. She looks like
a goddess, and—er—has all kinds of—of—qual-
ities. I don't quite know what they are, but she's
got them—you can see it in her walk. And then,
you're my sister, and I can't bear you to think
anything that isn't kind of any one, especially
of any one I care a lot about.

RHODA. Freddie, what's come over you? If
you go on in this way you'll become a country curate, or join the Salvation Army, or die
young.

FREDDIE. Perhaps I shall.

RHODA. [*Evidently thinking she has gone too
far.*] Don't be cross. Of course, I shall be very
nice if you marry her. I'll make up to her to-
night if I get a chance.

Re-enter GERALD.

GERALD. Margaret's getting nicely slanged all
the way to Wimbledon.

FREDDIE. Dear Margaret, it wasn't her fault.
It's so difficult to make mothers understand sometimes—even the nicest mothers.

RHODA. They outgrow things, you know.

Enter Mrs. Calson *alone, rather distraite. She
hesitates and looks round.*

Freddie. [*Aside to* Rhoda.] I'll go and look
for her now, our dance is the next but one. [*Nervously.*] I wonder if there's any champagne about.

Gerald. Plenty in there. [*Nodding to the
supper-room.*] Take Mrs. Calson in and give her
a bumper; they like it at that age, and with that
figure.

Rhoda. You mustn't say that sort of thing
to Freddie, or he'll go for you as he did for me
just now.

Freddie. Oh, I can't. [*Meaning that he can't
be worried with* Mrs. Calson.] I *must* go and
look for her—it's time—I might miss her. Look
here—I'll take you back, and Gerald can give
the old lady some supper.

[*Gives his arm to* Rhoda, *who looks back
triumphantly to* Gerald.

Gerald. I don't mind—they don't expect you
to talk.

Rhoda. [*Confidentially to* Freddie *as they
go off.*] You really are a lamb, Freddie, dear.

Freddie. I wish she thought me a lamb—
but what for?

Rhoda. Getting rid of Gerald for me. I do
think that a husband who follows one about a
ballroom or *any*where——

[*Exeunt* Rhoda *and* Freddie.

[GERALD *and* MRS. CALSON *left together.*

GERALD. Do anything for you? I believe there's food in there.

MRS. C. Well, I don't mind. I always like to make sure of things myself.

GERALD. They've put some tables here, but I think we'd better go in.

MRS. C. Why yes. Out here we wouldn't see much or get a selection, and I always want to see what your English ways are like.

GERALD. There isn't much to be said for them, but I daresay we shall get more to eat in there and that's something. Best of taking in a chaperone is that she appreciates a good supper—so do I.

[*They disappear through the curtains into the supper-room.*

WAITER *enters. Business.* BENSON *follows, they arrange table, evidently for* FREDDIE L. C., *business.*

[*Couple pass. Music louder and softer, &c.*

Enter DUKE *and* JENNIE CALSON *from ball-room.*

DUKE. It seems to be comparatively quiet out here.

JENNIE. Why yes, and it's lovely. [*Looking round.*] I do think you English people know how to do things. Why, this London is just one great show; but my! I wouldn't care to live here, it's all a sort of intoxication—like the champagne, not to be taken every day, though it does you good to taste it sometimes.

DUKE. Well—er—suppose we have some now —these little tables are meant for supper—this one will do——

[*Goes towards one arranged for* FREDDIE.

JENNIE. I'd like it, but I wonder where mother's got to. She's the only one here with a red feather on her head, and the last time I saw her it was waving along in this direction—that's the best of a red feather, you can always see it—it's as good as one of your post boxes.

[*Clatter is heard and laughter as of supper going on beyond curtains.*

DUKE. [*Dissatisfied.*] Do you want to go to her?

JENNIE. Not me, I'd like to have supper here.

Enter BENSON.

BENSON. Supper, your Grace?

DUKE. Yes. . . . You might put it at that table. [*Pointing to table* L.C. *To* JENNIE.] It will be cooler than going into a crowded room.

BENSON. [*Moving a table* R.C. *by palm.*] Your Grace will find this better—and that one has been taken——

DUKE. Oh—very well, it doesn't matter.

JENNIE. I'd like to look in. [*Looks in between the curtains when servants bring food, champagne,*

&c., to table R.C.] Mother's there. I see her— right at the far end. She's bent on doing everything there is to do. Going everywhere, seeing everything, eating everything. She'll be so pleased and satisfied when she gets back home she won't know what to do with herself. [*Sits down to supper at little table facing* DUKE, *business of supper. To* SERVANT.] No, I don't want anything. [*To* DUKE.] I'm too excited to be hungry——

> [*Another couple come and take table farther back so as to fill up scene.*

DUKE. [*Growing a little empressé in manner.*] Some champagne, eh? [*Pours some into her glass.*] And we'll have a quiet little talk, eh?

> [SERVANT *hands something.*

JENNIE. No, thanks. [*To* SERVANT.] Some fruit and a few crackers—biscuits, you call them I believe—or anything of that sort there is about, that will do for me. [*To the* DUKE.] At home it would be nearer our breakfast-time than supper-time, but I've been very much interested coming here, I can tell you—— My! What a time you have in London—I like seeing it.

DUKE. Though you don't want it—any more than that—every day?

> [*Nods his head at the glass she is raising to her lips.*

JENNIE. No, I don't.

[*Business, the* DUKE *is evidently considering something.*

DUKE. [*Bracing himself up.*] I'm sorry you don't like our English life.

JENNIE. But I do, it's London I'm speaking of—I thought Lexham just lovely. I'd live there always if it were mine.

DUKE. I hoped it might be yours some day when you were there, my dear young lady——

JENNIE. Why, Duke, what do you mean?

DUKE. My nephew was very much in love with you——

JENNIE. He's losing time falling in love with any one while you are round. [*It is said quite innocently, but the* DUKE *looks up.*] And in spite of being your nephew there isn't much in that funny-shaped head of his, yet—perhaps there will be—— Don't you think that experience is just so much seed that needs years to grow up before it becomes wisdom? I don't think your young men over here are half as charming as the older men.

DUKE. It never struck me—we older men feel ourselves to be merely the background of life.

JENNIE. I wish I could take a few over—it's our background that wants filling in. [*Business.*] I'd love to show you my home.

DUKE. [*Growing still more empressé.*] I
should like to see it—upon my word I would.

JENNIE. It will be spoilt soon, perhaps, but
all the world will, for they are making cities
everywhere—and there are always too many people in them, and some have too much to eat and
some too little, and a set of ways of their own.
I wouldn't like to be there when all the West is
like New York.

DUKE. Why don't you come over here?

JENNIE. But I wouldn't like to live always in
London.

> [FREDDIE *and* SYBIL *enter from ball-room
> at back, they come slowly down the
> stage towards the table laid for them*
> L.C.

> [SERVANTS *go in and out attending to the
> third couple, to* DUKE *and* MISS CAL-
> SON *and to* FREDDIE *and* SYBIL *as the
> scene goes on.*

DUKE. But you liked Lexham.

JENNIE. I just loved it.

DUKE. I mean—could you live there?

> [*Tries to take her hand.*

JENNIE. [*Surprised.*] Why——

DUKE. You said you didn't like young men,
I'm an old fellow, but—[*draws back as* SERVANT
.*comes forward.*]

FREDDIE. [*Stopping at the table* L.C.] I say, here's our table.

JENNIE. [*To* SERVANT *who offers something.*] No, thank you, I don't want anything more.

[FREDDIE *and* SYBIL *are behind them.*
[*The third couple, having finished supper, go back to ball-room.*

DUKE. This is a better place for a talk.

[DUKE *and* JENNIE *get up and sit down on the settee under the palms looking* R., *their backs towards* FREDDIE *and* SYBIL.

JENNIE. I like listening to that music in the distance—somehow it makes one think of home.

FREDDIE. [*Who has sat down with* SYBIL *at the other table* L.C.] I say, isn't this ripping?

SYBIL. [*Absently.*] Isn't it?

[WAITER *brings some soup, which she instantly begins; then as if she suddenly remembered* FREDDIE.

It's rather a good entertainment, eh?

FREDDIE. Ripping.

SYBIL. [*Busy with her soup.*] Ripping——

FREDDIE. I felt as if I couldn't live any longer if it didn't begin.

SYBIL. If what didn't begin?

FREDDIE. [*Nervously.*] Why—why—our dance you know, and supper, and everything. [*She goes on with her soup.*] I think of nothing but you all day and all night—you're just every-thing.

SYBIL. [*In a caressing but absent tone.*] You silly boy.

FREDDIE. I wish you wouldn't call me a silly boy. It doesn't matter, does it?

SYBIL. What doesn't?

FREDDIE. Being two years younger.

SYBIL. Not a bit—Royalties are awfully gra-cious to-night, aren't they? [SERVANT *offers champagne.*] Yes, please.

FREDDIE. P'raps they twigged, you know—often think they twig an awful lot.

SYBIL. [*To* SERVANT *who appears, hands a dish.*] Yes, please, some sole.

FREDDIE. [*To* WAITER.] No, thank you.

SYBIL. I always eat fish.

FREDDIE. So do I, awfully good, you know. But I like to think of 'em swimming about in the sea.

SYBIL. You funny boy.

FREDDIE. I wish you wouldn't call me a boy. I—I— Have some more fish? [*The dish has been put down between them, she nods and he gives her some more. Goes on nervously.*] You know I've been awfully afraid——

SYBIL. Afraid?—I am never afraid of any-thing. [*Laughs.*] What's the good?

FREDDIE. Oh, I say, don't laugh. When you

are like that you know—one knows you can't be thinking of—of—of what I'm thinking of.

SYBIL. What are you thinking of?

[*Looks up at* WAITER *who takes her plate.*

WAITER. Quail?

[FREDDIE *makes a gesture of impatience.*

SYBIL. Yes, please. [*Listening.*] I like that waltz—danced it last time with Harry Gregson.

WAITER. [*To* FREDDIE.] Quail, my lord?

FREDDIE. [*Impatiently.*] No, no, that'll do.

SYBIL. You must have some supper. I like men who eat—they are so good-tempered.

FREDDIE. [*To* WAITER.] Oh, say, quail—two.

[*Helps himself hurriedly.*

[*Exit* WAITER.]

SYBIL. Good, aren't they?

FREDDIE. Shall I tell you what I was thinking?

SYBIL. [*Still eating.*] Thinking—when?

FREDDIE. The other night when I broke your fan, do you remember?

SYBIL. Rather. I took it to be mended to-day.

FREDDIE. I wanted to say something then— it was so awkward breaking it. I wanted you to know and—[*She holds out her glass for champagne, he fills it*] I couldn't say it.

SYBIL. Why couldn't you?

FREDDIE. I don't know. I couldn't—I believe it broke itself on purpose.

[*Takes a long gulp of champagne.*

WAITER. Fruit salad?

[SYBIL *nods and is helped to some.*

[FREDDIE's *plate is taken away, he hasn't touched anything.*

[*She eats her fruit salad and sips champagne at intervals.*

[*He looks at her admiringly.*

FREDDIE. I told the mater this morning that you were like a goddess. Do you know what I think sometimes?

SYBIL. What?

FREDDIE. I think that you were once a marble statue in the British Museum, or that you are going to be one or something.

SYBIL. It would be awfully cold in winter, no clothes, you know—and nothing to eat or drink —[*sips champagne*]—wouldn't suit me.

FREDDIE. [*Nervously.*] I never thought of that.

SYBIL. What did the mater say?

FREDDIE. I like you to call her that. [*Pause.*] It was a bore breaking your fan, you know—I couldn't say it—I mean what I wanted to say.

SYBIL. Well, you can now. [*Reaches out her hand and helps herself to some grapes which are on a dish close to her on the table.*] Then perhaps I'll say something to you.

FREDDIE. [*Huskily.*] Do you mean that? [*She nods.*] You know what it is, don't you?

[*She shakes her head and pushes a grape into her mouth.*] I believe you do. [*She looks up at him with a little laugh.*] I'm awfully gone on you. [*He reaches across as if to take her hand. She pulls the left one back and with the right one holds up her little bunch of grapes.*] I've been feeling as if I should blow my brains out if it wasn't any good.

SYBIL. Oh, but you wouldn't, you know.

[*Goes on eating grapes.*

FREDDIE. But it's all right, it is all right, isn't it? [*Entreatingly.*] Do say it's all right.

SYBIL. [*Puzzled.*] Is what all right? I don't believe you know a bit what you're talking about.

FREDDIE. Yes, I do. I've been in love with you all the time, you know that. Look here, do you think you could marry me? I'm an awful rotter, but I'll do anything you like. You can't think how awfully fond I am of you.

SYBIL. You mustn't talk nonsense, dear boy. You are only a boy, you know.

FREDDIE. I am a man—and I love you—I love you.

SYBIL. You have said that.

FREDDIE. And I want you to marry me.

SYBIL. Fear I can't.

FREDDIE. Why not?

SYBIL. Don't want to. Besides, I'm engaged to Algernon Wake. The Prince was quite pleased

—we told him. No one knows—only you and the Prince.

FREDDIE. Oh, I say. You don't mean it. He doesn't care as I do. He has always been gone on Margaret.

SYBIL. He's gone on me now—[*triumphantly*] —and I'm gone on him—awfully gone. But we must be friends, Freddie, dear, you and I.

FREDDIE. I can't. [*Rising.*] I can't do it. You don't mean it, Sybil? Look here, you don't mean it, do you? I couldn't stand it. I'd give my life for you—I will.

SYBIL. I don't want it, my dear boy, no use for it.

FREDDIE. Oh, but I must.

SYBIL. [*Getting up.*] ' We'd better go back —I'll give you another dance presently.

FREDDIE. [*Gets up.*] I can't stay any longer —you made me think you cared—I can't face it.

SYBIL. Nonsense. [*With a laugh.*] Don't be silly.

FREDDIE. Oh, I say——

Enter from ball-room ALGERNON WAKE, RHODA.

ALGY. [*Coming forward.*] Oh, you're there. Been looking for you.

SYBIL. I've been having supper with Lord Gaysford.

RHODA. Luck for him.

ALGY. Come and have some more with us.

RHODA. [*Evidently remembering her talk with* FREDDIE.] Yes, do.

SYBIL. Shall I? I'm hungry still. Lord Gaysford doesn't believe in supper.

RHODA. Oh! But won't Freddie come too?
[*Turns to the table at back before he can answer. He doesn't move.*

SYBIL. [*At other table.*] This is splendid.
[*With a little laugh. Sits down at supper-table, with her back to audience and* FREDDIE. *A riotous supper begins.*
[FREDDIE *left alone, watches them, then sits down half concealed from them on seat well to the left, leans his head forward on his hand, and seems oblivious of everything.*
[*The talk is taken up by* JENNIE *and the* DUKE, *on the settee under the palm.*

JENNIE. [*To the* DUKE.] Well, I think you're just wonderful. What you should see in a wild Westerner girl like me I can't think—'tisn't even as if I were Anna.

DUKE. Ah, why is Miss Anna so often in your thoughts?

JENNIE. You see, she is my cousin. She lives in New York, and she's charming, and that generous——

DUKE. She can't be more charming than you, my fair Westerner.

JENNIE. Well, but I thought when you English married American girls, you expected us to come from New York or Chicago, or some other place where they raise great heiresses. That's why Anna wouldn't come herself.

DUKE. [*Uneasily.*] My dear—[*hesitating*]— Jennie—I am glad that your money has not been made in those terrible cities. Englishmen don't make it a fixed condition that American brides come from one of them.

JENNIE. [*Anxiously.*] But look here, I want you to understand I'm not rich; we've got miles and miles of land, and I don't know how many head of cattle——

DUKE. Ah!

JENNIE. But there are my four brothers, and they all come before me, they've wives and large families.

DUKE. But my dear young lady, I understood —that—that—um—well—people don't live as you and your mother have been doing if—if——

JENNIE. If they're poor? Why, we're not poor, but we're not rich. Perhaps we have got mixed up—it's Anna who is the great heiress of Calson's Trust. She sent us over; she was afraid to come herself, lest—well, lest she'd meet some one like you, Duke, and she said she didn't want to take her money out of her own country, so she wouldn't come over here till she was married—

—come for her honeymoon, maybe—meanwhile she
proposed that mother and I should see for her
what it was like; she insisted on giving mother
five thousand pounds, and made her promise she'd
spend it all in the four months we were away—
go to Court and do the whole thing—go back
and tell her all about it—carry back the frocks
and all. I didn't want to come—I'm quite content with my backwoods; but mother did, and she
wouldn't come without me—I'm glad I did now.

DUKE. [*Dismayed.*] I see—I see—I am
afraid that things have not been made quite clear,
and that you *were* mistaken for the cautious Miss
Anna.

JENNIE. Why—yes—I believe that's it.

[*Burst of laughter from supper-table at
back.*

[FREDDIE *starts as he hears it.*

DUKE. [*Coldly.*] I think it is.

JENNIE. Now I feel sure of it—for the num-
ber of—well I must have been pretty vain to
think it was done just for me. . . . I wonder
if you asked me to marry you because you thought
I was Anna. If you did, you needn't worry—
I'm not going to hold you to it.

[MRS. CALSON *and* GERALD *come slowly
through curtains on* R. *from supper-
room.*

DUKE. [*Formally, and evidently with a strug-*

gle.] My dear—Jennie, I am the most fortunate of men—[*Rises.*] Here comes your mother. Perhaps we won't take her into our confidence at this moment—the position is a little new—we might discuss it a little more fully first.

JENNIE. [*Looking at him anxiously.*] Suppose you come and meet me to-morrow at Miss Margaret Wake's—she's asked me to go and see her—we'll walk back from her house and talk it over—and till then I'll just say nothing to mother or any one else. Good-night, Duke. [*To* MRS. CALSON, *who has come forward.*] Mother, I'd like to go home, if you wouldn't mind—I'm tired—I want to be with you—let us go.

    [*Says it tenderly with a little break in her voice.*

MRS. C. [*To the* DUKE.] I see you and Jennie have been having supper out here. Well, she's missed something. That room filled with beautiful Englishwomen and distinguished-looking men, sitting at those little tables thoroughly enjoying themselves and the way that supper was served was a sight. Why——

DUKE. Ah!

MRS. C. Why, in New York they may be able to spend more money, but, compared with the way they do it here, it's like the child at school drawing on a slate compared to an old master. Of course, with us farther West—why it's different.

GERALD. Not quite so festive at this time of night, eh?

JENNIE. [*Wearily, putting her hand on her mother's arm.*] Let us go, mother—I'm so tired. [*Turning to* GERALD, *who has been standing listening to* MRS. CALSON's *talk with an air of derision.*] Mr. Massington, will you see us to our carriage? [*With a rather distant manner to the* DUKE.] We'll meet to-morrow afternoon. Goodnight.

DUKE. Mayn't I come——

JENNIE. Not now.

DUKE. [*Bows over her hand.*] Good-night.

MRS. C. Good-night, Duke, it's been a lovely ball, and we are very much obliged to you for getting us invited; the kindness of you English people is wonderful.

GERALD. [*To* RHODA, *at other table—he has just seen her.*] I'll be back directly—didn't know you were there.

[*Exit* GERALD MASSINGTON, *with* MRS. CALSON *and* JENNIE. *The* DUKE *remains near the settee lost in thought.*]

RHODA. [*At the supper-table.*] But it wasn't his own wife, you know. [*Laughter.*

VOICE. Then it didn't matter.

SYBIL. [*Laughing.*] Nothing matters.

DUKE. [*Hearing, and going a step towards table.*] Nothing?

Voice. Nothing, that is the best of it.

Enter Benson. *Business, with tables &c.*

Benson. [*Going up to* Freddie *and speaking in a low voice.*] Let me bring you a whisky-and-soda, my lord.

> [Freddie, *looking nervously over his shoulder and seeing that the palms virtually conceal him from the table at which* Sybil *and her friends are rioting, gives* Benson *a nod of assent, pulls himself together and sits up, evidently deliberating. Exit* Benson.

Rhoda. I didn't see you were there, Duke.

Duke. How do you do, Mrs. Massington?

> [*He goes over to the party at the other table but does not sit down.*
>
> [Benson *returns with the soda-water, which he gives to* Freddie, *who drinks, and evidently revives under its influence.*

Freddie. Do you know the nearest telegraph office that is open all night, Benson? I want to send a wire to Paris.

Benson. Charing Cross, my lord.

Freddie. I must go. [*Looking round uneasily*

Benson. Couldn't I send it for you, my lord? You look so tired.

Freddie. Er—I wish you would. [*Feels in his pocket, pulls out a letter, tears off blank half-*

sheet.] You must get it written out on a Continental form.

[*Feels for pencil, shakes his head.*

BENSON. A fountain pen, if your lordship can use it—[*pulling it out of his pocket*]—I always carry one.

FREDDIE. Thank you, Benson. [*Writes.*] "Tremayne, Hotel Bristol, Paris. No good, shall do what I said." [*To* BENSON.] It must go to-night, he starts for Constantinople at nine in the morning.

BENSON. I'll take it myself, my lord. Is there anything else I can do?

FREDDIE. No, I ought to write a note, but——

BENSON. I fear I can't find paper here, my lord, but I have a postcard in my pocket if that's any use. I find it so useful to have one about me. [*He pulls out postcard.*]

FREDDIE. [*Taking it with a tragic nod. Writes.*] "No good. Shall do what I said. Good-bye." [*Turns it over and directs.*] "Mrs. Merlin, 17B Bruton Street." [*Gives it to* BENSON.] Could you see that they go?

BENSON. I'll take them both myself, my lord.

[*Puts them in pocket.*

FREDDIE. Thank you, Benson. [*Hesitates.*] Look here, I should like to give you this. [*Gives him bank note.*

BENSON. [*Looking at him oddly, but evidently*

not suspecting what is in FREDDIE's *mind.*] Thank
you very much, my lord.

FREDDIE. [*Looking round nervously.*] Is there
any way out of this place except——? [*Nodding
towards ball-room and supper-room Exits.*]

BENSON. Through this door and the garden,
and you'll be home in two minutes. [*Unlocks the
door in conservatory on* L.] I'll come down and
lock the garden door after your lordship.

> [FREDDIE *goes a step towards the door,
> stops and takes a last look at the merry
> supper-party, which does not see him. While
> he stands thus, the* DUKE *comes back from
> the group supping to the seat beneath the
> palm, stands with his back to* FREDDIE,
> *whom he doesn't notice.*

DUKE. [*With a bewildered startled air as if he
can't believe it says to himself*]—Accepted!

FREDDIE. [*In a note of despair, as he turns to
go off by the garden door.*] Refused!

> [*A burst of laughter comes from the table
> at the back.*

CURTAIN.

ACT III

Scene.—Margaret's *sitting-room in Pont Street.
Small and pretty. Telephone os table, well
down stage; mullion window at back.
Green tree seen in back garden.*]

Time.—*Next afternoon.*

[Margaret *alone in out-door dress, hat,
&c., much agitated; reads a note, rings
the bell.*

Enter Servant.

Margaret. Are you *quite* sure that no one else
called?

Servant. No one, miss.

Margaret. And there are no more telegrams?

Servant. No, miss.   [*Exit* Servant.
[Margaret *alone. Takes off hat, &c.
Business. Re-enter* Servant, *announcing*

Servant. Mr. Algernon Wake.

Enter Algy; *looks rather foolish and
bothered through the interview.*

Margaret. Oh, Algy, I'm so glad you have
come.

Algy. Why, what's the matter?

Margaret. Have you seen Freddie Gaysford?

ALGY. No, haven't looked for him.

MARGARET. You don't know anything about him?

ALGY. Don't want to—I saw him last night.

MARGARET. [*Earnestly.*] Did he look happy?

ALGY. [*Almost with a grin.*] No—o. He didn't.

MARGARET. Oh!

AIGY. [*Still with a grin.*] Sybil refused him.

MARGARET. Oh! What *will* he do? [*Agitated.*]

ALGY. P'raps he'll go off his chump—he won't have far to go—he isn't up to much, you know.

MARGARET. Algy, you don't know Freddie; there's so much in him.

ALGY. No one would think it.

MARGARET. He doesn't wear his heart on his sleeve for daws to peck at.

ALGY. Keeps it in his manly breast, eh?

MARGARET. [*Earnestly.*] And it's full of the right feelings. He cares for the right things, and he does them. There's no one like Freddie.

ALGY. [*Irritably.*] I'm glad to hear it, we don't want another of them.

MARGARET. Algy! He's my friend.

ALGY. All right. Beg pardon. We're cousins —relations are always rude.

MARGARET. [*Forgivingly.*] Of course.

ALGY. Besides, I didn't come to talk about Freddie. There's awful news about Uncle Edward.

MARGARET. Uncle Edward! Oh, what is it? I've heard nothing.

ALGY. They say he's going to get married— it's all over the town.

MARGARET. Going to get married! You said it was something awful.

ALGY. It is, for last night I got engaged to Sybil Dolwyn.

MARGARET. *You* did!

ALGY. Of course I did.

MARGARET. I hoped she'd marry Freddie Gaysford.

ALGY. Well, she can't; she's going to marry me.

MARGARET. How *could* she refuse Freddie!

ALGY. Easily done.

MARGARET. Who is Uncle Edward going to marry? Mrs. Merlin?

ALGY. Not he! He's going to marry the American girl.

MARGARET. What, that nice Jennie Calson?

ALGY. Well, you may call her nice, and perhaps he does; I don't. . . . Don't you see that if Uncle Edward gets married, I may never stand in his shoes, and Sybil mayn't think the chance worth considering.

MARGARET. Oh, but you shouldn't count on dead men's shoes; it's so unkind.

ALGY. Sybil will——

MARGARET. But doesn't she love you?

ALGY. Don't know. She's going to marry me because she's thinks that some day I shall be a duke. I was going to marry her because she's rolling in money—corkscrew, you know.

MARGARET. Oh!

ALGY. I like her very well, and she likes me very well, but I've stated the main facts.

MARGARET. I think it's dreadful.

ALGY. I don't, quite fair, we shall each get what we want and jog along very well: nice girl, plenty of nerve—sha'n't be dull with her—never quite certain what she'll do next—I like that sort of woman, keeps one going.

MARGARET. Freddie loved her. [*Passionately.*] He didn't care a bit about her money——

ALGY. Didn't want it—plenty of his own—no uncle to worry him.

MARGARET. Yes, but if she hadn't had a penny, and he hadn't, it would have been just the same, he loved her. Freddie is worlds better than you, Algy.

ALGY. Very well, I really can't help it.

MARGARET. People think far too much about money nowadays. I wish there wasn't any in the world.

ALGY. I don't, and you'd be precious uncomfortable without it. But look here, do talk sensibly, there's a good girl; I came to consult you about Uncle Edward. I don't want Sybil to chuck me.

MARGARET. If she only accepted you for the reason you say, it would be a good thing if she did.

ALGY. My dear Margaret, I think you're going off *your* chump. Upon my soul, you're as bad as Gaysford.

MARGARET. [*Imploring and evidently unable to attend to what he is saying.*] Algy, don't be tiresome—but do go and find out if he's at his rooms, or at the barracks, if he's *any*where, and send me a telegram or ring me up, and—and— I'll find out about Uncle Edward for you. I'll telephone to Miss Calson, I can't very well ask her if it's true, but I'll ask her to come and see me and perhaps she'll tell me then. And Oh! I wish you'd be a real true man and marry for the right reason—the only right reason—because you love some one dearly, not because she has money —there's nothing so splendid in the world, Algy dear, as a great unselfish love—You are my cousin and——

ALGY. I say that'll do, I can imagine the rest. I'll go and find out about Gaysford and let you know—daresay he's only taking a day off and will turn up at the Lavingtons' to-night or somewhere else to-morrow.

Enter SERVANT, *announcing*

SERVANT. Mrs. and Miss Calson.

ALGY. [*Aside to* MARGARET.] Oh, I say, now you can find out. Perhaps she won't tell you before me——

MARGARET. Of course not—and do go and find out about Freddie—I'll do anything in the world for you if you'll find Freddie—and telephone anything you hear.

Enter MRS. *and* MISS CALSON.

MRS. C. [*To* MARGARET.] Miss Wake, I couldn't resist doing myself the great pleasure of paying you a visit. [*Shakes hands.*]

MARGARET. So kind of you.

[*She and* JENNIE *exchange greetings.*

JENNIE. Mother said she would bring me and——

MRS. C. Why, Mr. Wake, how do you do?

ALGY. How do? Been paying my cousin a friendly visit. How are you, Miss Calson? Enjoy the dance last night?

MRS. C. [*Before* JENNIE *can reply.*] I did. I thought it was a lovely house and the supper just perfect. When I go back to America I shall describe the way that everything is done here from beginning to end. Why, that ball last night was worth coming all the way to see. In New York they think they know what they are about when they entertain, but I can assure you——

ALGY. That we go one better, eh? Always

like doing that myself, so cheering. I hope Miss
Calson enjoyed it?

[*Looks towards* JENNIE.

MRS. C. [*Begins before* JENNIE *can answer.*]
Well now, I don't believe she did as much as she
ought. The Duke was very kind, but Jennie was
tired, and insisted on coming away before it was
over. He had taken great trouble to get us invited and he looked disappointed, [MARGARET *and*
ALGY *exchange looks.*] for he wanted to give us
a good time, as he always does, and he did me, but
I do think that here in London young people don't
enjoy themselves as much as we older ones——

ALGY. Awful shame, isn't it? I mean awfully
nice for the older people, young people come to
it by-and-by, you know; something to look forward to—[*edging towards the door.*] Sorry, I've
got to go. Good-bye. You shall hear from me
presently, Margaret, suppose you'll be here?

MARGARET. Yes—[*eagerly*] I shall—be here.

[*Exit* ALGY.

MRS. C. Jennie says you'd ask her to come and
see you one afternoon, and she wanted to come to-
day, so I thought I would pay my respects to your
Mamma who very kindly invited us one day when
we were not able to come. I am not sure that Jennie wanted me with her——

Enter SERVANT, *announcing*

SERVANT. The Duke of Lexham.

Enter the DUKE.

MARGARET. Uncle Edward—[*greeting him*] I am so glad to see you.

DUKE. How do you do, my dear? Safely back from the Wimbledon dance? [*Turns to the* CALSONS. JENNIE *is rather embarrassed but tries not to show it. They shake hands.*] How do you do, Mrs. Calson?

MRS. C. [*To* DUKE.] Why this is quite an unexpected pleasure and gives me a chance of thanking you again for getting us that invitation for last night. It's a pity Jennie was tired and we had to come away rather soon, but I can assure you that I enjoyed it just immensely.

DUKE. Ah?—[*To* JENNIE.] I hope you are better? [*Goes towards her.*

JENNIE. Yes, thank you—I'm better.

MRS. C. [*As if she saw that she would not get his attention, turns to* MARGARET.] I understand your Mamma was not at home—I hope she is quite well?

MARGARET. Oh yes, thank you, she is at the Albert Hall bazaar. There's one for her best charity and she has a stall.

MRS. C. Well now, isn't that lovely? I wish I had gone—what is she selling?

MARGARET. Wooden effigies of living celebrities —she has discovered a genius—no one else knows anything about him.

Mrs. C. Why! I'd give anything to be there
—did you hear that, Jennie? I'd love to buy
some; dead celebrities are so dull, but your living
ones just now are splendid and you have so many
to choose from, it's just wonderful.

Duke. Eh—why don't you go and pick up a
few before it is too late——

Mrs. C. I expect there'd be such a crowd I
wouldn't find my way to the stall and when I did,
perhaps they'd all be snapped up.

Jennie. [*Who while* Mrs. Calson *has been
speaking has edged towards* Margaret, *says to
her aside in an almost passionate tone.*] Oh, if
you could take her way—I want to talk to him
so——

Margaret. [*Surprised, looks round, then as if
she twigged the whole situation.*] Is your carriage at the door, Uncle Edward?

Duke. Yes, do you want it?

[*Turns to* Jennie *again, she has gone towards him after speaking to* Margaret.

Margaret. I know you'll lend it me. [*To*
Mrs. Calson.] Why shouldn t I take you to the
bazaar? Mother would be delighted, I know the
way to the stall—I should be back in ten minutes,
and I daresay Miss Calson would take care of
Uncle Edward while we went?

Jennie. But our motor is outside, it would get
there quicker still.

DUKE. *Splendid!* [*To* MRS. CALSON.] You'll be able to buy up every celebrity in London—and they are sure to be cheap—celebrities are nowadays.

JENNIE. It's a real chance for you, mother.

MRS. C. [*Rather surprised at finding herself hustled.*] Well, now——

MARGARET. [*Takes up her hat.*] Let us come at once, where are my gloves? We'll fly there.

MRS. C. Well—if you think she would be pleased——

MARGARET. She'll be charmed. (*To the* DUKE *and* JENNIE.) *Au revoir.* [*Opening the door.*

[*Exeunt* MARGARET *and* MRS. CALSON.

[DUKE *and* JENNIE *are alone. He looks at her inquiringly, she stands with her back to the mantelpiece facing him for a minute.*

JENNIE. I hoped to see you—I expect you had my note asking you to be here? [*He nods.* [*Going a step forward.*] It was splendid of Miss Wake to take mother away. I've been think all night—I've been thinking hard—— [*There's a note almost of emotion in her voice.*] I want you to understand that I like you for the way you stood by what you'd said last night—after you'd found out I wasn't Anna.

DUKE. My dear young lady—I stood by what I hoped might be my good fortune.

THE MODERN WAY 309

JENNIE. You must just let me do the talking for one minute—it was splendid of you; but I wouldn't marry you for all the world. You mustn't think I'm not grateful—most American girls like marrying dukes—I know one, Katherine Fiffer she's called, who says she owes it to her father to come over and invest his money in a title and lands and all that, and she'll do it. But there aren't many of you who would stand by a simple Western girl when they found out she didn't know for certain that she'd a thousand dollars of her own; and that you were one of them, and willing to do it just for the sake of your word——

DUKE. For the sake of a most charming woman——

JENNIE. [*As if she hadn't heard.*] I'll never forget. Since I came to England I've had nineteen offers of marriage of one sort or another, but now I feel that not one of them has been made to me, they've all been made to Anna's millions with which I got mixed up. It's a good lesson for one's vanity——

DUKE. My dear—Jennie—if I may call you that—let me speak—I *did* think you were an heiress, I own up. I told my nephew Algernon, that I should be delighted if you married him. He hasn't any brains, and he hasn't any money, and he'll never do a day's work, and I thought——

JENNIE. He might marry me? It *was* kind.

DUKE. I ought to be horsewhipped.

JENNIE. [*In a quick half-passionate, half-pathetic voice.*] And that was why you asked us to Lexham, I expect? Why it was like "'Will you walk into my parlour?' said the spider to the fly."

DUKE. [*Taking no notice.*] And when you came—or rather, when you had been there a day or two, I thought you the most charming girl I had even seen in my life, so fresh and natural, and unspoilt, that upon my life, meeting you after the London women was like walking out of a crowded ball-room down a country lane on an early spring morning. But it never occurred to me to think of you myself, I've had my day, I'm fifty-seven years old.

JENNIE. [*Still pathetic.*] It's just a lovely age —it's what makes you so interesting. I've thought you like no one else here, and haven't cared a bit about who you were or anything but just you, and those fifty-seven years you've lived—I knew how picturesque they must have been——

DUKE. Jennie! [*Goes on explaining.*] I don't pretend that I *haven't* thought of the—the fortune that I understood was yours. Er—er—I thought it would be a good thing for Algernon to have it——

JENNIE. It would be just the worst—he ought

to be made to work—it would make a man of him
—but they don't know how to do it over here.

DUKE.—And Lexham—what with the reduction
of rents and life charges and all the thousand and
one things that are a nightmare to property-own-
ers—is shrinking and falling to bits for want of
—of—of stoking—I think that is what you call
it——

JENNIE. [*With a little smile.*] For want of an
heiress to prop it up.

DUKE. Well, for want of money from somewhere, to put it plainly.

JENNIE. I see, I see—I was just the chance
for Lexham——

DUKE. Yes, I confess I wanted your money
for the place—but I wanted you for myself, I'm
more in love than I have been since I was twenty-
five—when I married—and had ten good years—
[*with feeling in his voice*] I've never seen any
woman I could put in her place till I met you, she
would understand your being in it——

JENNIE. If I were Anna I believe I would be
there——

DUKE. [*Going forward.*] Be there, without being Anna, if you can bring yourself to take me—
if you care——

JENNIE. Why, yes, I could care, but I'm not
going to marry you, it would just be the worst
mistake that either of us could make, and presently

we'd look at each other and we'd know it better than any one in the world. I couldn't live the life that all of you live over here.

DUKE. But you said you liked the life at Lexham.

JENNIE. I think it's beautiful, it's a living picture, but it isn't one that I want to be in. I've liked seeing it all, I'll like remembering it, just as I'll like remembering all I've done over here, living at Claridge's, wearing clothes such as I never had before, going to King Edward's Court, and your Universities and Ascot, and places like last night—why it's been a dream, but I couldn't take it as my life—I couldn't take even Lexham as that.

DUKE. Why not?

JENNIE. I couldn't do it. I couldn't live in a house with as many rooms, with all those beautiful things that have got to be just so, and just there; or with all that crowd of servants about. I couldn't wear my best clothes all day long; why they'd worry me, and as for sitting down to all those long meals every day with white table-cloths and servants dressed up waiting on me, or doing all the things that people do in that position— I'm not made that way. I'd feel as if I were in prison, or play-acting a piece that never came to an end, or in a wax-work—I wouldn't feel alive, I wouldn't feel able to breathe.

DUKE. But what sort of life do you live, my dear?

JENNIE. Why, we just live on the land, and our house is a long low one, and the room we are in mostly is a large one with high rafters and a stone floor and sheep-skin mats about, and a door that opens on to the world that stretches miles and miles away. We never use the best parlour unless strangers come or there's something out of the common going on. And no one comes over our threshold of the sort you see here in London.

DUKE. They'll come——

JENNIE. Yes, we know that. The cities are creeping nearer but they're not there yet. The planters and growers and cattle-ranchers know that the old life is coming to an end, but I wouldn't give up a single day of it—I couldn't—[*reaching out her hands.*]   .   .   .   I believe I love you a little. [*He goes a step forward but she keeps him back*]—but it's only as one loves in a dream or as one might love some one on Sundays. The man I live my life with must be for the waking time and the week-days. He must wear rough clothes and thick boots, and work with his hands and be ready with his fists, and love the open better than indoors, and know the sky and the ground and every sign of the weather, and every beast he owns and its name—and everything about it— [*struggles not to break down*]. I'm going back

to the life I want to live, but I'll remember you
—I'll just remember you all my life——

DUKE. Come to me for all my life——

JENNIE. No. I couldn't. And you'll get to see
how wise I am——

DUKE. Wise, my dear? I love you——

JENNIE. No, you're just surprised—you're
taken with the New World view—but you wouldn't
like it always——

DUKE. [*Reflectively.*] Perhaps——

JENNIE. [*As if it were all painful.*] Why no,
not perhaps—but certain—and now I'd like to end
all this—we're friends—and we'll always be
friends—at heart——

DUKE. You've taught me that money isn't everything. [*Takes her hands and kisses them.*] Some
day I shall come out to the West and see you—
if you'll let me.

JENNIE. Why yes, I'll let you do that. [*With
a pathetic laugh.*] You'll like it, but you'll feel
as much out of it as I would riding my rough pony
down Rotten Row, though I'd like that—[*Suddenly, as if unable to bear it longer*] I want to go
home, will you tell Miss Wake? Oh, but she's
gone off with Mother in the motor.

DUKE. Jennie, are you sure——

JENNIE. Yes, I'm sure and I want to go back
to the hotel right away. [*Turns as if to go.*]

DUKE. Let me drive you.

Enter SERVANT *with a telegram on a tray, looks round, evidently surprised not to see* MARGARET.

JENNIE. Miss Wake will be here directly.

[*Exit* SERVANT.

Oh! Here she is——

Re-enter MARGARET.

MARGARET. [*To* JENNIE.] Mrs. Calson has sent back the motor for you, but I hope you won't go just yet——

JENNIE. Why, yes, I must, the Duke was going to drive me, but now we can go along separately. Let me come and see you another day. [*To the* DUKE.] And I would rather you drove me some other day if you don't mind. Good-bye [*to* MARGARET.]

DUKE. I'll see you into the motor if I may. [*To* MARGARET *as he is about to go with* JENNIE] I'll come back in a minute——

[*Exit* DUKE *with* JENNIE, *re-enter* SERVANT, *hands* MARGARET *the telegram, and exit. She opens it, gives a little cry.*

MARGARET. [*Reads aloud with a puzzled air.*] "Am coming to you this morning, Freddie— [*looks at envelope.*] Redirected at Lancaster Lodge, sent first by mistake to Lansdowne Lodge." I don't understand. [*Agitated.*]

Re-enter the DUKE.

Uncle Edward, do you understand this telegram? It's from Freddie Gaysford, I expected a telegram from him this morning at Wimbledon, but it didn't come. He was to have come here this afternoon, but he hasn't——

Duke. [*Looking at telegram.*] Evidently forgot the address.

Margaret. And he's probably wandering about Wimbledon Common trying to find me, oh! Where is he?

Duke. He'll turn up, my dear, when he's tired of trying to find you there—I daresay he'll be here directly——

Re-enter Servant, *with another telegram.*

Perhaps this is from him.

Margaret. [*Tearing it open.*] " Just arrived at Folkestone, coming to you immediately, Tremayne." Mr. Tremayne! Why he started for Constantinople last night. [*Pause.*] Oh! do you think—— [*agitated*]—can it be about Freddie? I know he is miserable, for Sybil Dolwyn refused him last night.

Duke. It's lucky for him that she did.

Margaret. She accepted Algy——

Duke. I know—I thought she would do for him—but now—[*seriously*] I'm sorry for it, and Lexham will be sorry by-and-by, she's not the right sort.

Margaret. Algy heard that you were going to be married, Uncle Edward—to Jennie Calson.

Duke. I was last night.

MARGARET. Oh! I'm glad——

DUKE. But she has thrown me over—just now.

MARGARET. Thrown you over—Why?

DUKE. Because I'm not good enough for her, she wants a man who wears thick boots and rough clothes and a wideawake. She thinks that I am a loafer with too many luxuries—she's wrong; my class, if it does its duty, often works much harder than—than the one she admires. But she's a fine creature. I would rather not talk about it, though she's given me more to think about than I've had for twenty-five years.

MARGARET. [*Putting her hand on his arm.*] It's always good to love the best—be glad you have done that, dear Uncle Edward .   .   . [*Pause.*] I wish you would talk about Freddie, I am so anxious about him. [*Suddenly remembering.*] He asked me to shake hands last night—it frightens me, he meant—Oh! why didn't I understand?—[*Emotion.*]

DUKE. [*Looking round sharply, but speaking with tenderness.*] He's a nice lad—are you fond of him, my dear?

MARGARET. [*Half turning away.*] He's my friend—of course I like him——

Enter SERVANT *with a note on tray, which he hands to* MARGARET.

[*Exit* SERVANT.

DUKE. P'raps that's from him.

MARGARET. Oh no!—may I open it? It's from Mrs. Merlin. [*Reads.*] "I am so anxious about dear Freddy Gaysford, do you know anything about him? [*Agitated.*] Oh!—[*Rings the bell.*]

Enter SERVANT.

[MARGARET *goes to writing-table on* L., *and writes.*]

"Nothing, nothing, am miserable." [*To* SERVANT.] Send this note at once to Mrs. Merlin by hand. [*Exit* SERVANT.] [*To* DUKE.] Oh, *do* go to Grosvenor Place and see if Lady Gaysford knows anything—and come back and tell me —I would go myself but I can't—[*agitated*]—if she only had a telephone—but she won't have one in the house.

DUKE. Quite right—a telephone is as bad as a motor—I'll go this minute. [*Takes both her hands; kisses her forehead. Is going, then turns back.*] Don't tell Algy I'm not going to marry Jennie—I want to see what happens—don't tell him yet——

MARGARET. I won't. Come back and tell me about Freddie—I am so unhappy—and you are such an old dear—I love you, Uncle Edward.

[*Exit* DUKE.

[MARGARET *alone, takes off her hat, throws herself on a chair.*

MARGARET. [*Exclaiming passionately*]. Oh, Freddie, Freddie, if you would only come! [*The telephone bell rings. She flies to it. Business at the telephone.*] Yes, it's I, Margaret. Oh, Algy! He's not been there all day? I know that, he's been to Wimbledon, but I thought—he ought to have come back before this—[*listens to telephone*] —Oh, yes, I hope he'll turn up—thank you for going . . . Oh! yes. . . . *What* about Sybil? Oh! They've switched it off!

> [*Comes back centre of stage, sits down*
> *and evidently thinks anxiously.*
> *Enter* SERVANT, *announcing*

SERVANT. Lord Gaysford.

MARGARET. [*Starting to her feet.*] Oh!

> *Enter* FREDDIE.

> [*Exit* SERVANT.

Oh, Freddie, Freddie, I *am* so glad you've come. Oh, Freddie dear!

FREDDIE. [*Gravely, with a long sigh of relief.*] It *is* good to see you.

MARGARET. Oh, dear Freddie!

FREDDIE. Dear Margaret!

MARGARET. Your telegram to Wimbledon went to the wrong address—I only had it half an hour ago—sent back——

FREDDIE. *I* went to the wrong address— walked about the Common for hours, then I found the right place—you had just gone.

MARGARET. And then?

FREDDIE. Then I walked about the Common again to find a secluded portion to which—I could return—I'm going back there.

MARGARET. [*Anxiously.*] Oh! going back?——

FREDDIE. [*He nods.*] It's so quiet there. But I had to see you first.

MARGARET. I knew you would come.

FREDDIE. Rossetti and Browning didn't do much for me.

MARGARET. Tell me what she said.

FREDDIE. She's engaged to Wake.

MARGARET. [*With a sound of sympathy.*] I know. Algy has been here, Uncle Edward told him he ought to marry some one with money.

FREDDIE. She has tons—from the corkscrew. Still I could give her some things that he can't.

MARGARET. And you are so different—— Oh, I can't think how she could refuse you.

FREDDIE. That's only because you like me, dear.   [*Pause.*

MARGARET. What are you going to do?

FREDDIE. This. [*Stretches open his side pocket, lifts a pistol a little way out of it, and drops it back.*] I bought it in Wigmore Street this morning.

MARGARET. Freddie! You won't, really?

FREDDIE. There's nothing else. If there was

a war I should go to it; but there isn't—there won't be one in spite of the papers—there's only this.

MARGARET. Oh no, no, you mustn't!

FREDDIE. I've written to Mrs. Merlin.

MARGARET. I know, I had a letter from her just now, she's miserable.

FREDDIE. She's a dear woman; and I wired to Tremayne.

MARGARET. I know! He's on his way back.

FREDDIE. How splendid of him!

MARGARET. But your mother?

FREDDIE. Dear Mum! I must write to her— it's better that she should have the shock, it will at least save her the miserable anticipation. . .

MARGARET. But it's too dreadful. [*Reaches out her hands in despair.*] Oh, what *are* you looking at?

FREDDIE. Only at the tree in the back garden. I wonder how it got there. What tree is it?

MARGARET. [*Impatiently.*] I don't know—I don't care—we found it there when we took the house. [*Crosses stage.*] Freddie, you're not going back to Wimbledon?

FREDDIE. Not for an hour or two—it ought to be done in the dark, you know. There's no place nearer—the parks are overrun.

MARGARET. But you couldn't do it in the sub-

urbs [*shudders*] . . . And it won't be dark
for a long time. [*They hold each other's hands
and sit side by side. Pause.*] I can feel the im-
mensities near us. [*Pause.*] [*Very gravely.*]
Suppose we have some tea.

FREDDIE. I should like it.   [*She rings.*

MARGARET. You must give me that horrid
pistol.

FREDDIE. No . . . [*Firmly.*] I can't.

MARGARET. Only to hide in the coal-scuttle
while we are together, I am so afraid of it. You
don't want to kill me, even by accident, do you,
Freddie?

FREDDIE. No, dear, not for the world. Let
me put it there.

> [*She lifts up the lid of the brass coal-
> scuttle and he puts it carefully inside.*

MARGARET. [*With a sigh of relief.*] It can't
go off by itself?

FREDDIE. No—not in the coal-scuttle.

> *Enter* SERVANT *with tea.*

> [*They sit on either side of the tea-table,
> business of making it, &c.*

FREDDIE. It *is* good to be here. It's an awfully nice room. . . .

MARGARET. And this is its first week. . . .
Two lumps?

FREDDIE. Only one. . . . You'll see all
your own friends here?

MARGARET. I shall never have one like you. . .
Let me see, you do like cream?

FREDDIE. Not to much. [*Takes the cup. She
offers him bread and butter; he shakes his head.
He looks round.*] I shall never see it again,
Margaret.

MARGARET. We might have had such happy
hours here.

FREDDIE. Who did those pictures?

MARGARET. I forget his name—one of Whistler's disciples.

FREDDIE. He was an awful duffer.

MARGARET. What, Whistler?

FREDDIE. No, his disciple. And the books,
what are they? [*Nodding towards the little book-
shelf.*]

MARGARET. Modern poets. I collect them,
you know.

FREDDIE. Lucky chaps—but I wonder you
don't die—I found the big ones hard enough.
[*Pause.*

MARGARET. Freddie, don't you think it's
wicked to put an end to a great intellect—to a
great career, perhaps?

FREDDIE. What do you mean?

MARGARET. You might win some battle for
your country—you might be Commander-in-
Chief.

FREDDIE. They don't want one now. And they

are always wanting to reduce the army—I am helping—it's better than being disbanded—they only care for Territorials now.

MARGARET.   But it is wonderful how events seem to march out to meet each other.   .   .   . Perhaps the papers will manage to bring on a war.   Couldn't you wait and see?

FREDDIE.   No, dear—you can never trust them. [*Looking at her.*]   .   .   .   Your eyes are very blue, Margaret.   I thought so in the Park—do you remember how you and I went out to meet each other last Wednesday?   [*She nods.*]   It was that day you talked of some artist no one had heard of.

MARGARET.   [*Nods.*]   I told you of the picture in his studio at Hampstead, and you said Hampstead was the end of the world.

FREDDIE.   I wish we had gone.   .   .   .   We never shall now.   .   .   .   Primrose Hill is somewhere near it, Symonds told me he went there once.   .   .   .   I can't believe it's all over.   [*Gets up.*

MARGARET.   No, no—it mustn't be over.

FREDDIE.   It's time to go.

MARGARET.   Not yet, not yet.

FREDDIE.   And the worst of it is she won't care——

MARGARET.   Oh, she will—it'll kill her.

FREDDIE.   I don't believe it will even give her

neuralgia. She's not like you—if she had been like you, Margaret——   [*Turns away.*

MARGARET. You mustn't—mustn't go.

FREDDIE. It's time.

MARGARET. [*Passionately.*] You mustn't go, it would be wicked, cruel, cowardly—don't do it —don't do it.

FREDDIE. [*Surprised.*] I should look such a fool if I didn't—now; think of that, dear. Tremayne has chucked Constantinople, and Mrs. Merlin would never believe me again—and I bought it on purpose—[*nodding at scuttle*]. I should have done it last night if I'd had one by me.

MARGARET. Oh! What does it all matter? You mustn't throw away your beautiful life.

[*Puts out her hands entreatingly.*

FREDDIE. No one else thinks it beautiful— only you. [*Takes her hands, and looking into her eyes a change seems to come over him.*] There's no one like you, Margaret.

MARGARET. Yes—there's Sybil.

FREDDIE. She's heartless, and the strange thing is that to-day, when I ought to feel so much, it seems as if a wave had swept over me—it's Rossetti perhaps—it has carried all that I felt for her away—that makes it so hard.

MARGARET. Oh, but you loved her so only yesterday—you said she was like a goddess——

FREDDIE. A goddess has no heart, go and look at them in the British Museum—they are made of stone.

MARGARET. —or an Empress.

FREDDIE. She is a pig.

MARGARET. A pig!

FREDDIE. She ate too much supper. She ate two suppers—one after the other.

MARGARET. Women often do—you mustn't judge her so harshly, dear—I can't believe she doesn't care.

FREDDIE. *You* can't because—there's no one like you in the world. I never cared for her as I do for you—why didn't you love me, Margaret —Margaret, why didn't you love me? I should never have looked at her then. [*Telephone bell.*]

MARGARET. You never wanted me to—in that way——

FREDDIE. I always did. [*Sadly.*] I never really loved any one but you—if you had only cared for me—Margaret—*my* Margaret—why didn't you care—— [*Telephone bell again.*] It was because I thought you didn't—oh! damn that bell.

MARGARET. I did—I do. Oh, that bell! [*Bell rings furiously as they are in the act of embracing, and with a desperate exclamation* MARGARET *flies to it.*] [*At the telephone.*] Yes. . . . [*To* FREDDIE.] Oh, it's Algy.

[*To telephone.*] Yes, it's I, Margaret. Freddie
is here. . . . What. . . . Oh, how
cruel! Sybil says she was only joking? . . .
But she was not, she refused him! He was
broken-hearted—till just now. . . . Yes . .
What! She's not— Wait . . . I'll ask him,
he's here. Wait. [*Turning to* FREDDIE.] Sybil
says she's engaged to you; that she accepted you
last night at supper. And she was only laughing at Algy. [*With feeling in her voice, into
telephone.*] Ring me up again in five minutes
and I'll tell you what Freddie says. [*Gets up
and goes to* FREDDIE.] Freddie dear, you are
free, don't think that I will hold you. You must
go to *her*—you must go to her. You are free—
your are free——

FREDDIE. But Margaret! Margaret—it's you
I love—you——

Enter LADY GAYSFORD, *followed by* TREMAYNE
and MRS. MERLIN, *all agitated.*

LADY G. Oh, Freddie, Freddie, we've been
looking for you everywhere; I was afraid that——

FREDDIE. I've been having tea with Margaret.

TREMAYNE. But, look here, what does this
mean? They woke me up with your confounded
wire at seven this morning—only went to bed at
six—and instead of going to Constantinople, I
rushed back, because I thought you had put a pistol to your head.

MARGARET. [*Vehemently.*] He *was* going to
—he was, indeed; it's in the coal-scuttle.

LADY G. The coal-scuttle——

TREMAYNE. His head, or the pistol?
[*Going towards coal-scuttle. Business.*

FREDDIE. I carried it about all day, but I was
so bored with it. Mother, I was an ass!
[*Taking her hands.*

LADY G. Oh no, dear, I hope not.

FREDDIE. But for Margaret I should have
been.

MRS. M. [*Putting her hand on* MARGARET'S
arm.] I knew this dear girl would save him.

FREDDIE. She has—I'm engaged to her. [*Taking* MARGARET'S *hand.*] Margaret—my Margaret——
[*Telephone bell rings.*

TREMAYNE. [*Puzzled and savage.*] But it
was Sybil you were in love with——
[*Telephone bell rings violently.*

FREDDIE. Do let me answer the beastly thing.
It's Algy. [*Going to telephone.*] Yes . . .
It's Gaysford. . . . No. . . . Tell her
it was only a joke. I'm engaged to Margaret . .
I'm sorry she's thrown you over. . . . Yes,
of course—it's because she heard the Duke was
going to be married.

MARGARET. But he isn't—only don't say so.

FREDDIE. Oh! . . . [*To* ALGY, *at tele-*

phone.] Come and dine at the Ritz . . . good.

[FREDDIE *drops telephone and comes forward.*

TREMAYNE. You've made nice fools of us all round.

MRS. M. Yes. [*Shaking her head.*] You have, Freddie dear.

FREDDIE. But you've all been splendid, and I'm in the seventh heaven.

[TREMAYNE *grunts.*

MRS. M. [*Purringly.*] And not a fool's paradise?

FREDDIE. No. [*Puts his arm on* MARGARET'S *shoulder and looks into her eyes, and takes his mother's hand.*] Not a fool's paradise—in the one that Margaret has made for me.

CURTAIN.